ESCAPE FROM ZULAIRE

By Veronica Scott

Cover Art by Fiona Jayde

To my daughters Valerie and Elizabeth

Acknowledgements

Heartfelt thanks to the E-Book Formatting Fairies!

CHAPTER ONE

This is the most absurd thing I've ever done as assistant planetary agent for Loxton Galactic Trading—standing in as a bridesmaid in a borrowed puce dress because some other girl failed to show up. Andi Markriss sighed, feeling the garment binding too tight across her chest. *I didn't mind representing the company as a guest, but this is way outside the line of duty.*

Early afternoon on Zulaire was too warm for an outdoor ceremony, but the Planetary High Lord's spoiled daughter Lysanda didn't care to be ready any earlier in the day. Her guests' comfort wasn't a consideration.

An inch at a time, Andi shifted from her assigned spot into the shade cast by the towering stone pillars. *How did I get talked into this? Oh, yes, Lysanda wept, and her mother made vague threats about her husband reviewing our shipping contracts.* As the musicians played, Andi turned, watching Lysanda pace toward the dais in time to the music, smiling for her groom-to-be.

The local priest took a deep breath and launched into a lengthy blessing, invoking the deity and relating the history of the planet's three Clans—Obati, Shenti and Naranti. Andi chanted along with him under her breath. *Overlords, Second Class and Neutrals,* as her boss had told her when she'd arrived on Zulaire six years ago. Easy to keep them straight that way, he'd said, but don't ever slip and use the nicknames out loud.

"This young pair from two of the highest families will cement our peace," the priest proclaimed, lowering his arms and beaming at Princess Lysanda and her intended. "Their offspring will embody the union of Obati and Shenti blood."

Applause from the crowd, led by the bride's mother, made the officiant blush. As he bowed, Lysanda blew her mother a kiss.

That ovation will spur him to more oratory for sure. Andi smothered a sigh, wiggling her aching toes, held too tight in the borrowed silver sandals. *I thought the last three weeks of engagement parties, picnics and games out here in the summer compound were endless, but this ceremony tops them all.*

"The bride and groom will now light the symbolic candles." The priest led the pair to the side altar, where a trio of candles—blue, green and ivory—had been set into massive golden holders. Representing the three Clans, the candle ritual reinforced the political symbolism of this ceremony. Everything symbolic on Zulaire came in threes, Andi thought, watching the couple light each candle in turn.

Sneezing violently as the slight afternoon breeze carried colorful but pungent smoke from the burning tapers in her direction, she earned herself a glare and a hissed "Shh!" from the woman standing next to her. After taking a deep, cleansing breath of the fragrant bouquet she'd been clutching, Andi gave the other attendant a faint smile.

Lysanda had argued long and hard with her mother earlier about allowing Andi to substitute for the unaccountably missing handmaiden. Only the fact that without Andi to partner him, an important groomsman would be omitted from the ceremony swayed the decision. *Good for Loxton's business networking that I'm here. The Planetary Lord's family owes me personally now for preserving the precious symmetry of Lysanda's wedding party, at the cost of my aching feet.* With a flash of amusement at the ludicrous situation, Andi smiled. *Lucky for the princess, I accepted the invitation on behalf of Loxton, not my portly boss.*

Tuning out the priest's new recitation of more sacred writings, since the man had a nasal voice and a tendency to repeat himself, Andi studied the intricate carvings in the shiny black stone wall of the pavilion across from her, details brought to clarity by the slanting sun's rays.

The bas-relief depicted a stylized sun above a giant, multitrunked malagoy tree—each trunk symbolizing one of the three Zulairian tribes—Obati and Shenti locked in an eternal struggle to rule the planet, jockeying back and forth for thousands of years of bloody history. All the while the Naranti stayed neutral, filling a perpetual peacemakers' role, as their god, Sanenre, had legendarily decreed. Symbolic of their Clan's allotted role in the planet's history, the Naranti trunk was at the center of the tree, supporting the other two.

A skillfully carved herd of three-horned urabu grazed beneath the sheltering arms of the malagoy, the alpha buck depicted in a watchful stance, stone face staring at the occupants of the dais. The image of these legendary creatures, with their sweeping triple horns, was found everywhere on Zulaire, even on the Planetary Lord's seal. Beloved symbol of the god Sanenre, legendary bearers of good fortune and blessings, the gazellelike animals were extinct now, of course, hunted for the ivory of their sweeping horns.

Lysanda and her betrothed were repeating vows after the priest.

Apparently as bored as Andi was, the youngest attendant at the ceremony, just a toddler really, came across the platform with unsteady steps, reaching for Andi, her favorite playmate of the last few weeks. Missing her nieces and nephews, who lived far away in her own home Sector of the galaxy, Andi had been happy to skip a few adult entertainments to amuse the young ones of the house during her stay.

After a quick hug, the little girl plunked herself at Andi's feet, leaning against her legs. Pulling the flower garland from her glossy curls, she picked the petals off the blossoms while humming the processional tune off-key. The priest began to wrap up, raising his voice to override the toddler's song. Andi stared out over the crowd.

Quite a few empty chairs. A surprising number of high-ranking Obati guests had failed to arrive, which had driven the bride's mother into an angry tirade shortly before the ceremony. The failure of the missing bridesmaid and her family to show up had created another firestorm. Lady Tonkiln had a long memory for social slights.

It's been an odd summer, that's for sure. Andi would be glad to see fall arrive, when business always picked up and she could get back to the office, dive into the complexities of intergalactic trading and leave the socializing to others. *And decide if it's time to leave Zulaire for another assignment. Six years is too long to stay on one planet, if I want my next promotion. I wish I didn't love it here so much.*

Of course, no one had expected Planetary Lord Tonkiln to leave the important business of ruling Zulaire for his daughter's handfasting. He'd be at the formal wedding later in the year, held in the massive shrine at the capital, to accept the Shenti groom's petition for marriage to Lysanda. His oldest son, Gul, had been scheduled to stand in for the ruler today, but in typical Gul fashion, he hadn't shown up.

His careless attitude to responsibilities had been one of the reasons Andi had never let their casual, off-and-on-again affair become more serious. Charming as he was, Gul was unreliable.

Glancing along the fringes of the crowd where the invited Shenti guests were sitting, she saw everyone attentive, focusing on the glowing bride and handsome groom.

The Naranti servants clustered at the rear of the outdoor pavilion looked bored. *I suppose they just want to get this over with so they can clean up.*

Well, me, too. I want to get out of this dress. What a wretched color Lysanda picked! Andi sighed. *I'm glad I can wear my own clothing tonight at the reception, when I present the Loxton corporate bride gift.*

And still the ceremony continued. The bride gazed soulfully at her fiancé while he knelt, serenading her with a traditional Zulairian love song. *As if she hadn't been making fun of this very part of the ritual less than an hour ago. What a little actress.*

This was a coolly negotiated union of the ruling Obati family and an influential Shenti house to further cement everyone's power. *Lysanda and her groom are doing an excellent job of portraying lovebirds for the crowd. Both loving the spotlight. How fortunate he can sing—the family didn't have to hire someone to carry the tune for him.* Andi blinked, turning her full attention back to the couple as her own most favorite moment of the handfasting ceremony arrived—the giving of the bridal shawl. In the old days, she knew, these shawls had been hand-woven, selected by the groom with much care to symbolically enfold his chosen one in his love. Lysanda's shawl followed current fashion in the capital – machine-made, trimmed with three kinds of lace, the two family crests outlined in semiprecious gems—all about the show, not the emotion. Two attendants carried the unfolded shawl to the groom, displaying the embroidery and jewels for the guests to admire.

Still, it *was* the most romantic aspect of this particular ceremony. Andi suppressed a somewhat wistful mental picture of an unknown man wrapping her in one of the traditional, simple shawls. She took another deep breath of the flowers' perfume. *What is with me today, all this nostalgia for the dreams I had as a kid? Romance, a husband, children… Traveling around the Sectors doing business for Loxton is the wrong career if I want to settle down. I already made that decision, no looking back, no regrets. Maybe after I make Sector vice president, I'll decide on a different course.* No telling how old she'd be by then.

After adjusting the shawl to her satisfaction, Lysanda leaned toward the groom for a brief kiss before the couple turned to face the applauding audience. Scooping the bored flower girl into her arms, Andi juggled her own flowers, plus the toddler and her tiny basket. Arm in arm with the prominent Shenti man she'd been rushed into the puce dress to accompany, Andi walked down the aisle behind the happy couple, in time to the music.

As soon as the ceremonial party had left the pavilion, Andi searched for a maid or family member to take charge of the toddler. Another of the bride's attendants, a haughty girl from the capital, brought her the Tonkilns' youngest son, Sadu, who'd been a restless member of the wedding party too. "Here, you may as well tend them both, outworlder," the other girl said. "How do boys get so messy?" She turned on her elegant heel and walked away before Andi could protest.

"Hungry," Sadu proclaimed loudly, tugging at her skirt with one grubby hand.

Lady Tonkiln hurried by. "Oh, good, you have the children, Andi. Thank you."

"But I should be getting out of this dress, getting ready for the evening's reception—"

"You know the nurse left suddenly for her village this morning. I've no idea why, and she needn't bother coming back, begging to be rehired." Lady Tonkiln reached to untangle an errant flower from the girl's curls. "Do take the children to the house for me, won't you? The maids can watch them. No one will care if you're late to the dance as long as you're in time for the presentation of the gifts."

And with that barbed insult, her hostess was off to greet more guests before Andi could protest. Shaking her head, she stared after the older woman. *Typical. The "overbearing Obati" clan indeed!*

Giving Sadu an awkward pat on the shoulder, she tugged him in the direction of the waiting Naranti servants. "All right, Sadu, walk with me and we'll find Cook. I know I saw her earlier —she can take you both back to the house, get you a snack before you and your cousin here take your naps."

After handing Sadu and the flower girl over to the family's genial cook, Andi decided to walk back to the Tonkiln mansion, rather than take the shuttle. She'd had enough of the family and their guests for right now. *I need some time by myself.* Taking off the too-tight sandals, Andi breathed a sigh of relief and strolled into the forest that surrounded the ceremonial glade. The path was clearly marked, and the hard-packed dirt felt soothing to her abused feet.

When she reached the halfway point, out of sight of both the glade and the house, Andi took a detour to the east to a meadow she'd discovered a few days ago. Heedless of the borrowed dress, which she knew would never be worn again by anyone, Andi hiked the skirt up enough so that she could sit comfortably on the moss under a big malagoy tree and relax for a few moments. Leaning her head against the rough trunk, she closed her eyes and listened to the soothing hum of the pollen-gathering insects and birdsongs overhead. *Just have to get through this one last reception tonight, and then I can return to the capital. I can do that.*

Close to drowsing off in this peaceful spot, Andi suddenly became aware that the meadow had grown quiet. Opening her eyes with a flash of alarm, she found herself staring at a myth come to life.

An entire family of majestic urabu stood in the center of the lush meadow. To Andi's knowledge, no one had seen a living urabu on Zulaire in hundreds of years.

Behind the proud alpha male were three females, a younger buck showing nubs for horns, and a baby. *As if they came just to find me.* Andi chuckled at the idea as the buck swung his head in her direction, nodding once. Standing guard, he watched the perimeter of the small meadow as his brood spread out to nibble the dense stand of grass and flowers. From time to time the buck lowered his head to snatch a few mouthfuls of fodder, before going back on the alert. A vivid green, his eyes were fringed by thick, black lashes.

She wasn't sorry to claim this incredible experience all for herself.

Trotting forward a few paces, the fawn stopped to check on its mother's whereabouts, then wobbled straight to Andi on spindly legs. Amazed, she held out her hand for it to sniff before stroking the little urabu's muzzle and playing with the soft, tufted ears. The fawn's golden-brown pelt was warm velvet under her fingers.

The buck made an impatient huffing sound. Startled, jerking her hand back, Andi watched as the fawn took three awkward jumps, to press against the biggest doe's flank. Leaving the clearing, the herd bounded off to the northeast in a flowing line, buck first, fawn struggling valiantly to keep up at the end of the procession.

A wave of longing engulfed Andi as they left her. *I wish they'd stayed longer.* Taking a few tentative steps away from the tree, she peered hopefully into the jungle, but the urabu family had gone on their way without a trace.

With a breathless little laugh, she pinched her forearm. "No, I'm awake all right." She studied the imprint of the hooves in the rich soil. Crushed, fragrant grass was already springing back to hide the evidence. "When I think how many times I was told the urabu didn't really exist, or had been hunted to extinction—"

Well, this experience certainly redeemed my day. Frowning at a grass stain as she dusted stray twigs and leaves from her skirt, she shook her head. *I'm not telling the*

Tonkilns about this magical encounter or they'll be out here hunting the poor things. My secret, my gift from Zulaire's god.

Thinking of her imperious hosts reminded Andi to check the time. Whistling at how late in the afternoon it had become, she set out in a slow jog, skirt hiked above her knees. At the forest's edge, she stopped, planning to put her sandals on again. One of the gardener's legion of young helpers hailed her. Running along the center of the path, he made big summoning gestures. "Miss, miss, you're wanted at the house!"

"Why all the fuss? Were they afraid I'd gotten lost?" Andi said.

Coming to a halt in front of her, the boy tugged at her sleeve, trying to draw her along the path. "Men have come from the capital for you. Outworld soldiers."

"Soldiers?" Andi was startled, her heart beating faster. "What do I have to do with the military? There must be a mistake."

"We must go. The leader of these soldiers, he demands to speak to you." Lowering his voice, her companion intoned with relish, "At ONCE!" The skinny boy chortled at his imitation of the outworlder's less-than-exact accent. "He said it's important, a matter of utmost urgency."

Maybe something had happened at the office? Or to her boss? But why send the military out here with the message? The capital was hundreds of miles away, yes, but there were excellent comlinks between here and there. Breaking into a run, she covered the ground faster than the gardener's assistant's stubbier limbs could carry him.

Leaving the winded lad well behind, Andi sprinted the last few yards of the path, onto the main house's driveway. Skidding to a stop to catch her breath, she craned for a better look at a pair of military vehicles parked off to the side, between her and the mansion. One was a squat, two-passenger groundcar with an ominous-looking blast cannon mounted on the rear. Behind that was a much larger armored personnel carrier, also bristling with weapons, lights and scanners. Both vehicles were the gray, green and black camouflage design favored by Sectors troops on this planet.

Offworld troops seemed jarringly out of place in this idyllic playground of the Obati elite. *I can see why the kid was so excited.* Catching her breath, Andi put her shoes on before walking across the driveway.

Four Sectors soldiers sprawled on the blue-green grass beside the vehicles, taking advantage of the shade. Although armed, the men appeared at ease, happy for a break. Lounging against the back of the APC was a hulking Shenti warrior, who gave her a small nod as she drew even with him. Andi didn't recognize his sub-Clan insignia, which meant he was from the far western reaches of Zulaire, where Loxton didn't do much trade. *What's he doing with Sectors soldiers?* The Shenti wasn't a prisoner, and he probably wasn't a guide, not in this half of Zulaire. Western Shenti tended to be superstitious, didn't travel too far from their sub-Clan boundaries. *So why is he here?*

Studying the open engine compartment, a tall, lanky sergeant and a corporal bent together over the front flank of the APC.

Probably hearing her footsteps crunch on the gravel, the sergeant laid down his tools and turned to eye her in a friendly but distant manner. "Miss Markriss?"

"Yes. What's the matter? Has something happened at the Loxton office?" Andi's heart pounded as she voiced her greatest fear.

"Easy, ma'am, not that I'm aware of. Not exactly." The sergeant held up a hand to stop her next question. "I'm Sergeant Mitch Wilson. Pleased to meet you." Automatically, Andi shook the hand he offered. "Captain Deverane is waiting inside to explain the situation. I'm glad you're here because he has a short fuse this trip." Hooking his hands in his pockets, tilting his head, the sergeant eyed her up and down. "No one knew where to find you, ma'am. Upset them to admit it, too."

Lady Tonkiln's probably irritated at outworld soldiers intruding on her social event, along with everything else that's happened today. Hands on her hips, she leaned toward him. "It's no one's business to monitor my comings and goings. I wasn't expecting company."

"Well, you're here now. Problem solved." He grinned at her. "The captain wants to get going as soon as possible."

"Yeah, if this piece of junk holds together long enough to get us back to the capital." The corporal, who had been looking Andi over from head to toe with more appreciation than the sergeant had showed, kicked the APC's shielded wheel housing with his heavy combat boot. "It can slag itself then, for all I care."

"Go on inside, ma'am, please." The sergeant nodded toward the house. Then his attention switched to the engine and the swearing corporal, who was tugging at something deep in the guts of the APC. Wilson pushed back his hat with his thumb. "Yeah, okay, soldier, we all know anti-grav would be better, but the brass don't issue high-tech stuff to operators on a backwater planet like this. Find the damn problem before the captain's ready to leave, because I'm not anxious to tell him we can't."

"Might be tomorrow, Sarge. This engine needs a lot of work." The corporal held out a misshapen part. "I'll have to recalibrate this for sure."

"Miss Markriss!"

Hearing the familiar, stentorian voice, Andi flinched and walked away from the APC. Iraku, the Naranti who was chief of household staff for the ruler's family, stood at the top of the stone stairs, flanked by the massive, carved columns supporting the impressive facade of the "simple" summer dwelling. As Andi toiled up the steps, he steepled his fingers and glared down at her. "Lady Tonkiln has been looking for you. She was most displeased when you disappeared. *Not* the behavior we expect from a guest in *this* house." He sniffed.

Much to her own annoyance, Andi stumbled on the last riser, betrayed by the ill-fitting shoes. Iraku grabbed her elbow to keep her from falling, holding on too long, until Andi jerked herself free. Stepping onto the terraced patio, she moved as far away from the man as she could.

Something about him always sets my teeth on edge. Pompous, officious—as if he was the Planetary Overlord, not a servant.

For a moment, Andi was afraid she'd voiced her dislike out loud. Then Iraku did a jerky half-bow, rubbing his fingers on his robe as if to remove any taint from the contact with her. Biting back a smile at his instinctive reaction, she knew his antipathy toward her was as deep as her loathing of him. Iraku gestured at the stairs. "Polished yesterday. Perhaps the staff was too generous with the wax. My apologies, Miss Markriss. I'll have the entire job redone, to prevent any further such incidents. It would have been a tragedy if you'd fallen."

As if you cared. She was sure Iraku would have enjoyed the sight of her taking a header on the stairs. *The staff will hate me for having to redo the steps.* Massaging her tender elbow, Andi was conscious of the immense strength Iraku had in those long, slender fingers. She resolved to stay well away from him at all times in the future. *Thank goodness, the summer will be over soon.* "Where's this officer who's here to see me?"

"I put him in Lord Tonkiln's library. Follow me." Billowing silver and green robes made a graceful circle about the servant as he spun on one foot. Not bothering to see if Andi was behind him, he stalked into the house.

As a neutral Naranti, Iraku was well schooled in dealing with both the tempestuous, demanding highborn Obati and the subordinate Shenti population. He was also supposed to be expert at establishing cordial relations with any stray outworlders, such as her. *He must have missed that seminar.* Andi glared at Iraku's back.

Maybe running the household for the Planetary High Lord gave Iraku the right to be arrogant.

But does he have to walk so damn slowly? Reining in her annoyance, Andi paced behind him.

Iraku paused to adjust a spray of scarlet flowers in one of the urns beside the main doorway, shifting it an inch or two and bringing a second bloom up beside the first. Exasperated, Andi maneuvered around him. "I can get to the library by myself, thank you."

"Escorting you is not a problem, miss." Sidestepping neatly, Iraku blocked her path. She had to stutter-step and let him go ahead of her to avert an unseemly collision. This hallway was too narrow for Andi to walk anywhere but behind the chief servant as he continued his ponderous march to the library wing. Reaching for the elegantly curved brass door handles, he pushed the panels open. Muttering a curse, Andi brushed past him to step inside the room.

The Sectors Special Forces captain awaiting Andi in the library stood with his back to the door, hands on his hips, staring at one of Lord Tonkiln's prized abstract paintings. Well over six feet of hard warrior, he'd rolled his camouflage uniform sleeves up, revealing muscular arms matching the rest of his physique. Andi glimpsed the hint of an intriguing tattoo, a black sword wreathed in comets, on one bicep. His hair was sandy brown, a bit shaggy for military correctness. He tapped the toe of his boot against the expensive mahogany floor. The captain's whole attitude suggested a man poised for decisive action at a moment's notice, reinforced by the way he wheeled at the sound of the door opening.

"*Finally.*" His glance at the military chrono on his tanned wrist was an unconscious gesture of annoyance at time forever lost.

Green eyes in a tanned, ruggedly handsome face. Andi's knees went a little wobbly for a moment. *My particular weakness in a man.* Classic square jaw, straight nose, high forehead with a small scar on his cheek.

His eyebrows drew together in a frown. "Miss Markriss?"

"Why are you here?" Andi snapped out of her fascination with his features, feeling her cheeks grow hot. *Wow, was I blatantly staring or what?* "Has something happened to Dave Flintmay? The Loxton planetary agent?"

Flashing very white teeth in that tanned face, he smiled at her, but the too-easy grin didn't reach his tired eyes. "Don't you people get the news out here? Comlinks broken?"

She blinked, trying to follow this unexpected conversation starter. "What?"

Lady Tonkiln received a stack of messages each morning, from either her husband or friends in the capital. Lysanda also had many messages, filled with inconsequential social gossip. Nothing for Andi, but then, everyone knew she was on an extended vacation from the office. The Loxton operation was on its summer hiatus along with most of Zulaire. "Of course we get news. What does that have to do with anything? Captain, what are you *doing* here?"

Glancing at Iraku, the officer's lips tightened as if he bit back some hasty comment. Unabashedly eavesdropping, the Naranti servant remained by the open door. "Thank you, I think the lady and I can manage."

Andi stifled a laugh. The gardener's assistant had been right—the captain's accent was pretty bad, soft on the consonants and missing the required prefixes. *His hypnotraining must have been a rush job.*

Iraku stared at the outworlder, who glared back, jaw clenched, one hand resting on the butt of his blaster.

I never tried outright dismissal on the old dictator. Avoiding him sure doesn't work. Breaking the silence, Andi tried for a gracious note. "Thanks for escorting me, Iraku. Can you do me a favor and inform Lady Tonkiln I've returned to the house, since she was concerned?" Blinking at last, the servant bowed low. He left without another word but drew the door closed behind him in a leisurely fashion calculated to infuriate the impatient captain.

As Andi watched in disbelief, Deverane crossed to the door. Opening it a few inches, he checked to be sure Iraku hadn't lingered within earshot, before shutting the door again.

Offering no explanation to Andi for the cautious maneuver, he gestured toward the overstuffed chairs grouped in front of the fireplace. "Would you like to sit?"

"No, thank you, I want to know what's going on." She took a deep breath, trying to calm her frayed nerves. *Is all this mystery necessary?*

"Captain Tom Deverane, Sectors Special Forces." He walked to the chairs himself. To be polite, she joined him, shaking his proffered hand before seating herself. "Excuse my dust," he said. "But I've been in the Western Plains and the Abujan mountain range for quite some time now."

"Why don't you try telling me something relevant about why you're here?" Many a slow-moving clerk at the Loxton offices had jumped at that peremptory tone from her.

"I forget you've been out of the loop." Sitting down, Deverane leaned forward, putting his hands on his knees and taking a deep breath. "Two days ago I got urgent orders, relayed from Sector Command, diverting me from my primary mission. The new priority was to come five hundred miles out of our way to extract you for a safe return to the capital city." From the dry tone in his voice, Andi guessed how little he'd appreciated the change. "Now, if you could get your things together, I'd like to be on our way before dark."

She blinked. *Today? He wants me to leave now?* Andi shifted back into the chair's embrace, crossing her legs. "Get my things—what are you talking about? I'm the guest of Lord Tonkiln's family, and I'm expected to present a significant gift from Loxton at the reception tonight with due ceremony. I can't ride off with you on literally a moment's notice without some compelling reason. Why is your Command issuing orders concerning me anyway?"

The captain got up in one smooth motion, like a great cat uncurling, paced to the fireplace and back, then half sat on the edge of a sturdy table. *I bet he's a person in constant motion—discussing anything in patient detail doesn't appear to be his style. Well, I'm not one of his soldiers and I don't take orders from him, so he'd better explain himself.*

"Miss Markriss—"

"Call me Andi." *And let's get this discussion on a less military, more personal level so you stop trying to give me orders.*

The quick, meaningless smile crossed his handsome face again, never reaching his eyes. "*Andi.* In case you haven't heard, this entire planet is about to be embroiled in a devastating Clan war."

Andi didn't hesitate. "Ridiculous. The Obati and the Shenti have been at peace for four hundred years. Everyone has been satisfied with the status quo for four centuries. How long did you say you've been on Zulaire, Captain?" She raised her eyebrows, drumming her fingers on the arm of the chair. "You've been here—what? Two weeks?"

He drew himself up to his full height, probably a foot taller than she, hands clasped tight behind his back, and glared at her. "I've been here long enough to see that this place is approaching critical mass, which apparently escapes *your* scanners.

You're the only offworlder on Zulaire right now who isn't military, diplomatic, or mining personnel. And all of them are either safe in the capital or behind the defenses of the West Vialtin mine. *Except you.*" His index finger stabbed the air in her direction. "Along with my men and me. I intend to correct that situation in short order. Now, if you will please get your things—"

This is ridiculous. Not intimidated but curious, Andi shook her head. "We would have heard something out here. My office would have gotten in touch with me."

Deverane walked closer, leaned on the table. "Have you received any communications from the office, or anyone since you came out here?"

"No, but it's the summer slow period. Even the Loxton office is all but closed." She gave him a challenging glare. "Look, on the basis of what you've said so far, I don't appear to need rescuing. You still haven't told me anything to justify leaving tonight, missing the reception, insulting my hosts, and driving back to the capital like a prisoner." Wishing the deep upholstery didn't make rising such an ungraceful process, Andi left the chair.

"You aren't getting the picture." Jaw clenched, he took a few steps to stand next to her. The glare from his green eyes was scorching, and Andi recoiled from the intensity. Apparently taking note of her unease, the captain gentled his voice. "Though why that should surprise me, I don't know, considering the warnings Lord Tonkiln and the other members of the Council have ignored."

"Warnings?" Andi took a step back, crossing her arms over her chest.

"To get their families the hell out of this isolated, indefensible spot and into safety at the capital." Deverane took a deep breath. He walked over to stare at the carvings on the mantel. Andi got the impression from the rigid set of his broad shoulders he was trying to control his temper. After a minute, he came to sit near her again. "I was told your boss made numerous attempts to get in touch with you, right until the moment he and the rest of the Loxton staff took a ship offworld."

"Dave left Zulaire? They've all gone?" Now Andi fell back into the chair, raising a small puff of dust from the plush cushion beneath her. A wave of nausea rippling through her gut, she ran a hand through her hair, looping the tendrils behind her ear. "I don't understand any of this. Why would my boss and my co-workers leave without me? Why wouldn't the Tonkilns tell me? You're still not making sense."

Deverane came to hunker down in front of her chair, caging her with his arms, invading her personal space. Inhaling sharply, she caught a whiff of musk and forest and man, threaded with some delicious spicy note. She glanced down at his hands, strong, capable, locked on the chair close to her body. As if to calm an upset child, his voice was soothing and low. "Relax. We can get you offplanet in a military transport once you're safely in the capital."

She lifted her head, gazing straight into his eyes. Half-formed thoughts chased each other in her mind. The longer he talked, the more nervous she got, but it was still all too much to take in. Loxton only pulled staff offworld in the most serious situations. *I haven't heard a whiff of trouble. Dave wouldn't have left me behind. Would he?*

Deverane touched her arm lightly. "There have been incidents all summer. People disappearing, vehicles abandoned on the transportway with no sign of the occupants. There have even been some small-scale massacres in isolated villages, both Obati and Shenti. The violence keeps escalating. Command thinks a full-blown war is only a breath away, waiting for some convenient incident to touch it off. Lord Tonkiln and the others have chosen to keep things quiet, leaving their families at risk out here in order to demonstrate their belief in their own supremacy. Putting on a pretense of things going along as usual. Or else they refuse to see what's coming. *Civilians.*"

He might as well have said *idiots*.

Deverane frowned at her, three deep wrinkles marring the strong sweep of his forehead. "Are you prepared to take the same risk?"

He's invading my personal space, damn it. I don't intimidate that easily, pal. She pushed at his rock-hard shoulders. Standing, he moved away a pace or two, still keeping his eyes locked on her. Licking her lips, Andi smoothed down her silky skirt. "You're insinuating my hosts have deceived me and deliberately put me in harm's way? I find that insulting."

Eyes closed, he pinched the bridge of his nose. "You're a pawn to them." Now he reopened his eyes and flung his arms out, hands wide open. "You mean nothing to them. If you're going to refuse my offer of evacuation, then you'd better be ready to take care of yourself, because I guarantee you the Obati won't."

"Give me some specifics to back up your claims, Captain," Andi said. "So far I only have your word there's a problem. No insult intended."

He nodded. "All right," he said, his voice crisp. "Fair enough. One of your own Loxton agents was murdered in the southern region, along with all his Shenti guides and workers. The cargo wasn't even stolen, just left to rot in the haulers. I'm told that was the incident that spooked your boss to close the office and leave the planet."

"One of the Loxton crew? Who?" As deputy agent, she knew and worked with all of the Loxton staff. Mentally reviewing who might have been in transit, seeing the faces of men and women who were her friends as well as co-workers, Andi felt a wave of nausea.

"Someone named Kane. I'm sorry to be the one to tell you all this."

She felt as if he'd thrown ice water in her face. Kane was one of her favorite crew chiefs on Zulaire, always laughing, even while he ran a highly organized local operation. *Massacred*? Andi's thoughts were racing and she began to tremble. She swallowed the bile in her throat and said, "When did this happen?"

"Two weeks ago."

"And no one thought I needed to know? No one saw fit to tell me?" Her voice rose as she got angrier.

"I told you, the Obati were keeping you in the dark, blocking your company's attempts to communicate with you out here," Deverane said. "I know it's a lot to take in."

She shook her head. "Why would the Obati keep information from me?"

Deverane shrugged. "Maybe it's good propaganda to have the Loxton deputy agent still on Zulaire, still at the social event of the summer. Signals things aren't as out of control as people might think."

"Using me?" The idea revolted her.

He nodded. "There have been other incidents, although the slaughter of Kane's caravan was the worst. The victims have primarily been Sectors citizens associated with either Obati or Shenti interests in some way. As a guest of the Tonkilns, you fit that profile."

"But if this is a Shenti attempt to take over rule of Zulaire, why did they kill Kane? He was honorary Shenti. It doesn't make sense." Andi's stomach was in knots, vertigo making her senses swirl. *A tragedy beyond anything I could have imagined.*

"Someone commits a crime, someone else takes revenge and the innocents get caught in the middle, because of who they are, who they were with, who they know. Sometimes being in the wrong spot at the wrong time gets a person killed," Deverane said, his tone gentle. "I don't want it to happen to you."

A vision of the atrocity committed on her friend battered Andi. *What would I do if I got caught in a similar situation? I didn't even bring my personal blaster.*

She stood, resting her hand on Deverane's arm for a moment. "I'll go back to the capital with you in the morning. And…thank you."

"*In the*—" He glared at her, eyebrows drawing together in an impressive frown, forehead wrinkles deepening even more. "Have you been listening, Miss Markriss? This planet is in a precarious state. We can't wait for your convenience. We need to leave tonight. The sooner the better."

Andi walked to the door. "I don't think we *can* leave tonight, Captain, no matter what you want."

The door handle moved under her hand. Startled, she released it, falling back a pace or two. When the door opened, Iraku stood there, condescending as ever, face contorted in a sneer, lips pursed in disapproval. Hands on their curved belt knives, two of the armed household guards stood a few steps away. Startled by their hostile expressions, Andi retreated a step.

Addrerssing her but staring at Deverane, Iraku asked, "Is there a problem, miss? Lady Tonkiln wishes to speak with you regarding the presentation at tonight's ceremony."

Andi shook her head. "No problem, I'll be right there." She turned to Deverane, holding out one hand, palm up. "Better ask your sergeant what's wrong with the APC's engine."

"What are you talking about?" Deverane strode to her side.

"He told me there was an engine problem. The corporal said it was going to take all night to fix. Listen, assuming your men can't repair the APC tonight, I'll go to the reception, do my duty for Loxton, and leave with you in the morning. No problem."

What Deverane would have said next, Andi didn't wait to hear. After all, the Tonkilns had a small army of Naranti servants and household guards. Every Obati household in the summer colony did. The well-trained security force ought to be enough protection from any hotheaded Shenti warriors bent on making mischief.

Rolling her shoulders as she walked down the hall, she took a deep, calming breath. *We can't leave now anyway, so I might as well stick with protocol. Nothing's likely to happen tonight, not here in the middle of the Obati stronghold.*

CHAPTER TWO

Although she packed a single suitcase with essentials before dressing for the reception and driving over with Lady Tonkiln, Andi refused to let herself worry too much about Captain Deverane's dire news. Although the massacre of Kane's team was a heartbreaking, shocking tragedy, the crew had been half the planet away. Surely whoever was trying to foment rebellion in the south didn't affect the situation here. *Dave always was an alarmist. Loxton won't appreciate his abandoning the planet. Can you say career-ending move?* Yes, she'd travel back to the capital with the Sectors soldiers tomorrow, but for tonight, she couldn't find a reason good enough to shirk her duty.

Despite a nagging headache, she got through the dinner and made her well-practiced, flowery speech as she presented the Loxton gift, which was well received by Lysanda and her groom. When the dancing began, Andi stood on the sidelines, remembering the end-of-summer party last year, when she and Gul Tonkiln had been together. Although their breakup had been mutual, she still felt a brief flash of regret, tempered by the sure knowledge nothing long term would have developed between them. Careless, handsome Gul Tonkiln, oldest son of the ruler, who'd sworn he'd be here this weekend. He hadn't even bothered to show up for Lysanda's handfasting ceremony earlier in the day. *Well, what did I really expect? This is classic Gul behavior. Obviously, nothing's changed.*

A deep, rich voice spoke to her in Basic. "Waiting for someone? Or will I do?"

Deverane stood in front of her, his wide shoulders blocking her view of the room. He bowed very slightly, but his intense gaze never left her face.

A hot little tingle of electricity ran through Andi's nerves. *I never expected to see him here.*

"Don't tell me you were invited?" *How did he manage that?* Looking down on anyone not in their noble caste, the Obati made their parties hard to crash. Outworlders weren't normally included on the guest lists, but Loxton was important to Zulaire's intergalactic credit balance, which explained Andi's access.

Deverane still wore his camouflage fatigues but had pinned on his silver captain's bars. Riding his hip was a Mark 27 blaster.

Andi pointed at the weapon. "You always wear a sidearm to formal occasions?"

"On this planet I do." He rested his hand on the blaster's butt. "I invited myself, and the doorkeeper didn't quite know what to do, so she let me in. With Mawreg incursions in the adjoining Sectors, we're an important presence on Zulaire. Nobody wants to piss off the Sectors when the enemy might just decide your planet is a tempting target." The captain glanced around the crowded room, full of laughing, dancing Obati and Shenti. The pounding music was fast, with a heavy bass line. "Pretty good turnout. Took me a few minutes to work my way over here. I saw you dancing when I came in."

Andi's cheeks flamed. *He was watching me? Wasn't at my most graceful, not doing that awkward step.* She hoped the subdued lighting would hide her embarrassment. "I was dancing with a business acquaintance." *Right, a jerk trying to get certain personal fringe benefits from throwing large shipping orders Loxton's way. Won't be dancing with him again.* Not after what she'd told him to do with his order.

"I see." Very slowly, the captain's gaze traveled from her head to her toes and back again. "Great dress, by the way. Nice shade of blue." The pupils of his eyes were huge, sparkling.

Could all-business Captain Deverane be trying to get on my good side with compliments? Hers was a knockout dress, though. Much better than the borrowed, overfussy getup she'd had to wear for Lysanda's ceremony earlier in the day. Low-cut, sheer, pale-blue offworld silk with subtle flowers woven into the fabric, the dress flowed over a tight, blue bodysuit. This outfit could hold its own with any other woman's at the party. The dress cost her a chunk of last quarter's salary. *I wish Loxton's accountants understood the necessity of blending in with the clients.*

"You don't strike me as the type to notice what a woman is wearing, unless she's a soldier out of uniform," she said. Teasing Deverane seemed safer somehow than acknowledging the compliment outright.

"Hey, I'm serious." His genuine smile and twinkling eyes took ten years off his face.

"Well, thank you, sir." *Why is this new side of Deverane making me tongue tied?* Andi cleared her throat, fidgeting with her necklace.

"Let's declare a truce." He held out his hand, palm up. "I recognize this song the band is attempting to play. It was popular at Sector Hub when I was last posted there. I do know how to dance." This last was said directly into her ear. His breath whispered over her skin, tickled her cheek in a way that gave her butterflies. The captain nodded toward the dance floor and winked.

The orchestra had switched to a slower, more romantic tune, and the lights dimmed to match the shift in mood.

"I never thought of dancing as a military skill." Still a little flustered, she stepped onto the polished hardwood floor. Her fingers trembled ever so slightly as his closed around them.

Deverane encircled her waist with one arm, tugged her close and swirled her into the throng of couples. He was smooth and sure at following the intricate patterns demanded by the music. "Command believes we should know all about maneuvering in tight situations. I learned at Star Guard Academy as a cadet. Some skills stay with you for life." The captain avoided mishap by swinging her around a couple doing exuberant, sweeping turns, hogging the floor. Twirling Andi out, then back, he held her tight for the next series of steps.

He was warm, solid against her, all muscle. Catching a whiff of his intriguing scent, she inhaled, trying to ignore the way her nipples pebbled and tightened. *I'd better watch myself, this officer is affecting me on more than one level.* Andi relaxed as the music played on. They moved so smoothly together, as if they'd been dance partners before, maybe in another life.

He grinned down at her, green eyes gleaming. "I'm sorry I was so abrupt this afternoon."

"Apology accepted. Why are you here at this party, though? To kidnap me? After all, you do have orders, right?"

Deverane looked away for a second. "Not orders to kidnap civilians under the protection of the Planetary High Lord." The words were clipped, bitten off, his voice low and tense.

Andi decided to ignore the odd undertone. "Not that I'm ungrateful for the dance, but I never expected to see you here."

"I never expected you to leave the house and *be* here." He sounded annoyed. "The situation is unsafe, you're unprotected, vulnerable—"

"You don't think the Tonkiln's protection will be enough?" She was surprised.

"No." Breaking off the dance, he stared into her eyes, still holding her close. Annoyed couples bumped into them on both sides. Andi staggered, and the captain steadied her, but another somewhat inebriated couple jostled him. Shielding her from the impact, Deverane fended off the other dancers with his hip and elbow. "Look, we can't stand here to discuss it. And we sure as hell can't dance and have a debate. Agreed?"

She nodded, but with a sigh. He was the best partner she'd ever danced with. It had been effortless to follow his lead, like flying. *Why couldn't this have lasted longer before reality broke in on us?* "We don't have to go back to the Tonkilns' yet, do we? Is the APC repaired?"

"No, my men are working on it. Let me get you something to drink, and we'll step outside where we won't draw so much attention." Deverane led her by the hand through the throng of onlookers, back to the intimate groupings of small tables along the wall. Giggling, a cluster of the younger Obati ladies talked animatedly, stealing glances at her. The scrutiny made Andi tense, on edge. She could imagine what trend the gossip was taking.

What would Gul say?

Does he know about this good-looking offworlder?

Is she trying to make him jealous? Clever girl!

She dropped Deverane's hand. "I'll meet you at the western door," Andi said over her shoulder, already walking away along the line of tables. Deliberately, she kept her pace slow and unhurried. *One never exhibits undue haste in front of the Obati nobility.*

Slipping outside, Andi waited in the gloom by the vine-covered pillars. She hummed under her breath, the song they'd been dancing to, trying to block the amorous sounds coming from couples sprawled on the double-wide lounges scattered outside the ballroom. As soon as Deverane walked out, she went to meet him, accepting the cold drink he offered her. She waved her free hand toward the tree line just off the patio. "Can we walk down to the lake? With the two moons out tonight, it's clear enough, and this is one of my favorite places on Zulaire. If what you've told me about an impending war is true, I may never be here again."

"All right, but we're not going to stay long." Taking her elbow in a light clasp, Deverane guided her down the shallow stairs toward the lake.

"I can leave," Andi said, sipping her drink. "Lady Tonkiln went home with a headache right after all the gifts were tallied. And I haven't seen Lysanda and her groom since the dancing started. My duties are complete."

Arm in arm, they strolled past a reflecting pool. The captain kept gazing around, checking the area for threats, apparently. *Military reflexes, no doubt.* His actions reminded her why she was really here in the moonlight with this handsome man—politics, not pleasure. Sighing, she chose the flagstone pathway toward the lake, which gleamed gray blue in the moonlight ahead of them. Not far from shore, the trees on a small island cast odd black shadows onto the calm waters. Misty clouds were coming to rest on the distant mountains.

They walked for a few minutes, not touching but companionably close. She was very conscious of him at her back, ready to shield her from any danger they might encounter. Pausing at the lakeshore, Andi savored the peaceful scene, allowing the lapping of the waves to calm her nerves a bit.

"A beautiful place." Deverane moved to stand right beside her, his hip brushing hers. Even the slight contact sent sizzling sparks through her nerve endings. Apparently unaware of the effect he was having on her, he gazed out over the lake. "Serene."

Andi laughed. "You should have seen it during the day, when the children were riding their personal aquatic craft. *So* much noise. I pity the poor water creatures."

He glanced at her sequined dance shoes gleaming in the moonlight. "Your feet must be tired. Are there benches?"

Warmed by his attentiveness to her comfort, Andi couldn't help wishing just a little that they weren't out together because of the unsettled circumstances between the Clans. *Why couldn't I have met this intriguing guy some other time?* "Over here."

He followed her onto another path made from crushed white rock. Artistically rustic, but still comfortable, wooden benches were placed at intervals along the shore. Selecting one a few yards from the entrance to the path, Andi sat down. Taking a longer swallow from her drink, she savored the fruity taste, berries and citrus with a biting alcoholic kicker. Raising his glass, Deverane took a sip, rolling it around in his mouth to appreciate the blend. She watched the muscles in his throat work as he finally swallowed. He smiled. "Good stuff. Packs a punch but smooth."

Sipping her own drink, she stared unseeing at the silvery waters. Conflicting thoughts warred in her head – an increasing interest in, and attraction to, the man beside her versus the memories of what he'd told her about the atrocities going on elsewhere, the death of her friend Kane…Rubbing her forehead, she felt a headache coming on.

A pair of night hunting birds called from the woods behind them. In the parking area on the other side of the celebration hall, a groundcar alarm blared then abruptly cut off.

Andi stood up, putting her glass down on the bench before resting her hand on Deverane's arm. "I think we'd better go. Everything you've told me today is making me nervous, although I still find it hard to believe there's danger to Lord Tonkiln's family, or any of the others out here."

"Maybe the Naranti mediators can reduce the tension levels. I understand it's worked before," he said. "Not my problem, however. Command doesn't want any Sectors citizens caught in a Zulairian concern."

She turned her head away from him. Even with their own citizens getting killed in the crossfire, the Sectors would take a hands-off stance, leaving the people of Zulaire to solve the problems. The offworld government didn't care if it meant years of local bloodshed. "Sectors doesn't want to have to get involved, you mean."

"Right." Crisply, Deverane nodded. "Zulaire provides some essential minerals, from the Abuzan Range, but we've secured and supplied the mine to withstand a two-year siege."

Andi took a last look at the lake, trying to imprint the quiet scene on her memory. "What did Lady Tonkiln say when you decided to spend the night?"

"A lot of gracious nonsense. The old harridan didn't mean a word of it. She left it to Iraku to decide where to quarter us. He must dislike outworlders even more than she does, because he stuck us in the big transport barn with our vehicles." He smiled, but his clenched jaw betrayed his true feelings on the subject.

"You're not serious?" Andi did a double take. "You're an *officer*. Weren't you provided a room in the main house?"

"Iraku offered a room to me. But I'll be damned if I'm going to sleep in a posh mansion while my men bunk in a garage." Tossing the remainder of his drink into the shrubbery, Deverane set the heavy, engraved glass on the bench.

She shivered, rubbing her arms, trying to soothe away the goosebumps brought on by the night breeze.

Giving her a concerned look, he stood up. "I'm an idiot. I should have thought to ask if you had a wrap before we came out here."

"It's all right. I'll be fine. I'm upset about my friends and concerned about everything you just told me."

"The situation report was a lot to take in, I know." Deverane moved closer to her, heat radiating from his body. Slowly he reached out with one hand to circle her wrist, tugging her gently closer, until she was right up against him. "Better?"

Andi nodded, placing her hands on his chest, enjoying the feeling of their bodies together, the implicit intimacy holding promise for what might happen later.

The lights along the path and beside the benches flickered and went out, plunging them into darkness.

Glancing around, Deverane frowned in the moonlight. He released her, keeping one hand around her wrist and putting the other on the butt of his blaster. "Is that normal?"

"The generators have been known to be troublesome in the summer. Probably nothing." The moment was gone, the spell she'd been under broken. *Am I disappointed? Relieved?* Things had been moving way too fast between them for people who had just met. "Fortunately, we still have enough moonlight to see the path." Andi took a step toward the clubhouse.

He tightened his grip on her wrist, forcing her to stop. "Wait."

Yelling broke out in the large building on the rise behind them. Glaring, sporadic flashes burst from the general direction of the parking area and from the main wing of the celebration hall itself. Making the forest brighter than day, a sizable explosion obliterated the light of the two moons for a moment. Clapping her hands to her ears at the concussion, Andi ducked, crowding into the reassuringly hard-muscled captain.

In one fluid motion, he had his blaster in hand. Still keeping his grasp on her wrist, he drew Andi farther away from the path, taking cover behind a wide, multiple-trunked tree. Placing himself between her and the building, he leaned out, reconnoitering the pathway. The screams and shouts were increasing in intensity and number.

Andi huddled against the tree, rough bark scraping her arm. *He was right, this sounds like the beginning of war.* Trembling, she had to lock her jaw to keep her teeth from chattering as one piercing shriek rose above the rest of the general uproar.

"I'm afraid we missed our deadline for a clean escape." His voice was harsh, the words angry. "Come on." Pulling Andi to her feet, he laced his fingers in hers and drew her from the safety of the tree, setting a course around the edge of the lake to the east. Andi stumbled in her high-heeled dancing shoes over rocks and branches.

"*Wait.*" Digging her heels into a softer patch of ground, she forced him to stop, yanking her hand free. "Shouldn't we go back, try to help?"

"We're overwhelmingly outnumbered." He frowned at her, nostrils flared as if he could scent the enemy forces. His stare was unblinking.

Eyeing the blaster in his hand, Andi raised her eyebrows.

Deverane sighed. "Even with a blaster. This was a well-planned, well-timed attack. You and I can't afford to be caught in the middle of it. We've got to get back to the Tonkiln house and my men."

Across the lake, one of the Obati mansions on the far shore exploded into flames. Andi gasped. "The attack is spreading."

"This is worse than I thought." Grabbing her shoulder, he turned her toward the lake and gave her a gentle push. "Are there any boats? We need to keep this head start. No time to creep around the edge of the lake."

"The boats were drawn up on shore late this afternoon for the end of the season. This way." She led him to the lakeshore, where the going was easier. Kicking off her stiletto heels as soon as the ground changed to beach sand, Andi ran faster than she'd ever managed in her life.

Not even breathing hard, the captain kept pace. Swiveling his head, he evaluated the situation. "I don't like us being so exposed in the open."

"There are the boats." Andi pointed to the line of gaily painted pleasure craft resting in the sand about ten yards ahead. Holstering his blaster, Deverane sprinted, grabbing the first boat in the line. He dragged the small craft across the sand into the lapping water. By the time she skidded to a halt, his hand was stretched out to her as he gestured impatiently. "I'll boost you in. *Come on.*"

Holding her shoes above her head, she waded out, gasping a little at the coldness of the water. With one hand he helped her shimmy up and over into the boat, where she landed with a thud. Scrambling on hands and knees to the stern, she sat at the control panel, trying to remember the simple instructions she'd received earlier in the week. As Deverane fell over the side, she had the motor revving to the red line. Leaving a broad wake gleaming in the moonlight, the little pleasure craft shot straight across the lake.

He crouched low on the bench amidships and ran his hand over his hair. She hoped he was planning their next move. Blaster in his hand again, he reconnoitered the shore with deep suspicion. "Any obstacles in this water?"

Chilled in her half-drenched party clothes, she shook her head, wishing her expensive dress could shed water the way his uniform was engineered to do. "Not this direction. Can you contact your squad?"

"I'm trying right now." He showed her the tiny comlink cradled in his other hand. "No answer, which could mean anything or nothing, but probably isn't good."

"Do you think the Tonkiln house has been attacked?" Andi worried about heading into an even worse situation than the one they'd left behind.

Not looking at her, he just shook his head. "Let's deal with that when we come to it. Don't steer straight to the dock—we'd be too obvious, sitting ducks. We need to land and work our way to the house without attracting attention."

Angling the boat off to the east, Andi set a course to avoid the dock as ordered. "I never considered an attack on the family's home. Lords of Space, what about the kids? Sadu and his two little visiting cousins—their Shenti nurse went home to her village last night—there's only old Iraku and a few of the housemen there to protect them." Worry about the younger family members gnawed a pit in Andi's gut. "Lady Tonkiln must be terrified."

"I have to extract the Sectors citizens, not risk my men trying to rescue anyone else against overwhelming odds. The Tonkilns aren't my concern, understand?" His voice was flat, the words dismissive.

Andi jerked her head around to stare at him. "We can't ignore the danger to them."

"Lady, I have orders." Shaking his head, he grabbed the wheel and yanked it, sending the boat veering away from its route to shore. "Cut the engine and get down. Someone's moving by the dock."

Cold flooded her body at the thought of enemies watching them. With fumbling fingers, she flipped the switch. Drifting through the dark waters, their craft floated in silence, slowing as the momentum died away. Andi crouched in the bottom of the boat, Deverane's body warm and reassuring beside her.

"Can you swim?" He tucked his blaster and the small com unit away, sealing a pocket with a quick motion.

"I can swim." She stared at him, trying to read his expression in the moonlight. "Can you?"

"Now's as good a time as any to learn," he said with a tight grin. "I've been told it's like zero-grav exercise. Any major predators in this lake?"

"Well, there are two varieties of snake and a large fishlike thing with razored jaws, but none of them are active at night. Supposedly." Andi peered over the side of the boat. The opaque surface of the lake was impenetrable in the dark. Only too well aware of what could be lurking there, Andi remembered hooking one of the snakes on her fishing line. The Shenti guide had had a terrible time killing the reptile without toppling them all into the lake, where its nine-foot-long mate had been waiting, swimming easy circles around the small boat. *Not a reassuring memory right now.*

"Let's go." Reaching past her, Deverane rocked the boat with a sudden violent motion. Taken completely unaware as the craft tipped over, Andi flew through the air for a moment, instinctively arcing her body into a flat dive into the chilly water. Surfacing, she searched for her companion. The captain was already swimming at a fair pace toward the shore, using a strange overhand stroke. His bobbing head was much less visible in the light of the moons than the boat had been. He glanced back once to make sure she was all right.

She treaded water for a minute, hampered by the clinging silk folds of her gown. Unfastening the tabs, she let the garment fall away in the water. *No time to waste bemoaning my expensive dress.* Left in the sleek one-piece undersuit, freed from the extra layers, Andi could swim efficiently, catching up to the captain. His unusual stroke was forceful, propelling him through the water as if he was fighting an opponent. She followed him, reaching the shallows, then wading to a spot on shore where an immense tree had fallen into the lake, providing some cover. A steep hill lay between them and the looming Tonkiln mansion. Raising her head above the rotting tree trunk, she risked a glance.

The huge house was dark and silent, every light off. *Probably a very bad sign. There should be lights on in half the house right now. Especially the kitchen and the servants' wing.* "Where are your men?"

"With our vehicles in the garage." He rolled over onto his back, reaching again for the com unit. Glancing at her, he did a pronounced double take, swallowing hard. "Got rid of the finery, eh? Much better for crawling around and avoiding enemy attention."

The wet garment was plastered on her body, outlining every curve for him. Andi was glad the moonlight wasn't any brighter. Now was *not* the time for physical distractions. Halfway serious, she said, "Well, I thought dark blue was more suited for combat situations. What are we going to do next?"

A reverberating explosion shook the hillside as flames shot from the roof of the mansion, followed by a smaller eruption where the garage stood. *Lords of Space, are rebels attacking here as well?* Flinching at the sudden high-pitched whine of Sectors blasters somewhere in the darkness, Andi hugged the ground.

From her prone position she stared at the mansion, trying to figure out exactly where the fire was blazing. Flames were licking at the walls in a number of rooms, including the far end of the third floor. Adrenaline coursed through her. "The fire's on the top floor where the nursery is. I can't leave until I've made sure the children are safe, Captain." She held up a hand as he drew a breath. "I know, you've mentioned your orders enough times, but we're talking *children*. I'll never forgive myself if I don't at least check the nursery." Before he had a chance to stop her, Andi was on her feet and running. *He'll have to follow me since his precious orders are to protect me, so if I can just get to the house, I'll have him—and his blaster—for backup.*

Sure enough, she heard Deverane give chase, but she had the advantage of a head start and familiarity with the grounds. She sprinted to the side door, entering the house through the kitchen. One dim light glowed from an emergency panel in the ceiling. A half-eaten meal sat on the table. The chairs were toppled, one broken as if it had been used as a weapon in a violent struggle. A bloody knife lay on the floor.

Andi barely glanced at the knife. *No time to be ill, just RUN.*

Carefully, she stepped barefoot through the mess to the emergency supply cabinet next to the pantry, where she grabbed a hand lamp. Pointing the cone of light ahead of her, she jogged into the service corridor to the main part of the house. Fear of what she might find made her lightheaded, and she took a few careful breaths to calm her nerves. *I've got to make sure the kids aren't trapped upstairs in their cribs. With the nurse gone, there may not be anyone else but me to double-check.*

Tripping, Andi fell headlong. The body she'd stumbled over cushioned her fall for the most part, although her right elbow smashed into the floor. Sitting up, she rubbed her elbow, looking for the hand lamp she'd dropped. Instead, she saw the bloody face of the elderly cook, starkly outlined by the beam of light. The elderly woman's sightless eyes were wide open in death. Stifling a scream, Andi scrabbled away from the corpse of the cook, who'd been stabbed multiple times.

When she felt her back against the wall, Andi reached for the lamp, then used the wall to lever herself to her feet. After sidling past the corpse, she ran down the hall and opened the door to the main entryway. Curling like a living thing, a thin layer of smoke drifted across the foyer, about ten inches off the floor. The flicker of reflected flames in the library tinted the area in orange light.

A piercing shriek echoed from the second floor. Increasingly terrified but determined to help whoever was in trouble, Andi launched into a dead run across the slick stone floor, taking the wide, curving, carpeted stairs at high speed. Past the first curve she stopped abruptly, right before she would have stepped on another corpse. It was the gardener's helper, sprawled across three risers. Hugging the wall, Andi tiptoed carefully past his outflung hand.

She burst onto the second level of the house and stopped short at the sight of Lady Tonkiln struggling with a burly man. Screaming obscenities in a harsh voice, the lady was clawing her attacker's face and chest. Unfazed by her blows, he wrapped his hands around her neck, squeezing as he cursed her.

Retreating two steps, Andi set her lamp down, grabbed a heavy bronze urabu statue in a wall niche and ran to attack the assassin. She stabbed the man in the back with all her strength, driving the bronze horns of the statue deep into his shoulder muscles. Adrenaline gave the blow considerable force. He dropped Lady Tonkiln, who fell against the wall and slid to the floor, wheezing. A broad smear of blood coated the elaborate tapestry where she hit it.

The man swept his beefy arm back, hitting Andi in the chest, knocking the wind out of her and sending her staggering. The urabu statue fell, bouncing over the edge of the stairs. She grabbed at the wrought iron railing to keep herself from tumbling headlong to the first floor. The would-be killer strode to where Andi lay on the top stair, stunned from her fall. Fisting his hand in her hair, he yanked her to her feet, scattering hair pins as her elaborate chignon loosened. Andi fought to get away, but her arm was numb where he'd struck her. Black spots danced in her vision.

Deverane launched himself up the last few stairs and tackled them both, breaking Andi free of the attacker's hold. A clump of her hair tore from her head in the process. The pain radiated through her body, paralyzing her for a minute. Pressing the muzzle of his blaster into the other man's stomach, the captain fired. The stench of burned flesh filled the hallway as Deverane rolled away and came to his feet, looking to Andi.

Tears of pain in her eyes, she crawled to Lady Tonkiln to check how badly the Obati matriarch was wounded.

"Leave me. Save Sadu, save my baby," the lady moaned, her words slurring.

Swallowing hard, Andi averted her eyes from the wreckage of Lady Tonkiln's severely beaten face. She put an arm under the older woman's shoulders and tried to get her to sit up. "We'll go get him together."

"No time, I—I'm dying. You must save him." Lady Tonkiln grabbed Andi by the shoulder in a viselike grip, shaking her in a final surge of strength before falling against the wall in a violent convulsion. Some of the dark blood staining the woman's garments spread onto Andi's jumpsuit.

"Are *you* hurt?" Deverane pulled her to her feet, looking at the bloodstains. Andi shook her head, numb, unable to say anything. She kept staring at Lady Tonkiln's body. *I can't believe she's dead. I can't believe any of this—it has to be a nightmare.*

Coughing from the increasing smokiness of the air, he gave her a little shake, tried to get her to meet his eyes. "Come on, Andi. We have to get out of here."

He was tugging her toward the stairs leading down.

"No." She wrenched away from him. "We can't leave. You heard her—I have to get the children—Sadu and his cousins, in the nursery."

A woman's voice cried out in agony from the level above. Deverane didn't say another word but jerked Andi behind him and started climbing the stairs two at a time, before dropping to his knees to crawl the last few. She matched his pace on the top risers, chest tight and hot as she moved, choking on the smoke infiltrating this level from the fires. By staying a few inches above the carpet, she could still find some breathable air. The corridor ahead was lit by roaring flames in several of the rooms.

A man emerged from one of the side doors.

Iraku.

Andi rose to her feet despite the choking smoke. "I never thought I'd be so glad to see you," she said. "Come with us to get Sadu from the nursery." She'd taken an automatic step toward the chief of household before she noticed the jagged, bloody knife in his hand. Her gaze traveled to his face, which was contorted in rage, eyes wild. Hands up in self defense, Andi skidded to a halt, averting her eyes, only to see the bodies of several women lying just inside the room Iraku had come from. Paralyzed by horror, crumpling to her knees, Andi screamed as the Naranti took a step in her direction.

Deverane fired his blaster from behind her, but the angle was off. Iraku dodged the beam, running across the hall into another chamber, slamming the heavy door. Andi heard the locking mechanism slid into place. She knew there was a balcony, with a tree growing right next to it under that room's window. *If you try to escape that way, you son of a bitch, I hope you break your neck.* Hands pressed against her eyelids, she tried to blot out the mental picture of the corpses of the women he'd obviously just murdered. Head spinning, she thought she was going to pass out under the nonstop onslaught of horror.

Deverane squatted beside her, jaw clenched, his face expressionless. "Andi, we have to keep moving." He pulled her to her feet. "Which way to the nursery?"

Andi braced herself with one hand on the wall for a heartbeat, before running down the hall, counting off the doors to herself as she proceeded in the increasing smoke and heat. The nursery door swung open under her touch. Coughing, covering her mouth and nose against the thick smoke, she advanced into the center of the room, the captain on her heels.

"Stay here for a second." Deverane stopped her with a hand on her shoulder, before striding over to the nearest crib, his face set like stone. Andi held her breath as she watched Deverane peer into the small bed. Turning, he shook his head. "Empty." He glanced at the other beds with the same result. "Time to go."

"Thank the Lords of Space." Wiping tears from her cheeks, she said, "Maybe their parents have been and gone already. Maybe they took Sadu to safety with their own kids."

A faint whimpering sound caught her attention. She stepped further into the room. "Wait, I heard something, I know I did." Andi ran to the storage area at the back of the room, finding the door ajar. Breathing a tiny prayer, she knelt and slid the mirrored panel open, shoving aside the hanging clothes, tossing large plush toys out into the room to crawl inside. Homing in on the whimpering, she felt around on the floor in front of her as she went deeper into the spacious closet, until she touched a toddler's chubby legs. Locking her grip on the boy's ankles even as he tried to kick her, she dragged him free of his hiding place. "Sadu, it's okay. It's Andi, I've got you." Taking a quick look, she confirmed that he was the only child in the small space. No sign of his cousins. Clumsily, off balance, she reemerged into the room with the toddler, his arms locked around her neck.

Repressing an *I told you so*, Andi gave Deverane a triumphant look. "It's Sadu, Lord Tonkiln's youngest son."

"I don't care who he is, we've got to get out of here *now*." The captain's whole body was tensed for action, his face stern, jaw set and eyes narrowed. "Follow me and stay close."

He led her back into the hall, where flames now fully engulfed the ceiling. Doing her best to shield the toddler in her arms, pushing his face against her shoulder, Andi made it to the top of the stairs and sprinted down, staying close to Deverane. Sadu clung to her for dear life. In the foyer, Deverane held up a clenched fist and signaled her to wait while he checked the side corridor. She had to force herself to stay where he'd left her, listening to the great house creak and groan as the fire attacked its supporting timbers. She was coughing nonstop by the time the captain returned, carrying a stack of dripping towels.

His eyes streamed from the smoke, and there was a scorch mark across one cheek. "All clear this way. I think maybe the bastards have moved on to the next set of victims. Here, let me carry the boy."

But Sadu screamed, clutching at Andi's neck and hair and refusing to go to an unknown person. She warded Deverane off with her hand. "*Never mind*, I can carry him. Let's get out of here."

"Wait, I've got some wet towels, let me drape them over you and the boy. Smoke's pretty heavy and this'll help you both breathe while we escape. I don't need you to pass out from smoke inhalation." As he was talking, he placed one of the towels over her head and Andi felt some immediate relief from the cool, wet cloth against her lower face. She did her best to cover Sadu's mouth and nose as the toddler wheezed and coughed.

"Stay as low as you can and keep close," Deverane said before he rewrapped the towel draped on his own head and moved off.

She kept a hand on Deverane's back as he worked his way past the cook's body and through the kitchen, out into the cool night air. He didn't give her a chance to get her breath, but led her all the way into the landscaped garden, settling her and Sadu behind a low, ornamental shrub.

"Stay here." He pointed at her for emphasis. "Don't make a sound, and don't show yourself to anyone but me. Got it?"

"Don't worry. Seeing Iraku…" She swallowed rising nausea and shook her head. "I will not be trusting any Zulairians tonight, of any Clan."

Deverane held up his blaster. "Can you fire one of these?"

"Yes, I'm trained on the civilian model." Her voice sounded hoarse to her own ears, her throat sore from the smoke. "Won't you need it?"

"I have other weapons." He handed her the blaster. "Keep the kid quiet, whatever you have to do."

He watched her check the charge level before crouching low and moving away into the night. Andi supposed he was going to look for his men or transport, or both. Settling into a more comfortable position against the main stem of the shrub, she let Sadu curl up in her lap, his thumb hooked in his mouth. He didn't make a sound, save for some great silent sobs. Murmuring a soothing lullaby, Andi rocked back and forth, trying to give him some comfort. *I wish someone could do the same for me right now.*

Her low-cut garment had dried in the heat from the fire, but the thin fabric offered little protection against the night wind coming from the west. Shivering as the breeze cut across her body, Andi curled more closely around Sadu. The ongoing whine of shots filled the night, punctuated by intermittent screaming. She tried not to think about what must be going on in each of the mansions around the lake—nor about what horrors had all too likely happened in the ceremonial house after she and Deverane escaped.

Sadu snored like a baby pig, drooling on her lap, poor little guy. She shifted him to a more comfortable position, still keeping her grip firm on the blaster. *This weapon's not leaving my hand.*

As a low cry sounded from behind her, Andi stiffened, a fresh spurt of adrenaline jolting through her veins.

CHAPTER THREE

Andi whipped her head around in an attempt to locate the source of the moaning. The mewling groan came again, hoarse and low, raising goose bumps along her arms.

Captain Deverane would take violent exception to what I'm about to do. Managing to get Sadu onto her shoulder without waking him and, clutching the blaster, Andi left her hiding place to investigate. Working her way toward the pitiful sound, she stayed within the shadows of the ornamental hedges. The nightmarish keening came from the small gazebo at the far end of the garden. *Well, the rebels aren't likely to waste the night hanging around to ambush any latecomers…*

I hope.

She took a deep breath then another. Ready for instant retreat if necessary, Andi stepped into the open space at the gazebo's entrance, where the two moons provided some light. A body lay sprawled there, facedown, but she knew from the signet ring on his hand that it was Lysanda's fiancé. The girl was lying crumpled a few feet away, bronze satin dress in stained shreds. Curled in a fetal position on the stone floor, she was crying in heartrending sobs.

Andi set Sadu on a cushioned chaise to the left of the entrance, careful not to wake him. Kneeling, she turned Lysanda over, choking back a curse at the cuts and bruises. Grabbing a filmy scarf that lay across the railing of the gazebo, Andi ran to soak it in water from the ornate fountain so she could bathe the woman's injuries. She started to daub at the princess's bloodstained arms when Lysanda sat upright, drawing in a deep breath, preparing to scream. With one hand Andi covered her mouth while reaching for the blaster with the other.

The intruder stepped forward, and the moonlight gleamed on his captain's bars.

Lowering the weapon, Andi sank back on her heels with a sigh of relief. "Oh, it's you—thank the Lords."

"I told you to stay put, damn it, not go off on search-and-rescue ops. Where's the little boy?" Radiating tension and anger, Deverane spoke barely above a whisper. Three Sectors soldiers and the tall Shenti warrior followed him. Assessing the cringing Lysanda in one rapid glance, the captain gave an order. "Wilson, diagnostic, on the double. Will the girl live or do we leave her?"

After the events of the night, Andi hadn't thought anything could still astonish or appall her. Deverane's order did both. "*Leave her?* You can't be serious. What if the raiders come back?"

"We have to move fast, and we have to leave the area now. No time for a dying woman." The captain's face was emotionless. He barely glanced at Andi before he went back to evaluating the surroundings for any threats.

"But this is Tonkiln's daughter." Andi smoothed Lysanda's hair away from her face so Deverane could see for himself.

"I don't care if she's the Outlier Empress, we're in a bad situation. I can't carry dying locals out of here with me." He scowled at Andi, eyebrows drawn together, eyes hooded. "Will you please try to remember the Sectors doesn't want to get involved? My orders are specific. We're here for you, not for them." He turned on his heel, cradling his weapon. "Wilson, damn it, double-time here!"

Murmuring reassurance into Lysanda's ear, Andi clutched the girl's trembling hand as the sergeant ran a quick med diagnostic. Weeping, Lysanda hid her face on Andi's shoulder. When Wilson didn't immediately report to the captain, Andi felt hopeful. Plucking a medinject from his supplies, the sergeant gave the injured woman a dose of something. *That's got to be a good sign. He wouldn't waste his supplies if she was dying. Would he?*

Glancing around, she noted how the Shenti warrior and the other two men had taken up positions around the perimeter of the gazebo. Hyper alert, weapons at the ready, the soldiers were scanning for any sign of renewed enemy presence. Deverane walked back, waiting for the sergeant's report.

"No life-threatening injuries, sir. She's in shock," Wilson said as he closed his medkit.

"Hardly surprising." Deverane tapped the fingers of his free hand on the blaster he'd apparently acquired somewhere during his reconnaisance. His eyes flicked from the sergeant to Lysanda and then back to scanning the perimeter. "Tell me something I don't know from looking at her."

"I've given her a tranquilizer and some antibiotics." Sergeant Wilson stood, shifting his pack onto his back again. Taking a closer look at him, Andi realized he was the same man she'd met on the lawn earlier in the day, his cheerful, easy going demeanor a victim of the night's tragedies. He was in combat mode now, grim faced and edgy like the others.

Taking another look at the traumatized woman, the captain clenched his jaw. "Can she walk?"

Wilson shook his head. "Not right now. I think I can carry her, sir."

Deverane nodded curt permission. "All right. We take her. She's going to be *your* responsibility," he said to Andi. "Like the kid."

Taking a deep breath, she relaxed, relief flooding through her like a cool wave. The task of minding the two Tonkilns would be a challenge, but she'd do whatever it took to get these survivors to safety. She wanted to achieve something good to balance the overwhelming horror of the massacre. "Fine."

"Give Miss Markriss a pack, Latvik." The captain summoned the nearest soldier, who wore one pack on his back and carried another looped over his free arm.

The man slung his weapon over one shoulder, holding out the spare pack to Andi. The bag was heavy, dragging her hands down before she realized how much it weighed. She looked at the sergeant. "What do you have me carrying? Ore from the mines?"

"Supplies, ma'am. Field rations, water, blaster charges, things like that. No rocks, I promise." Wilson gave her a fleeting, tired grin.

Deverane reclaimed his blaster from her, trading her an extra from one of the packs. He also handed her a pair of sandals. "Figured you'd need something for those bare feet. Took these off one of those poor bastards in the house." He shoved them at her when Andi hesitated. "There's a shirt in the pack. Put it on. Can't have you freezing."

"And Lysanda? Her dress is half torn off." Andi struggled into the oversized camouflage shirt she found in the backpack. Trying not to speculate who had owned the sandals before tonight, she tugged the simple leather shoes on. *These are going to chafe my feet, but anything's better than going barefoot in the jungle.*

The captain gestured to the other soldier, summoning him. "Rogers, give An—Miss Markriss your extra shirt."

Shucking his pack, Rogers rummaged through it then offered a second shirt to Andi. Working as fast as she could, she got the garment on Lysanda, who offered no help but also no resistance. *This is like dressing an oversize doll.* "Ready."

"None too soon." The captain's voice sounded clipped and tight. Edgy. He looked her up and down once, with none of the appreciation he'd shown earlier at the dance, then turned away to issue crisp orders.

Andi felt reassured. *He's all warrior now, which is what we need to get us safely out of here.*

"All right, Latvik, take point." Deverane pointed at the Shenti warrior. "Abukawal, watch our backs. Let's move it, people, before those terrorists get organized and sweep for survivors."

He helped Andi get the drugged Lysanda to her feet so Wilson could hoist her over his shoulders. Next, Andi retrieved Sadu, still napping on the cushions where she'd left him. As the captain hurried them out of the gazebo and through the length of the garden, Andi breathed a heartfelt sigh of relief. Crossing the boundary into the jungle proper with no sign of roving renegades was even more reassuring.

Deverane set a fast pace. Andi walked beside the sergeant, taking three steps for every one of his long-legged strides, despite his double burden of pack and injured woman. Annoyed by the way the straps of her pack dug into her shoulders with every step, Andi made futile adjustments. "What's your secret, Wilson? How come you aren't winded yet?"

"Special Forces training, ma'am," he said. "Best conditioning in the Sectors. I've carried wounded men three times the size of this little lady."

"Where are we going?" Andi asked. As Deverane came up behind her, she startled.

"We're going south for now," he said, squeezing her shoulder for reassurance. "How are we doing back here?"

"Fine, sir, no problem." Wilson wasn't even breathing hard.

"Andi?" The captain eyed her.

"Yeah, we're just great." She thanked the Lords of Space for the compulsory grav training her company insisted agents keep up. She might not have the conditioning of the soldiers, but she could hold her own for now. "So you're telling me we have no destination in mind?"

Falling into step with her, Deverane pulled branches out of her path as she worked her way through a stand of large, fernlike bushes. "Too much likelihood of running into the rebels again if we try for the main transportway. I need another plan, but south is the right direction, no matter what."

"What happened to the APC? Why can't we just escape in it?" Andi tripped over a vine. His hand shot out to steady her.

"Remember the big explosion in the transport garage? That was when the APC slagged. It was sabotaged." Even in the moonlight, Andi could see the captain's grim expression.

"Not many ways to sabotage an APC." Sergeant Wilson shifted Lysanda on his shoulders. "Terrorists on backwater planets normally wouldn't even know how to try."

"Yeah. Something doesn't add up here." Deverane was frowning again, head tilted. Rubbing his forehead with one hand, he sighed. "We don't have the luxury of time right now to figure it out."

Their ragged column emerged into a clear space in the forest.

"I'm going to check with Latvik." Deverane broke into a quick trot and pulled ahead of Andi and the sergeant.

She watched him go. *Which reminds me, where is everyone else?* "Sergeant, can I ask you a question? Something's been bothering me."

"Yes, ma'am?" Wilson's voice was neutral.

Not sure she wanted the answer, Andi hesitated a second. "Where are the other men? Are they meeting us somewhere?"

The sergeant spared a second to glance sideways at Andi. His eyes were narrowed, his lips tight. "They're dead. Poisoned, I think. The Tonkilns' snooty butler…"

"Iraku." Uttering that murderer's name filled her with revulsion and disbelief. *Why did he turn on the Tonkilns? He's Naranti, sworn to neutrality and service!* She blotted out the chaotic thoughts running through her head to listen to Wilson's answer.

"Well, he came around at dinnertime, all apologetic for the inconvenience we were suffering, bunking in a damn garage. As if it hadn't been his idea in the first place. He offered to have the maids bring food so at least we wouldn't have to eat field rations." Wilson snorted. "I didn't partake. Fancy stuff doesn't agree with this boy's stomach, not on any world, even my own." He rubbed his flat abdomen, shaking his head, apparently remembering some unpleasant past experiences. Pushing past a stubborn bush, turning his body to shield Lysanda from the prickly branches as he walked, he went on with the story. Gesturing at the two soldiers trudging ahead of them, he said, "Rogers and Latvik were asleep on the second floor, catchin' up on rack time. They pulled the all-night-drive duty after we were diverted here to find you."

Wilson marched in silence for a few yards. "Abukawal was off hunting his own dinner. Said he couldn't abide field rations *or* Obati food. My other three men took a break from working on the APC engine to eat. When I came back from squaring away some gear, I found them dead. Not a good way to go."

Unsure what to say, Andi made herself keep walking. *This whole night has been one long horror story.*

Doggedly, Wilson continued to fulfill her request for information. "Next thing I know, we're under attack. I go to the stairs to yell for Latvik and Rogers, which saves my life, because I'd been standing right next to the APC. If it had blown one minute sooner, I wouldn't be here, carryin' your little lady friend to safety."

What small things make the difference between living and dying. Andi shivered. *I was so lucky not to die myself tonight.* "Then what?"

"Well, the three of us were trapped on the second floor of the garage, which was burning down around our ears, and the terrorists were waiting for us to pop out. We got ourselves and as much gear as we could onto the roof, and we were having some luck picking off attackers stupid enough to show themselves."

"I thought I heard blaster fire." Andi adjusted Sadu more comfortably on her hip and kept walking.

"Yes, ma'am, we gave a good account of ourselves." He bared his teeth in a wolfish smile. Shifting Lysanda a bit on his shoulders, he stood up straighter as he strode forward. "It discouraged the bastards, and they decided to go somewhere else to have their fun. Probably figured we'd die in the burnin' building. They left two men on guard to make sure. Abukawal snuck up behind and slit their throats. Handy guy, Abukawal."

"What is a western Shenti doing traveling with Sectors soldiers? Is he a recruit or something?" *How can they be so sure they can trust him? Although if he saved their lives, I guess that's a point in his favor.* The world as she knew it was upside down if the Neutral Naranti were murdering Overlord Obati now, while the Shenti Seconds were stepping in to be heroes. She glanced ahead, at the broad back of the Zulairian warrior.

"We don't recruit locals, ma'am. He's comin' to the capital with us to testify to the Planetary High Lord about dirty dealings the Naranti in his area was up to. So anyway, ol' Abukawal helped get us off the roof. I was ready to take a recon run around the lake to find you and the captain, when he comes up on us from the direction of the big house." Chuckling, Wilson shot Andi a sideways glance. "Latvik almost shot him. We was pretty keyed up. Sure glad you and the captain made it out of the ambush in one piece."

Andi glanced ahead to where Deverane led the column. *If I'd been inside the dance hall when the terrorists attacked, could I have gotten myself out somehow? Would he have been able to rescue me?* Having seen the captain in action, she figured he would have found a way, even against dismal odds.

As if the mere mention of his name had conjured him out of the air, Deverane circled back to check on them. "Save your breath, Sergeant, Miss Markriss. We need to make serious time here, not discuss current events."

Unable to argue with his logic, Andi trudged onward, obeying orders not to waste energy talking. Between the weight of the toddler and the pack on her back, her shoulder muscles burned and ached. *I'm going to ignore that stitch in my side until it just goes away or I fall down.*

When Deverane called a halt somewhere in the early hours of the morning, she sagged in relief, sitting on the nearest flat rock. Latvik came to hold the sleeping Sadu for her while she slipped the pack off. Then, cradling the toddler in her lap, Andi leaned against a convenient tree, closing her eyes.

The captain shook her awake. "Sorry to disturb you." He kept his warm, reassuring grip on her shoulder as Andi tried to reorient herself. She'd been sound asleep, even past the dreaming stage.

"Are we moving again so soon? I don't know if my arms and legs will take that command right now, Captain." Determined as she was, Andi couldn't keep the exhaustion out of her voice.

"No. Relax, I just need a small favor." He gave her the easy smile, accompanied by a warm glance from his brilliant green eyes. "Wilson and I want you to look at the map. We can't aimlessly march through the jungle for too long. We need a specific destination."

She sat up, disturbing Sadu, who whimpered. Deverane lifted him smoothly out of her lap and deposited him on the pile of packs. Scrunching his small body around like a puppy making a warm nest, Sadu went back to sleep.

Andi ran her hands through her now-tangled black curls. Embarrassed to mention such a mundane concern in desperate times like these, she said, "I need a comb or even a set of clips. Don't suppose you have anything like that in these two-ton packs?"

"Hardly." Quietly, Deverane laughed, putting his hand under her elbow to help her stand up. He rubbed his other hand over his head. "Hair's not an issue for us."

Andi walked with him to where the sergeant waited.

"What kind of destination?" Yawning, Andi rubbed her eyes, stumbling a little. She tried to put herself into a businesslike mind frame, be professional to match Deverane's competence. Not be some helpless person he rescued. "What are the priorities?"

Deverane ticked them off on his fingers. "Transportation. A comlink strong enough to reach the capital. Anywhere around here we might find one?"

Stopping in front of Wilson, Andi pushed her hair off her face again. "Where's this map?"

Holding out a flat disk, the sergeant pushed a button, and the holographic representation of this half of the Zulairian continent spread out in thin air. The sheer speed with which it appeared made her eyes cross. Each major feature glowed in a different color. "We figure we're about here." Wilson pointed with one long, thin finger. The spot was achingly far away from the green dot of the capital, which promised absolute safety.

Even on the map, home is a long way off. Closing her eyes, Andi concentrated on visualizing landmarks.

"Are you all right?" Deverane put his arm around her shoulders and pulled her to lean on him. "Do you need to sit down?"

"No. I'm just so tired, and everything is so damn far away from where we are." Andi opened her eyes. "Let me take it in for a minute, okay?" Despite the overwhelming temptation to stay within the reassuring circle of his embrace, she forced herself to move away, to study the map readout details. She snapped her fingers. "I just remembered, Iraku told us the nurse had gone home to her village last night."

"So?" He invested a lot of hope in that one syllable.

"Don't get your hopes up too far, but the nursemaid was proud of her village because it has a major shrine to Sanenre. Their priest has a comlink to the capital because he has to confer with his church hierarchy about the conditions at the shrine, the number of religious pilgrims, the donations…" Andi paused, trying to remember scraps of half-heard conversation about this nameless village. "There might even be transportation available. The place is remote, but it receives quite a few visitors from the lowlands during the pilgrimage season."

Deverane was so pleased his face lit up, crinkles of good humor around his green eyes. "You could join the Sectors Intel staff any time. Nice job." He nodded at the map. "You see the shrine, Wilson?"

"Local shrines in red. Let me look." With his index finger the sergeant skewered a ruby dot all by itself. "This must be it. Nothin' else this side of the mountains."

The captain squinted, apparently estimating the distance, then looked over at Wilson. "Maybe another four or five hours to march?"

"Good guess, sir. Considering we're carrying a baby and a tranked noncombatant." The sergeant shot Andi a sympathetic glance. She massaged her aching calves and grimaced.

"Best I can do for you, sorry," she said.

"All right then." Deverane stood with his hands on his hips. "Five more minutes, Miss Markriss. Wilson, set the destination on your tracker and take point when we move out. I'll have Rogers take over the duty with the Tonkiln girl." He was gone, striding off before Andi could say anything.

Wilson walked away and returned with her pack, which he dropped by her side. "Better eat something, ma'am." The advice was given in a kind but firm tone. "Field rations in your pack will give you an energy boost. And be sure you wash it down with water from the canteen."

Automatically, she reached out to fumble with the flap of the pack, her dry throat aching at the thought of water. "Thank you."

Putting his hand on top of hers firmly, Wilson stopped her as she lifted the water bottle. "Now you promise to eat a ration bar with that?"

Surprised, she nodded. Reaching into the bag he brought out one of the bars, unwrapped it for her and handed it over with a flourish. She laughed and took a big bite, chewing ostentatiously and swallowing hard. "I can see why Abukawal preferred to go hunt his own dinner. Now I need that water, okay?" Grinning, the sergeant walked away as Andi opened the canteen. The cold water was wonderful going down her parched, raw throat.

All too soon, the column was moving again. Rogers, now carrying Lysanda, didn't offer to make conversation, so Andi put one foot in front of the other as required and allowed herself not to think.

***

Deverane called for two more breaks during the night, each longer than the previous one. Andi was walking slower and slower, her companions adjusting their pace to hers. By the second halt, Lysanda was coming out of her tranquilized state.

"No, ma'am, I ain't giving her anything else right now. Best we let her wake up and walk a bit," was Wilson's reply when Andi asked.

"Do we dare let the drugs wear off? What if she gets hysterical on us?" Andi lost her grip on Sadu's hand. Running to his big sister, the toddler begged to be picked up. Lysanda greeted the baby with a cry of delight.

"She's still in shock to a large extent, ma'am." Wilson and Andi watched the Obati girl tickling her younger brother and playing peek-a-boo as the baby shrieked with laughter. "It's a mercy."

"How long will she be in shock, do you think?" Andi looked away from the huge bruises on Lysanda's face and arms, revealed by the morning light.

Wilson rolled his shoulders. "There's no tellin'. I'm sorry. I'd say let's hope she stays this way until we can get her back to her father in the capital. And proper doctors. I've had the sergeant's course on field medicine, nothing advanced. This *ain't* my specialty."

"As far as I'm concerned, you're doing a terrific job." She gazed around the small clearing, counting heads. "Where's Rogers?"

"Captain sent him and Latvik ahead to scout the village. We're nearly there. Didn't you know?"

Andi shook her head. "I'm so tired, you could make me walk all the way to the capital, and I'd never realize it until I ran nose-first into the gates."

Moving quietly through the dense jungle, the two soldiers returned in a few minutes. Both men were keyed up, holding their weapons at the ready. *Lords, now what?* Andi's muscles started tensing for fight or flight in anticipation of the next problem.

"It's real ugly, sir," Rogers reported to Deverane. "I think the entire village has been massacred."

Andi's knees buckled, and she staggered a step. *More carnage? This can't be happening, not on Zulaire.*

"You're sure? Any hostiles still around?" Eyebrows drawn together, the captain was intent on the men and their assessment.

"We're sure, sir." Rogers bobbed his head. He swallowed hard, his Adam's apple prominent. Glancing quickly at Latvik, he added, "There's quite a few bodies in the village square. Nothing moving, though, other than some big carrion birds."

"Whoever did this hit and ran maybe two days ago, is my guess, sir," Latvik chimed in. "Judging by the condition of the bodies in the square. We didn't go all the way through the town."

Wilson and Deverane exchanged a look. The sergeant shrugged. "We *do* need supplies."

"Milk or juice for Sadu, if at all possible," Andi said. *Can't let him get dehydrated.*

"Someone set fire to the big shrine and some of the houses, but pretty much everything else is intact," Rogers added to his previous, terse report.

"Oh?" Deverane tilted his head, raised his eyebrows slightly. "Any vehicles?"

"No, sir. Couple of beat-up tractors that had been set on fire. Pretty poor farming village by the look of things."

"And you say the shrine was burned?" The soldier nodded. Deverane cursed. "Damn, we needed the comlink."

"Rebels must have been in a hurry. Maybe they did a half-assed job and left something we can use," Wilson said.

Andi sat cross-legged on the ground, leaning on her pack, waiting in tired silence while Deverane considered options. *I don't care what he decides. I just want to be on the move again, and I trust his judgment. Being in the open makes me nervous.* Skin crawling, the spot between her shoulder blades itched, as if she was in the sights of a sniper's weapon. *I hate this waiting. Gives me too much time to think about what happened back at the Obati summer compound.* She shivered, trying not to focus on the memories, unable to really process the brutal reality of the events that had happened. Part of her still wanted to somehow believe this was all just a horrific dream.

Drawing his blaster, the captain checked the charge level. "All right, we go in. Weapons hot. We make it fast, in and out, take what we need and be on our way. No one wanders off on any unauthorized explorations." He stared straight at Andi.

The men all nodded. Lysanda remained oblivious, sitting on the fallen log she'd selected, playing aimlessly with her hair and crooning a soothing tune to herself. She was braiding and unbraiding the same thick plait in a repetitive motion. The fixed look on her face and the blank stare in her eyes was unnerving. Andi had the sudden urge to catch Lysanda's hands and force the girl to be still and calm. Sitting big-eyed but quiet at his sister's feet, Sadu reached out to bat at the long, swinging braid as if it were a toy.

"Sir, maybe the women should stay here?" Latvik said. "It's about the worst atrocity I've ever seen."

"We can't afford to separate." Deverane met Andi's gaze across the small clearing. "I'm sorry, but you're all going to have to come with us. It's not safe to split up. I don't want to spend time backtracking to collect you."

I don't want to be left behind in the forest anyway. Drawing her blaster, Andi nodded. "I understand. Let's get it over with."

"All right then. We need food, more water—"

"The well is…polluted, sir." Latvik swallowed hard, stared at Andi briefly and withheld the details.

"Check the first few intact houses or the marketplace, see if anyone has water stored in jugs. At least we can fill our canteens." The captain's next remark was said directly to Andi. "Can you look for something else to wear? I can see those sandals I picked out in the dark are too small. We can't have you going down with ruined feet. And your clothing isn't practical. Pretty, but not practical." The lopsided grin came and went, before she registered his attempt to tease her.

She knew her answering smile was weak. "The last thing I feel right now is pretty, but thank you. I'd like to change into something else but I—I hate to help myself to some poor person's possessions like a common thief."

Walking over to her, he extended his hand, palm up. She laid her hand in his, and he carefully tugged her to her feet. He was gazing down into her eyes, and Andi had to raise her head to look directly into his face. His eyes held a gentle, warm expression, and his words were soft, meant for her ears alone. "There's really no choice, if we're going to make it back to the capital and bear witness to their fates. They won't mind. Trust me." Without shifting his focus from her face, he reached down and scooped up her pack.

Sighing, she took the strap of the bag from him, allowing him to adjust the weight on her shoulders. "I'll look for some things for Sadu and Lysanda, too."

"Good." Deverane gave the backpack one final tweak, patted her shoulder and stepped away. Raising his voice, he commanded everyone's attention. "All right, let's get this done. Rogers, Latvik, lead the way. Wilson, take rear guard. Abukawal, can you help with the girl and the baby?"

The Shenti warrior nodded, moving to snatch Sadu off the ground. He tossed the toddler high into the air, catching him easily, much to Sadu's chortling delight. Abukawal repeated the game one more time before handing the boy to Lysanda with a wide smile. Hooking a hand under her elbow, Abukawal assisted Lysanda, now holding her brother, from her mossy perch. Andi held her breath, but in some corner of Lysanda's mind she'd apparently accepted Abukawal as part of their group—and therefore a friend. Her bruised face was relaxed, calm, a small smile on her lips. She held out her delicate hand to Abukawal and the big warrior clasped it carefully, as if he was afraid of crushing her birdlike bones.

When the column moved out, Andi toiled up the ridge behind Rogers and Latvik. As the forest thinned, a stomach-churning combination of smells assaulted her nose—stale smoke with a sickly sweet odor overriding everything else. *I hope I can deal with this. Lords give me strength.* Nausea roiled Andi's gut, and her head swam.

"Close up, close up. Stay together." Deverane's impatient, harsh reminders kept coming.

Reluctantly, she trudged the last few yards into the village, past the fringe of houses and small kitchen garden plots. Domesticated animals grazed in their pasture around a burnt tractor, displaying supreme indifference. Andi stopped for a second as she approached the first pitiful cluster of bodies, then averted her eyes. *I'm never going to get this out of my nightmares. Lady Tonkiln, the cook, these poor people—so much senseless suffering and death. And for what?*

Crossing to the opposite side of the dusty street, Andi covered her mouth and nose with her hand. Resolutely, she stared at the rutted track they were following to the heart of the settlement. *I can't look at anymore pitiful scenes, I just can't. My heart aches for everyone who's suffering and dying in this conflict.*

Andi walked into the large circular gathering place at the center of the village and stopped. A line of eight bodies lay crumpled against the wall of the largest building. Streaks of dried blood painted the clay bricks where the victims had been placed for this execution. The signs of violence and hate were all around her whether she wanted to see them or not.

"Obati." Startled by the guttural hatred in Abukawal's voice, Andi turned to the warrior.

"The Obati did this." Abukawal pointed at the graffiti painted with blood in sprawling loops on the walls. He kept a tight grip on Lysanda's hand. Oblivious, she remained in her own little world, could have been on a stroll through the gardens back at her home for all the emotion she displayed. The Shenti warrior stared around him, a muscle in his cheek twitching.

"Calm down." Deverane was unemotional, his tone contrasting with the anger in Abukawal's voice. "I doubt if the Obati have even had time to think since the massacre at the summer compound. And this appears to have happened at about the same time, judging by the condition of the corpses. Someone is setting up a nice little double play, to make it look as if the Shenti and the Obati in this region have been at each other's throats. *We* know better."

"I saw Naranti Clan killing members of Lord Tonkiln's family last night," Andi said, walking closer to Abukawal, keeping her tone low and steady. "You claim you have proof about the Naranti involvement in all this."

Abukawal nodded, but the veins still throbbed in his thick neck. Face flushed, eyes narrowed, he clenched and unclenched his fist. "We must stop this before the whole planet erupts in flames and death." Thick and clogged with emotion, his voice rumbled.

"We're working on it, but first we have to get ourselves safely back to the capital. That's my focus here." Deverane marched up to Abukawal, forcing the warrior to take a step back. The captain kept his eyes locked on the Shenti's face, even though he had to look up to do it. "My only focus here. Clear?"

There was a long minute before Abukawal lowered his gaze. "Clear." His shoulders slumped.

Deverane watched him for another minute before turning away, apparently satisfied. "All right then, Rogers, you and Abukawal have the guard duty here in the market square. Latvik, Wilson, foraging detail. You know what to look for."

"How much time, sir?" the sergeant asked.

He checked his wrist chrono. "Ten minutes and we meet back here. No exceptions. We have to keep moving."

Andi looked at the carnage around her. *Lords, I can't stand here just thinking about what happened. I need to do something, too. We're wasting time.* "Any suggestions where I should start my search?"

"I'll go with you." Deverane came to her side. "*You* don't go alone."

"I don't need a guard. I know how to use this—" She waved the blaster. "I can take care of myself. Didn't you want to check out the com room at the shrine?"

"Well, yes." He looked her up and down. "You're stubborn at all times, aren't you?"

"Better believe it." She gave him a tiny push. "Go on, I'll be *fine*. We need to know if there's a working comlink." Andi walked away, heading for the nearest house that had no corpses anywhere near it.

"*Watch the time,*" he yelled.

Waving a hand to acknowledge the reminder, she kept walking. She was glad to have a few moments alone, since Abukawal had volunteered again to watch over Lysanda and Sadu. Halfway down the street, she forced herself to select a house to search. Avoiding contact with the blood-smeared threshold, she stepped through the half-open door of the dwelling. As her eyes grew accustomed to the gloom inside the front room, she whispered a small prayer for the dead to the Shenti household spirits and made herself keep walking. *One foot in front of the other, Markriss. Find what we need to help us survive. That's your priority.*

Great gouges had been hacked in the walls of the house. The furniture lay piled in the center of the main room and had been set on fire but had burnt itself out, probably from lack of proper air circulation. Passing through into the kitchen, Andi found all the drawers had been emptied onto the floor, the storage baskets dumped out. Smashed dishes crunched under her feet as she walked cautiously through the debris.

Andi squatted by a likely pile of fruit and vegetables, picking out a few that weren't too spoiled then stowing them in her backpack. From her vantage point on the floor, she spied an unbroken clay jug lying where it had rolled under the table. When she unstoppered it, the sharp scent of cider reached her nose. Taking one cautious swig, Andi found the cider tart on her tongue, although warm. As she pushed the cork back into the mouth of the small jar, she noticed a yellow, webbed carryall hanging from the back of the kitchen door. Grabbing it, Andi tucked her finds in the bag, scooped up half a dozen hard rolls that had evidently come out of the oven right before the attack. Munching one, she retraced her steps to the stairs leading to the sleeping quarters on the second level. Blaster in hand, Andi peeked slowly over the top riser before standing up and hurrying into the bedroom.

Quickly, nervous as a cat, Andi picked through the storage baskets and a cabinet. She found a pair of stout, thick-soled walking sandals close to her size. Sliding them onto her feet, Andi breathed a sigh of relief. *Much better.* Looking further, she selected a long, green skirt fringed at the bottom and a wraparound tunic for herself and a similar outfit in blue for Lysanda. These she bundled into the webbed carryall to change into later. She discovered a basket of baby clothes, unfortunately too small for Sadu, and a stack of clean, folded diapers, which she did take.

As she passed back over the threshold into the open again, Abukawal and Rogers waved at her as she walked to the next more or less intact house, further along the street. Quickly ransacking the kitchen, she found some supplies and filled her borrowed canteen. Leaving the house, Andi felt she couldn't face another destroyed home, so she retraced her steps.

As she hurried through the jumbled marketplace, she saw baskets of fabric spilled in a crumpled heap at a weaver's stall. Thinking about the cold nights facing them on the trail, she bent to pick up a shawl woven through with glints of silver thread. The material flowed through her fingers like silk, and she recognized the wool of the rarest highland grazing animals. Abstract lavender, green and turquoise patterns twined around the silver thread accents. *Probably would have been sold to be someone's bride gift.* Folding the fabric into a small square, Andi stowed it in her pack.

Wilson and Latvik arrived at the gathering spot just as Andi walked up. There was no sign of Deverane and it had been exactly ten minutes. *Where is he? I hope nothing's happened to him.*

Tipping his hat back with his thumb, Sergeant Wilson sighed, assuming command as the next in rank. "I'll go after him, see what's so interestin'. Rogers, Latvik, you pack this lot up and get ready to move."

"I'll keep you company, Sergeant." Andi set down her carryall.

"And what if he's gotten into a tight spot? An ambush? Do you think he'd appreciate me bringing you into danger?" Wilson had a skeptical look on his face, one eyebrow raised.

Andi lifted the blaster. "In that case I'll back you up. But we didn't hear any explosions or weapons fire, did we?"

Reluctant grin on his face, the sergeant shook his head. "No, we surely did not. Okay, then, but stay behind me and follow my lead." He set off on the street leading to the village shrine.

Two minutes' brisk walk, interrupted by a short pause to adjust the straps of her sandals while the sergeant forged ahead, and Andi came around a curve in the road to run right into Wilson's outstretched hand. "Stop, don't look." He made an effort to grab her around the waist and turn her back.

Annoyed, she evaded him then saw the burnt-out hulk of the shrine straight ahead. Charred bodies lay everywhere, in and beside the ruins. She realized the rebels must have herded all the remaining survivors into the shrine and burned it to the ground, shooting any who tried to escape. Doubling over as cramps assaulted her, Andi threw up the hard roll she'd eaten earlier, retching until she had the dry heaves. Wilson supported her, keeping her hair out of the way.

"Andi?" Deverane had come from somewhere to stand beside her. He gently touched her arm. "You all right?"

"No, I'm not *all right*. How can the rebels do such unspeakable things?" She rubbed her abdomen gingerly, sore from the vomiting.

Deverane gathered her against his broad chest, wrapping his arms around her in a comforting embrace. "Go ahead, let it all out. You've been so stoic. I figured the emotional dam would break sooner or later. *Shh*, it's okay." His hands stroked softly through her hair. Andi sighed, lowering her head, listening to the reassuringly steady beat of his heart through the uniform shirt. Shuddering, she concentrated on breathing in and out slowly, regaining her self-control.

"I'll get the others, sir." Wilson draped the two packs over his arm and left.

"We'll be going out by the west," the captain said, over Andi's head. "No need for anyone else to have to look at this today. The three of us are enough."

Deverane tightened his arms around her. Andi was acutely conscious of how the two of them stood pressed together, their bodies meeting. *I want to linger in his arms forever. Let him keep all the bad things of the world at bay. But we need to be going. I'm not staying in this village after dark.* She took a deep breath, the constriction on her chest easing, and moved away. "Hadn't we better get going, join the others?" She risked a look at him. He still watched her with a warm, tender look in his eyes. Andi made her voice stronger, more positive. "I'll be all right."

"Take your time." Deverane reached out and tilted her face with a gentle hand on her chin. His gaze locked onto Andi's for a long moment before his hand fell away, and he looked at the trail beyond her. His impassive military demeanor snapped back into place. "I want to be well away from here by dark."

"My thoughts exactly." She walked down the dusty street behind him, hurrying to catch up with the rest of their party.

Andi found Sadu, cooing and laughing as he rode in a complicated harness on Abukawal's back. The toddler was clearly delighted by this newfound perspective on the world.

Latvik saw Andi eyeing the carrier. Grinning, he pointed his thumb at his own puffed-out chest. "Found it next to one of the overturned carts. I figured it had to be for a baby."

"Makes managing him on the trail much simpler, yes?" Abukawal said with a wide smile, apparently enjoying Sadu's happiness.

Deverane said, "I checked the shrine thoroughly. Whoever did this made a special target of the priest and his comlink. What happened here was a well-planned attack, not random, mob-driven slaughter. Doesn't look like these poor people had any warning and little chance of defending themselves. A few tried—I found the bodies of several Naranti rebels. The Shenti villagers managed to exact a little payment before they died."

Andi took a swig of water from her canteen, swirled it in her mouth then spat it out into the dust. "Good."

Chapter Four

Hours of hiking later, Deverane approved Latvik's choice of camp site. The place was a small, rocky plateau jutting from a sheer cliff with a peaceful lake rippling on two sides. An unlimited field of vision from the summit allowed the soldiers to watch for any raiding parties, or anyone on the trail. "This is the most defensible place I've seen all day," he said.

Wearily, Andi set about feeding Sadu some dinner off to the side of the plateau so the others could construct a camp without a toddler underfoot. Sadu dined with noisy satisfaction on fruit that Andi sliced in small bits, using one of the deadly combat knives. She mixed the raw juice with water from the canteen and got him to drink some. He toyed with a hard roll, enjoying the process of shredding it into crumbs, a few of which made the journey into his mouth. In the middle of tearing at the roll, the toddler fell asleep and the bread fell from his chubby hand.

"He needs a nap, Andi." Lysanda picked up Sadu and stood. "Where is his bed?" Her voice was querulous and thin. "Where's the nursemaid?"

Surprised, Andi shook off a flash of irritation. *She can complain all she wants, if it means she's coming further out of shock.* "You're the nursemaid tonight, Lysanda." Putting her arms around the woman's shoulders, Andi guided her to the bedrolls. Making sure the Tonkiln siblings were safely curled up on a shared sleeping bag well away from the edge, she tucked them both in under a lightweight but warm military-issue blanket. She sat next to them, holding Lysanda's hand, crooning the only Zulairian lullaby she knew over and over, something about fuzzy baby birds, until both were asleep.

Tired but satisfied, she joined the others around the small fire that Deverane had reluc-tantly agreed to let them light as the sun started to set. Andi scrubbed a hand tiredly over her face. "I feel like an instant mother."

"You do it well, ma'am." Wilson handed over a cup of steaming soup.

The metal cup warmed her chilled hands, the return of feeling soothing. Before sipping, she inhaled a deep, appreciative breath of the steamy tomato aroma. "I have younger brothers and sisters. I practiced on them." Andi glanced around, Deverane's absence making her uneasy. She'd come to rely on his calm presence. "Where's the captain?"

"He and Abukawal went to cover our back trail for a mile or so before it gets completely dark." Wilson poured himself another cup of the soup and blew to cool it off. "He's concerned about pursuit."

Pulse skyrocketing at the idea, Andi said, "Does he actually think the insurgents will be determined enough to come all this way after us?"

"Hard to say." Dipping half of a roll into his soup, he took a bite, apparently considering her question. "Depends if they think you and the captain survived the fire, and if they had some agenda about capturin' you."

"Me?" Andi swallowed a generous mouthful of the savory soup, the warmth and spice taking away some of the inner chill.

"We were specially detailed to extract you," Wilson reminded her. "Someone somewhere in the chain of command must think you're a high-value target. Deverane doesn't believe in takin' chances, which is one reason he and I've survived so long in the field. He's always three jumps ahead on what the enemy might do. Drink up, ma'am, and then you should probably turn in, too. Lot of hard ground to cover tomorrow. Captain'll want to start at daybreak."

Andi finished her soup, draining the last drops. She clambered stiffly to her feet. "I want to help with guard duty tonight."

Wilson cracked a slight smile. "You've done a nice job, ma'am, for a civilian. You managed to keep the Tonkilns from causin' us any difficulty on the march. I know the captain appreciates it. I think we can cover the duty for tonight. Better you get some sleep."

"All right then." She couldn't summon the energy to protest. *This is one time I'm going to give in gracefully. I'm almost too exhausted to stand up.* "Good night, Sergeant."

***

Somewhere after midnight, Andi woke from a terrible dream, sitting upright before she was even fully awake, clutching at her throat. She'd been dreaming about Lady Tonkiln's death, reliving the fight with her attacker.

Disoriented, she stared around at the campsite for a full minute until the night air calmed her racing pulse. Lysanda and Sadu lay curled up together. Two soldiers slept across from her on their portion of the plateau. Somebody was snoring. Andi shook out her makeshift pillow, shut her eyes tight, trying to quiet the riotous thoughts in her head by thinking of something else. The scenes of the slaughtered village kept re-running in her mind, interspersed with the memory of witnessing Lady Tonkiln's shocking murder. Finally, she cursed and sat up, pushing her hair off her face. Captain Deverane perched on the edge of their rocky plateau, alternating between gazing off across the lake and out over the jungle on the other side. The twin moons laid down silvery paths on the water's surface. One of the big pulse rifles lay across his lap, and his blaster was close by his side.

His turn for guard duty, apparently. One of the others must be out patrolling in the jungle, watching the trail.

A breeze stirred her hair. *Clearly, I'm not going to get back to sleep for a long time. If at all.* Wrapping herself in the shawl, she picked her way through the other sleepers to join the captain.

Deverane looked up as she walked over, patting the rock beside him in invitation. "Can't sleep?"

Shuddering as she sat, Andi rewrapped her shawl more tightly. "You're surprised I'm having bad dreams? After everything we saw today? What time is it?"

Reaching over, he tucked the fabric more securely around her shoulder. "Still middle of the night, I'm afraid. A long time to go until sunrise chases away the nightmares."

"That's what I was afraid of. I'm drowsy but scared to risk closing my eyes for more than a second. There are a lot of vivid images forming a queue in my subconscious tonight. These kinds of things don't affect soldiers, I suppose." Leaning back, she tilted her head to look at him, eyebrows slightly raised in query.

He continued to gaze across the rippling water and said nothing for a long minute. When he did speak, his voice was low and measured. "I went into the military because the abuse and slaughter of innocent civilians *do* bother me. At least in the service, I can do something to prevent atrocities."

Biting her lip, she looked away across the lake. "I'm sorry. Was I being rude? Maybe I'd better go back to bed and leave you alone."

"No, please stay." He grabbed at the shawl, which promptly came off her shoulder again. Their hands met as he tried to reposition the wrap and she tried to keep it from falling off. "I apologize if I sounded abrupt."

She stared at him for a minute then smiled as she settled back down. "It's all right. The last few days have been…rough. For both of us."

Deverane set his pulse rifle on the rocky surface and picked up the metal cup that had been sitting on the other side. "I'd offer you a cup of coffee, but since wakefulness is your problem—"

Andi smiled ruefully. "I'd love some, but you're right. That won't help my insomnia."

He drank before setting the cup down, steadying it with one hand as it rocked on the uneven surface. "I have nightmares sometimes, but from my own private collection. Have you ever heard of Merenia 12?"

"Sounds familiar." Racking her brain, Andi chased down the reference. "It was one of the first worlds the Mawreg attacked in Sector Fourteen, wasn't it? A long time ago?"

"Right. I'm the sole survivor." He stacked a couple of small stones on top of each other, then toppled the tower with a flick of his finger.

"You must have been very young." *What could it have been like, going through an ordeal like that as a child?*

"Maybe a year or two older than Sadu." Deverane's smile was the one Andi had come to read as a social gesture only, containing no amusement. He looked at her briefly, his eyes hooded, then turned his attention back out toward the lake. "My mother made me crawl into the storm cellar—Merenia 12 has huge tornadoes. Anyway, she shut me in there, and she ran to decoy the Mawreg away from me. She told me to wait until Dad came to get me." Falling silent, Deverane picked up the blaster rifle again, checked the safety and the charge level.

"Then what?" Andi reached out from under the enfolding shawl to lay a hand on his arm, squeezing gently. Maybe he needed to talk about it. *And I have to admit I'm curious about the man beneath the taciturn warrior façade.*

Raising his coffee cup to his lips, Deverane gave her an unsmiling sideways glance. "Are you sure you want to hear this?"

Andi nodded. *If it helps me understand you better, I'll listen all night.* "I'm a good listener."

"Well, the Mawreg slaughtered all the colonists. The old star destroyer *Cassiopeia* had been detailed to escort the next colony transport ship from Sector Command to Merenia. Her captain engaged the enemy cruiser in battle, which he eventually won by ramming those Mawreg bastards, sending them all to hell. Our ships at that time didn't have the armament to do the Mawreg much damage any other way, you know? Suicide runs were the only solution."

Andi huddled inside the shawl, pulling it closer around her. *The Mawreg are one scary subject.* "I've read some journals of the early encounters. I know things were grim. At least now we have a new class of battleships capable of taking on the enemy and winning. What happened to you?"

"The colony ship landed, put out a distress call," he said. "While waiting for evac escort, her crew and the new colonists buried the victims."

"But they found you?"

"I'd gotten out of the storm shelter somehow. I was sitting next to my mother's body, holding her hand." Deverane shrugged, but Andi thought maybe she saw a glint of unshed tears in his eyes. Next second, he brushed a hand across his face, cleared his throat and sat up straighter. "I remember that. I've no memory of how I got out of the shelter or much of anything else."

Andi sat silent. *I wish I dared to hug him. Or hug the little boy he had been. Sad, so sad.* His closed-off body language didn't suggest that he'd welcome any demonstration of her sympathy.

The captain flicked the remnants of his coffee from the cup into the lake below. "After the Sectors authorities abandoned the effort to start a colony there, I was shipped to the Star Guard Orphanage. Standard procedure back then. I swore I'd get revenge on the Mawreg someday." Coming out of his reverie, he gave her the more genuine, lopsided Deverane smile. "The Special Forces gives me plenty of opportunity to even the score."

Andi tried to do the math in her head, working back from the age she guessed he was. "So you've been in the Special Forces for what? Twenty years?"

He shook his head. "Twenty-*three* years. The duty burns you out. I'm already past the average age for being deployed in the field, but I'm not interested in a rear-echelon desk job on some cushy planet."

Andi laughed out loud, then clapped her hand across her mouth, mindful of how sound carried at night. "No, I can't see you sitting behind a desk. Not at *all*."

"I could retire. Ranch maybe, try farming. I don't know. We get veterans' acres as part of our pay. And bonus acres for certain assignments. Plus, I have a special allowance for being a survivor of a Mawreg raid. I could have quite a homestead. I can take my acres on any open planet." He shook his head. "But the idea of putting roots down doesn't appeal to me much. I feel safer on the move."

Wow, he is kidding himself if he thinks he'd be any happier farming than at a desk job. Guess I was right, here's a guy who has to stay in constant motion. Why does that disappoint me so much? Andi stretched, tired of sitting curled up. "Well, if you can't choose, Loxton buys veterans' acres rights."

"Are you serious? They can do that?" He looked askance at her. "How is that legal?"

"Don't be so surprised. It's a lucrative sideline for them. Loxton found, or created, some loophole in the Veterans' Benefits Act." Andi stretched again, easing the kinks in her back and loosening the tightness in her shoulders before yawning. "Listen to me, talking business with you after all we've been through."

"Don't *do* that."

At her startled look, he smothered a yawn of his own. "See, it's catching, and I have another hour on guard duty before I can turn in." Deverane laughed. "Think you can sleep now?"

Andi made a dramatic show of closing her eyes, only to pop them wide open in exaggerated fashion.

Face serious now, Deverane eyed her. "You really need to go try for a few more hours of shut-eye. A lot of hard territory to hike through tomorrow."

"Oh, my sore feet. And my aching back. I don't want to think about more marching with that boulder you call a backpack." She stood, dusting herself off. *If he's giving orders again, there isn't going to be anymore personal chitchat. Maybe that's just as well.* "See you in the morning, Captain."

"Call me Tom." He made the request in a casual tone and avoided meeting her gaze. "Special Forces doesn't stand on too much ceremony, not like regular troops."

Andi nodded, pleased by his request. "Goodnight, Tom." Enjoying the sound of his name on her lips, she walked away, toward the sleeping area. *What am I thinking? Not a good idea to get too interested in a roving, hard-living military man. He just warned me himself he isn't going to settle down. That came through loud and clear. And I have to move on from Zulaire for the good of my career anyway.* With a sigh, she lay down, closed her eyes and strove for sleep. *Mustn't let these dramatic circumstances affect my good sense.*

***

In the morning, Andi and the others packed the supplies and headed into the thick forest for a long day's slow march. By midmorning, Tom told her they were less than half a mile from the transportway. "I have hopes of capturing or commandeering some vehicles, but we've got to avoid roving groups of rebels. Wilson, you and Rogers scout ahead. Check out the situation on the road and report back."

Working their way into the brush, the two soldiers disappeared from view. Grateful for the break, Andi sank down in the grass, getting out her canteen. *I hope Wilson takes his time on that recon.* She was lightly dozing when Wilson and Rogers crashed back into the clearing at a dead run. Rubbing her eyes, she sat up with a start, grabbing for her blaster.

"Trouble ahead, sir," Wilson reported crisply. "Party of hostiles has four civilians stopped on the transportway. Looks like things are going to get ugly *fast.*"

"We should go help them." The urgent thought impelled Andi to her feet, and she took a step or two in the direction the scouts had just come from.

Tom moved fast, grabbing her elbow hard and glaring down at her. "I thought I told you—*more than once*—my primary orders don't allow me the discretion to go around the countryside rescuing everyone in distress." He spaced out each word for emphasis. "I have to get back to the capital. We've got vital information that could stop the entire planet from descending into war. I can't conduct firefights and rescue individuals. You were an exception because someone somewhere pulled a lot of rank and got special orders issued. Okay?"

Biting her lip, Andi flushed and jerked her elbow away from him. *I wish he wouldn't keep rubbing it in my face that I got special treatment. I didn't ask for him to come rescue me.*

Apparently satisfied she wasn't going to argue, Tom's next remark was addressed to the waiting sergeant. "How many hostiles?"

"Fifteen. Armed with standard planetary-issue weapons, from what we could see." Rogers nodded his agreement with Wilson's rapid assessment. "No heavy stuff. No Sectors contraband. We could take them, sir."

Brow furrowing, Tom glared at Wilson. "We have to stay on mission here. You're starting to sound like her." He jerked his thumb at Andi. "I need a reason to break our rules of engagement."

Wilson looked at Rogers, getting no help from him beyond a sheepish shrug. Turning back to the captain, the sergeant continued to plead his case. "They're roughing up a bunch of *priests*, sir. Defenseless noncombatants. Don't seem right to walk away, orders or no orders. I...can't explain it any better."

Tom pulled out his blaster and checked the charge. "All right, I'll commit to going and assessing the potential for intervention." He fixed Andi with a stern gaze. "I am *not* promising to intervene. So don't push it, Miss Markriss."

Afraid to say anything and risk changing his mind, she simply nodded. From what she'd seen of Tom so far, he'd intervene all right. *Soft heart inside a very tough exterior.* She bit her lip, realizing he and his men would be going in harm's way, based mostly on her request. *I hope we won't all regret my urging them into danger. There aren't any good choices, only risky tradeoffs right now.* She breathed a little prayer to the Lords of Space to watch over Tom and his men in the coming moments, especially if the situation turned into a firefight.

"If they have vehicles, we could use a lift. The whole point of tracking us back to the transportway was to beg, borrow or steal a ride home." Having found a military rationale, the captain wasted no time in moving out. "Abukawal, keep Sadu and Lysanda well to the rear." He motioned for Wilson and Rogers to lead the way.

Andi crept southward behind Tom, moving through the brush and scrubby trees lining the ridge. Soon, she was high atop the ridgeline itself, at a vantage point opposite the roadblock where the unwary travelers had been caught. The road was clogged with vehicles and a large mass of people.

"Looks like they forced the passenger vehicle off the road." The captain stared at the scene below them through his distance-viewers. Slowly, he tracked along the line of the transportway.

"How can you tell?" Andi eyed the road. *All I see is a wrecked car and an angry mob.*

Wilson leaned in on her other side, speaking quietly right at her ear. "See how the two cargo haulers and the smaller car are angled on the near side of the road? They double-teamed the driver, boxed him in, caught nice as you please."

Tom lowered the viewers. "Priests weren't expecting any trouble. Their vehicle looks like the high-end luxury model. Not built for speed."

Things have obviously deteriorated in the short time since Wilson and Rogers first reconnoitered the site. Andi scanned the scene. Two of the black-robed Sanenre priests now lay unmoving, covered with blood in the muddy roadside ditch. Two priests—one young, one elderly—remained standing on the elevated road. A half circle of jeering Naranti rebels loosely surrounded the pair, turning on these defenseless members of their own Clan. Trying to shield his companion from their assailants, putting his body in front of the older man, the younger priest extended his arms wide in a blocking motion. Judging by his gestures and attitude, he was arguing with the rebels.

Burning fiercely, the boxy passenger vehicle was sending thick black smoke skyward. Andi eyed the car warily. *I'm surprised the fuel tank hasn't blown yet from the fire.*

Next minute, she stifled a scream as one of the men in the throng below raised his weapon and shot the younger priest at point-blank range, sending him staggering across the pavement. The old man tried unsuccessfully to catch him before he tumbled off the raised transportway into the ditch with his luckless fellows, coming to rest against their bodies.

The remaining priest rose from where he'd fallen. Smoothing his robes, he stood quiet and calm in a half circle of shouting, heckling tormentors. There was no avenue of retreat.

He looks really familiar. How do I know him? "Let me have the viewers." She tugged at the strap around Tom's neck. With some reluctance, he unlooped the viewers, ducking his head to get disentangled and then handing them over. After a moment fumbling with the adjustment, Andi peered across the ravine, focussing on the priest's face, one glance confirming her suspicions as to his identity. "Serene Holiness Rahuna."

She dropped the viewers, clutching at Tom's arm. "We have to save him." *Think, think, what can I say that will give him grounds to act?* Taking a deep breath, Andi spread her fingers in a self-calming gesture. "Look, Rahuna is the Pontiff of Sanenre, head of the planetary religion. He's one of the few people on Zulaire respected by *everyone.* All three Clans trust his word. If this war is going to be stopped, he's the only man who can do it."

"She's right, Captain." Andi shot Abukawal a look of pure gratitude as he spoke up. "If Rahuna dies, there will be chaos. In time of Clan warfare, the Obati and Shenti are required by our gods to turn authority over to Sanenre's Serene Holiness, who is always of the Naranti Clan. His neutrality is unquestionable." Abukawal nodded toward the ugly scene on the road below them. "If the rabble kills Rahuna, there will be no one able to neutralize this crisis. It takes fifty days and nights of intense ritual for Sanenre to manifest the signs identifying the new religious leader."

"Anything could happen to Zulaire in fifty days." Anxiety nipping at her nerves, Andi's voice rose. "How can the rebels do this? They must know who he is, he's one of their own people."

Tom took the viewers back from Wilson, who'd retrieved them from the ground. The captain had a half smile for Andi as he dusted the lenses off with his shirt. "Are we ever going to run into anyone in distress you don't want me to rescue? No matter what my orders—my very specific orders—say?" He took another look himself. "If this guy is so important, killing him would be a logical strategy for the rebels, Clan loyalties aside. Classic destabilizing move. Buys them more time to solidify their gains." Lowering the viewers, Tom drew the sergeant aside a few steps for a semi private conference. "Mitch?"

"I say go for it, rescue the guy, sir. It's worth doing. Fits into our mission on Zulaire in the first place. We can stretch our orders a little more." He winked at Andi.

She held her breath.

Tom nodded, and Andi exhaled in a rush as he issued his orders. "All right, we move in. Rogers, Latvik, target the men closest to the two trucks. The sergeant and I will pick off the ringleaders. The guy with the pockmarked face, the one with the drop on the old man, is mine."

"I'm coming, too." Andi checked the charge on her borrowed blaster. *They're going into danger at my urging again and I need to be there, do my part.*

"I expected nothing else. Stay beside me. Choose your targets from the rear fringe of the mob over there." He pointed. "And we want the trucks in one piece, if at all possible." Without waiting for her acknowledgment, Tom turned to Abukawal. "Stay here with the girl and the baby. If we don't succeed, make your way to the capital. Stay low, travel at night, don't get involved in anything. Your priority is to get there in one piece."

Abukawal drew himself up, tightening his grip on his weapon. Eyes flashing, jaw jutting, he shook his head once. "Staying on the sidelines is a hard thing for a warrior."

"I know, I get it. I'm sorry. Your eyewitness information is too important to risk." Tom clapped Abukawal on the shoulder, then nodded to his own team. "Move out."

The small party crept down the ridge, utilizing every bit of sparse cover, trying not to draw any attention. Andi tried to match her movements to those of Rogers, whom she followed, and not blunder into Tom next to her. Although she understood the tactical necessity for creeping up on the enemy, the slow pace frayed her nerves. *I just hope we won't be too late.*

The captain signaled a halt about halfway, where a long, rocky outcropping provided limited cover. The soldiers deployed, Andi taking a spot in the middle of the line, still next to Tom, per his instructions.

She was now close enough to hear the discussion going on below, at the edge of the road.

The Naranti mob leader taunted the old priest, an incredible lapse of cultural norms—to berate an elder and one of his own Clan, at that. "You're powerless to save your companions or yourself."

Taking a step forward, the ringleader of the mob pushed the old man hard with each sentence he spit out. "Your day has passed. We don't need you to talk to the Obati and Shenti for us. It is *our* Clan's turn to rule Zulaire. We're done bowing and serving. We'll make them tremble at our war cry, bend their necks to our knives. They'll have to respect us. The Naranti can carry war banners and fight better than the Obati or Shenti ever did."

"This is to be the accomplishment of our Clan?" Scorn colored Rahuna's powerful voice. "The killing of innocents? Taking what isn't ours?"

The rebel spokesman struck the priest across the face with the butt of his weapon. Spinning from the force of the blow, Rahuna crumpled in a heap, his small shiny black hat skittering across the road.

"*Enough.* We waste time," declared another Naranti man, who appeared to be the final authority over the ragtag squad. "Kill him and have done. We must be at the rally point before nightfall."

Tom half raised his hand, on the verge of signaling his men to fire.

Rahuna struggled to his feet, hand pressed to his bleeding head. "I warn you, and those who launched you on this path of hate and destruction, your crimes are the shame of Zulaire. It's a betrayal of all we Naranti have stood for as a people, for the last four hundred years of peace. The evil you do will return to haunt you a hundredfold. You won't gain what you seek from these unholy acts."

Andi shivered at the power in his voice, in his words, even though the message was not meant for her. *It almost sounds like he's cursing them.* Uneasily, a few men on the edges of the crowd glanced at each other. She hoped they were reconsidering their involvement with this episode of hate.

"You break the peace with unspeakable horrors. You'll be called to answer for these acts, whether in this world by the authorities or by Sanenre in the next." Rahuna raised his hands to the heavens, palms up.

"I said be quiet. Your smooth words serve no purpose here today." The rebel leader took a half step forward.

"The Great Sanenre Who Sees and Judges will decide whether you're right, or whether *I* speak truth." Lowering his arms, Rahuna stared straight at the man opposing him.

A broad smirk puckering his pockmarked face, the rebel lieutenant raised his weapon. "Shall I kill you at once, or shall we see how long you can endure pain, old man? How long does the Serenity last?"

Rahuna made a sign with one hand. The leader of the mob hesitated. Speaking softly, the elderly cleric said, "One more moment, I beseech you, to make my peace with Sanenre before I die, one moment to ask his blessing on your souls and mine."

"Is this guy for real?" Wilson whispered. "He's hypnotizing them."

"Yeah, maybe he doesn't even need our help," was Rogers' half-serious rejoinder.

"I think the rebel leader is losing some support from his own men." Andi glanced over the mob again, noting more than a few ashamed faces and slumping shoulders.

On the roadway below, the Naranti gestured with the weapon. "All right, say your damn prayers, old man. But be quick about it! And don't concern yourself on *my* behalf. I don't follow your tired, irrelevant Sanenre." Noisily, he hawked and spat.

Rahuna raised his bleeding head with an effort, eyes seeking the sun, in whose flames of purity Sanenre was believed to dwell. Sinking to his knees in the dusty road, facing the proper direction, he recited the prayer for the dying.

"*Now.*" Tom's order was a curt whisper.

Andi jumped, lost her grip on the blaster. Swearing under her breath, she got the weapon firmly in her hand again, scrambled to her feet. Adrenaline and anger swept through her, making her aim deadly, as she thought about what the rebels had done at the compound and in the village. *These men don't deserve mercy.* Beside her, the soldiers fired at the designated targets in economic, efficient bursts. The energy charges flashed in a whining barrage, wreaking havoc on the mob.

"They're trying to get away!" Tom shouted. A small knot of the remaining Naranti Clansmen made a mad scramble for the nearer of the two vehicles. "Concentrate fire on the red truck."

Andi switched her aim to the designated cargo hauler, joining her fire with a stream of energy coming from her companions' blasters. The target vehicle's power source detonated in a resounding explosion, sending deadly metal fragments flying for dozens of yards. Dazed and deafened by the explosion, Andi hardly felt Tom pulling her behind the rocks, shielding her from the shrapnel screaming through the air. A second explosion shook the hill as the other cargo hauler blew up.

Above her head, the captain swore in a steady stream. *"Damn it.* There goes our hope of getting transport." Andi buried her face in her arms, conscious of the reassuring weight of Tom's two hundred-plus pounds shielding her. He wrapped himself tightly around her as more explosions went off.

The moment of silence stretched, and Andi heard her own heartbeat thundering in her ears.

Tom raised his head to check out the scene. Then he rolled off of Andi, putting his face next to hers for a second. "You okay?"

"My ears are ringing, but I'm fine."

Tom got to his feet. "All clear, men. Get down there and see if we screwed up enough to kill the guy we were trying to rescue. Rogers, go tell Abukawal to be ready to move out fast. We're going to have to get away from this mess with all possible speed."

He extended a casual hand to help Andi to her feet, but kept her in his grip, allowing the soldiers to go in first. Not until Wilson signaled an all-clear from the roadway did the captain lead her to the bottom of the hill, pausing at the edge of the ditch, where the three younger priests lay in a tangled heap.

Tom checked to see if any of the men still lived. Rejoining her, he shook his head. "We were too late to help any of them. Sorry."

Shaking a bit from the aftereffects of the battle, Andi clambered to the roadway. *At least at the village the violence had happened before I arrived on the scene. Horrific as the devastation was, I didn't see the events as they occurred. But here, I killed a few of these people.* Her stomach heaved, and she stopped walking, bending over, hand across her abdomen.

"Are you all right?" The captain put his arm around her shoulders.

Not trusting her voice, she nodded.

Tom gave her a half hug before moving away. "Hey, you did a good job for your first time in combat. Once we engaged, it was them or us, you know."

"I know." Andi resumed her climb up the last few feet of the slope.

"The reverend is still alive, sir," Wilson called as she and Tom stepped onto the black surface of the transportway. Medkit open, the sergeant crouched on his knees next to Rahuna, checking for injuries. "Shrapnel blew right over him, I guess. I think he passed out."

"Help him take care of your priest, would you, please?" Tom directed Andi in Wilson's direction. "Latvik, come on. You and I need to make sure none of these rebels are still breathing."

As Andi knelt next to Wilson, Rahuna's eyes flickered open. Arching his pencil-thin eyebrows, he cleared his throat. "Are you winged messengers of Sanenre?" He looked from her to the sergeant and back again.

"Not exactly." Smiling, Andi patted his shoulder. She grabbed the folded shawl from her pack and slid it under his head to serve as a cushion against the hard surface of the road.

"No matter. I'm not disappointed." Rahuna got his elbows under him and tried to sit.

Not unkindly, Wilson pushed him back. "Not yet, sir, if you please. I need to finish dressing your head wound."

The priest eased himself down. "Who are you and where did you come from?"

"We escaped a massacre at the Obati summer colony." Andi sat cross-legged on the road to get more comfortable, resting the blaster across her lap. "These soldiers are the survivors of a Sectors patrol detailed to escort me home. We got caught in the attack, and now we're trying to get to the capital to let the authorities know what's going on."

"Sanenre sent you to this spot at this moment." Rahuna's voice sounded stronger, less raspy. "My fellow priests? What of them?"

"I'm sorry, sir." Andi took his hand. "We were barely in time to help you. Too late for the others."

"My nephew was the last to fall, trying to defend me." He blinked hard, biting his lip, and closed his expressive brown eyes for a moment. "How shall I face my sister with this news?"

Thinking about her own family, about the Tonkilns, Andi blinked back some tears herself, squeezing his hand in silent sympathy.

Opening his eyes, Rahuna studied Andi. "I think I know you. From the capital?"

"Yes, we've met. I'm Andrianda Markriss, deputy agent of the Loxton Galactic Trading station. This is Sergeant Mitch Wilson of the Sectors Special Forces."

"Glad to meet you, sir." Wilson finished the last bandage and started putting away his supplies. "You can sit now, but take it slow, okay?"

With Andi at one side and the sergeant offering support on the other, His Serene Holiness managed to sit upright. "My head spins most alarmingly." Wincing, he put his hand to his forehead.

"A normal reaction to a head wound, sir." Wilson was reassuring, calm as always. "It was a glancing blow. You're going to have a spectacular bruise but no concussion. You've got a couple of superficial cuts and bruises and one flesh wound to the lower leg. Guess you didn't manage to duck all the shrapnel when the truck blew."

"I'm so relieved you're going to be all right, sir." Andi smiled at Rahuna. "Bruises and a headache are much better than what could have happened."

"I think the captain needs me over there by what's left of the truck, ma'am. Can you keep an eye on your friend here?" Wilson asked.

"Of course. Go on." Andi waved the sergeant on his way, then helped Rahuna to his feet. A bit portly, the cleric was about her height, somewhat short for a Naranti. "Sir, what were you doing way out here without an escort?"

"I'd been to the meditation pools at Quanjiran. I heard tales of the unrest in the countryside, but I didn't want to believe the four hundred-year peace had been broken. A few hotheaded young Shentis, perhaps, but nothing the Obati couldn't solve on their own. So I took my pilgrimage to Quanjiran, as always in this time of year. Then, two nights ago, I received an urgent summons to return to the capital. We…we set out at once." He put his head down, scuffed one toe at a piece of shrapnel on the roadway. Andi felt him shiver.

"If you'd rather not talk about it—"

"I regret to the bottom of my soul that I didn't listen to those who urged me to wait for an armed escort. Lord Tonkiln offered to send guards. My impatience and foolish belief in my own immunity as Serene Holiness cost three good men their lives today. I'll bear the burden until I, too, go to my grave." Rahuna stared at a pile of rebel corpses across the roadway. "Did you see the mob was Naranti?"

"Yes, sir. The men who attacked the Obati summer colony were all Naranti, too. The ringleader there was Iraku, Lord Tonkiln's chief of household," Andi said.

"Unthinkable." Rahuna's voice sharpened. He rubbed at his eyes, then stared at her. "Iraku had been a loyal servant to the Tonkilns for thirty years."

Yeah, till he started murdering them. "Iraku is a key figure in this rebellion. I'm sorry to have to add to your distress about the identity of the rebel forces, but the truth is plain." She gestured at the carnage around them. "An unknown number of your Clan's people are at the bottom of this."

"What drove my Naranti brethren to madness?" Rahuna leaned all his weight on her for a moment, closing his eyes, whether in physical or mental pain, she couldn't hazard a guess. She staggered a little under the burden, and he stood up straighter.

Andi put a supportive arm around his waist as he wavered off balance. "They're trying to make it look as if the Shenti and Obati Clans are committing these crimes on each other," she explained. "We're traveling with a young Shenti warrior who's going to the capital to give firsthand evidence. Abukawal heard Naranti Clan members planning attacks on various outlying areas."

"You speak of a massacre at the Obati summer colony? No wonder Tonkiln offered me armed escort," Rahuna said in a wondering tone. "I hadn't heard of this fresh atrocity—he didn't speak of it in his message. How bad was it?"

Andi shivered, breathing rapidly, pulse skyrocketing. The memories rose all too readily to her mind's eye, the events still too raw and fresh for her to suppress. Rahuna put his dry, warm palm on her forehead. At his touch, the sounds and sights of the massacre faded. Peaceful calm stole over her, radiating through her body from the center of her forehead where his fingers rested. She'd heard of the ability His Serene Holiness was said to possess, to ease mental or physical anguish with his touch.

"Sanenre's Serenity be upon you, child," Rahuna chanted. "I'll hear the details another time, when both you and I are more prepared to cope. Thanks to Sanenre for preserving you and your companions from evil."

"Yes, thanks indeed," Andi echoed the common phrase of gratitude. Although she was not a believer in the local religion, she respected the beliefs of the Zulairians. *Maybe Sanenre is watching over us, who knows?*

Tom strode back across the transportway, Wilson and Latvik trailing in his wake. Andi focused only on the captain, studying his face, tired and lined, but resolute. His wide shoulders were set, his bearing military. *Just the warrior I want at my side when things are going all to hell.* He flashed a smile at her, and she knew she blushed a little.

Turning to Rahuna, she said, "Sir, allow me to present Captain Tom Deverane of the Sectors Special Forces." Given Rahuna's exalted position on Zulaire, Andi didn't want to skip the formalities even in such an unusual situation.

Tom gave the priest a crisp salute. Rahuna made a small bow in return, holding out his hand. "I can never offer you adequate thanks for risking your men and yourself to rescue me, Captain."

Shooting Andi a look that was half teasing, half annoyed, Tom shook the cleric's hand firmly. "Miss Markriss was most insistent Zulaire couldn't manage to solve this crisis without you. She gave me no choice—we had to come to your aid. How well can you walk, sir? We have to get away from here before someone sees the smoke and comes to investigate. I doubt if there are any friendlies left in the area."

"The trucks?" Rahuna put a hopeful lilt into his question.

"Useless. We had to slag one during the firefight to keep the survivors of the mob from getting away. The fuel tank blew in the other from the intense heat, so we're still a foot patrol." Tom's brow furrowed as he exchanged a glance with Wilson.

"Let us walk then." Rahuna squared his shoulders and adjusted his robes. "Can someone find my hat? Oh, yes, thank you, Sergeant." Letting go of Andi's arm, he set the shiny black cap on his closely cropped, dark-red hair. "I used to hike all day when I was a boy in the southern hill country. I won't delay you."

"*Oh*, my shawl…" Andi had left it, forgotten on the roadway after using the generous length of fabric as a pillow for Rahuna.

"Right here, ma'am." Wilson held it out to her. "I grabbed this when I went back to get my medkit."

"Thank you." She took it from the sergeant's outstretched hand. The afternoon breeze flung the shawl open like a banner while the sun glinted on the intricate patterns of the silver, iridescent green and lavender threads woven through the creamy wool fabric.

"A beautiful bridal shawl indeed." Rahuna helped her reel the garment in from the wind's grasp. "I'm honored you used it to cushion my poor broken head. You and the captain are to be wed, then?"

Andi shook her head. *Look at the appalled expression on poor Tom's face. Keep it together. Don't make this worse by laughing at his embarrassment.* "No, *no*, I found this in a de-stroyed Shenti village where we stopped for food and water. The nights are so cold, and I didn't have anything to wrap up in." *And I still feel a little guilty about taking it, but, oh—it is so beautiful.*

The priest steepled his fingers. "You're trying to help Zulaire heal itself. No one could begrudge you a little comfort and warmth along the journey." The comment had the ring of a blessing.

Warmed and cheered by Rahuna's understanding remarks, Andi stowed the now-refolded shawl in her black pack.

"We need to go. *Now.*" Tom's tone sounded crisp, no-nonsense. Hands on hips, he frowned at Wilson and Latvik, who were still smothering wide grins at the priest's initial comment about the shawl. *"Move out, people."*

The captain led the way down the slope away from the transportway. Andi guided Rahuna's descent of the crumbling, brush-covered hillside. When they reached the three corpses lying in the muddy ditch at the bottom, the priest halted. "I must say the prayer for the dying."

"Sir, they're already dead and we need to move. We'll join them if we don't get going." Tom glanced at the bodies and shook his head, mouth turned down. "I don't have time for burial detail."

"A moment only, Captain. It's for the benefit of their eternal rest in Sanenre's arms." Rahuna met the captain's stern gaze with calm assurance, before falling to his knees in the mud. Thinking at first he'd collapsed from his injury, Andi rushed forward.

As Rahuna chanted, she drew away a yard or two, standing in silent respect with the others. When the last sonorous, heartfelt syllable of the cleric's prayer faded away, Tom motioned for Wilson and Latvik to aid the priest in scaling the next hillside.

Climbing alongside Andi, the captain provided a quick hand to her elbow when she slipped or fell behind.

True to his word, Rahuna jogged up the steep hillside with incredible agility for a man of his advanced age and recent injuries.

Tom stopped at the rocky line where they'd hidden prior to the ambush. Pausing beside him, Andi took deep breaths, leaning over, hands on her knees, trying to rest for the remainder of the climb. Her leg muscles were knotted in pain, and she couldn't catch enough air.

"His Holiness is pretty amazing," Andi said between deep breaths. "He's doing better than me, and I'm probably thirty years younger."

"He's running on adrenaline, I bet. We'll be carrying him by nightfall." Tom shook his head.

Andi straightened, arching her back. She watched the other men climbing the hillside for a minute. "Thanks for changing your mind, for going in after him."

"Hey." Grasping her shoulders lightly, the captain swung her around to face him. He leaned closer. "I'm not a heartless guy, you know. But my orders have to take precedence over anything else. Personal agendas get you killed in a war, which is what we have here. Okay? I can't go off trying to rescue everyone we find being attacked by these Naranti bastards. We have to reach the capital."

"I understand that." She was mesmerized by his green eyes, so intensely focused on her. "You don't owe me an explanation. I'd be dead if you hadn't had orders to come get me. So I'm the *last* person to quibble with you for following orders." She didn't relish the tension between them in the last few minutes. *Where did this come from? I wonder if he's still touchy about the shawl comment.* "I'm sorry if His Holiness embarrassed you with his remark about the bridal shawl."

"It's all right." Blaster raised, he turned and let loose a sustained barrage, sweeping over the dry brush on the opposite hillside. Startled, she withdrew a few steps up the hill as flames licked at the ground cover. "Little diversion," he said in response to Andi's questioning look. "Burn the evidence, confuse whoever comes to investigate. Maybe cover our tracks, too. Come on, we'd better catch the others." Tom headed up the hillside. Andi made short work of the climb to join him and their companions.

"We're going to have to travel inland for a while." He joined Wilson, who was studying a map readout. Looking a bit pale, Rahuna sat on a boulder, blue around the lips and not as spry, despite his earlier boasts.

"If we stick to the transportway, it'll be too easy for anyone who wants to find us. And I'm guessing someone will decide to come after us. It's going to be pretty obvious His Holiness didn't do all the damage to the raiding party himself.

I figure we cut inland a few miles, work our way through this valley between the two foothills and come back out here." Tom stabbed at a spot close to the black ribbon where the transportway began a straight run across the Mdaba Plains to the capital.

"No cover anywhere in the Plains, sir," Wilson said.

"I know. I'm hoping we can steal vehicles someplace along this route." The captain released the map, which disappeared in a blink. "How are you in the small-miracles category, sir?" he asked Rahuna with an engaging smile. "Can you conjure up a cargo hauler? Or even a big personal vehicle?"

Chuckling, Rahuna shook his head. "Sanenre is known to approve of those who don't ask for much beyond their true needs. I'm grateful for my life, but I can't promise, Captain. I think your arrival was my appointed miracle for this journey. But I'll include your request in my prayers."

"Fine, then we'll all be counting on you to get us a ride." Straightening, Tom lost his momentary air of good humor, his face reverting to a frown. "All right, folks, time to move out."

***

The group hiked all afternoon through a valley between the two foothills the captain had indicated on the map. Even with no sign of any pursuit, Andi couldn't relax, no matter how peaceful the surroundings appeared. Midway through the afternoon, Tom allowed one break. The soldiers sprawled out in all directions underneath the multiple trunks of an ancient tamaril tree. Lysanda sat, resting her head on Abukawal's shoulder, and appeared to drowse a bit, while Sadu played with twigs and pebbles, building a fort and knocking it down.

After Andi and Wilson divided up the combined rations, Rahuna blessed the food as if it were a holiday feast before he would let anyone eat.

After the meal, as the group moved out again, Andi excused herself to the old priest so she could walk with Tom.

"Have a nice lunch with His Holiness?" The captain gave her a lopsided grin and a quick sideways glance.

He noticed. Pleased, Andi smiled. "Rahuna's an excellent companion. People pay bribes to be his seatmate at state dinners, and here I had him all to myself for an hour."

Stumbling, Tom caught his balance again with a jerk. Pausing to collect himself, he hitched the pack up better on his shoulders and resumed walking.

"Are you all right?" Andi reached out, but he shook off her helping hand.

A fine sheen of sweat beaded his forehead. There were dark circles under his eyes. "I'm fine. It's warm this afternoon." Tom wiped at his brow.

Lords, he's shaking like a leaf. What's going on with him? She grabbed his hand and was unable to still the tremor running through it. "You are *not* all right. Let me look at you."

Fists clenched, red-faced, Tom pulled away again. "I said I'm fine, now drop it. If you have to worry about someone, then maybe you'd better go keep an eye on Rahuna." He stomped off. As he moved away from her, she saw that sweat had soaked through the back of his shirt.

That's not right. Worry nagged at her, jangling her nerves. She searched along their straggling column for Sergeant Wilson.

He was pulling rearguard this shift. Andi worked her way through the rest of the group to meet him. Wilson was idly whistling another of his endless, on-and-off-key tunes. "Pleasure to see you, ma'am. Seemed like you enjoyed your lunchtime chat with—"

Curtly, Andi interrupted the flow of remarks. "Something's wrong with the captain. I want you take a look at him, because he won't even talk to me."

Stopping in the middle of the trail, Wilson craned his head, trying to see the front of the line where Tom was leading. The captain was out of sight, around a bend in the narrow valley. Wilson fired questions at Andi. "Sweating? Got the shakes?"

How does he know that? Speechless, she nodded.

Shucking off his main pack, Wilson jerked the medkit out, spilling some of the other contents onto the trail. "Can you stand rearguard until I can send Rogers back to relieve you?"

Not even waiting for her answer, the sergeant rushed off, running and darting through the group. Andi waited to be relieved of duty, uneasy thoughts welling up inside her. *He clearly knows something I don't. And it doesn't seem to be good.* Taking cover behind one of the broad-trunked trees, she faced the valley they'd hiked through and scanned the tree line, blaster at the ready. *Thank the Lords of Space, we haven't had any rebels on our trail.* She had her orders. She had to wait and guard, although every instinct in her screamed to go see what was happening with Tom.

Rogers brushed past her, startling Andi. "I've got the lookout, ma'am. Sergeant Wilson's compliments, and could you join him at the head of the column right away?"

"What's going on?"

"I couldn't say, ma'am, but the captain had some kind of seizure. He's down."

Feeling like she'd been kicked in the gut, Andi stared at Rogers for a split second then ran as fast as she could toward the head of the column. She skimmed past Abukawal and Lysanda. A short distance farther down the trail, she pushed Latvik unceremoniously out of the way, skidding to a stop next to Rahuna. The priest reached out a hand to steady her.

Tom lay full-length on the ground on his back, his eyes closed. His hands rested at his sides, twitching from time to time. Beads of sweat rolled down his temples, pain contorted his handsome face, deep wrinkles marking his forehead. Dismay lanced through Andi like a knife as her heart skipped a beat. Wilson sorted through the contents of the medkit. Discarded in the grass, one used medinject already lay by his boot.

"What's happened to him?" She fell to her knees next to Wilson. "How could his condition deteriorate in just a few minutes?" Reaching with one hand to touch Tom's cheek, she was shocked to find his skin cold under her hand. "He was talking to me and walking when I left to find you. And now he's *unconscious?*" Andi grabbed Wilson's sleeve and tugged on it to make him look at her. "How can that be?"

"Bhengola fever." The sergeant's lean frame was tense, his shoulders hunched. He wouldn't face her. The vein at the side of his throat throbbed as he rummaged through the medical supplies. "The captain gets these attacks from time to time. We were hopin' to get back to the capital before the next one hit. You know of any local remedies?"

"Bhengola fever?" Andi covered her mouth with both hands and gasped. "Did I hear you correctly? *Bhengola?*" Wilson nodded once. Chewing her lower lip, she ran one hand through her hair. "He never caught it on Zulaire. We don't have that here."

"He's had it for years, ever since an assignment on Panamilla 2," the sergeant said. "It ain't a contagious thing, not after the first attack has passed, thank the Lords of Space."

"Isn't bhengola usually fatal?" Stepping backward, Latvik swallowed nervously and glanced around, probably to see how everyone else was reacting.

"Can be over time," Wilson confirmed. "Attacks get more intense. Not more frequent. They're pretty predictable, as a rule. We carry off-the-books doses of aliquinalone on every mission."

"Off the books?" Andi repeated the phrase softly, a question in her voice. *Does he mean illegal?*

Wilson shot a hard glance at her. "Soldiers with bhengola fever get mustered out, ma'am. No ifs, ands or buts. No cure, you know? And the military is all Captain Deverane has. We've used most of the quine we brought because we never expected to be stuck here so long. I haven't been able to get more on the black market, although I might have a shipment waitin' when we get back."

How can he be so matter of fact about admitting to black market activity in front of all these witnesses? Andi felt the blood pounding in her temples. Trying to will away a headache, she rubbed her forehead.

"So do you know of anythin' local that might help or not?" Wilson's face was pugnacious, jaw jutting, eyebrows drawn together. He gathered up the discarded injects and stowed them in a side pouch of the pack.

She'd studied the symptoms of the major interplanetary infectious diseases one semester at the Loxton Academy. Often the agent on an isolated planet would be the only medical resource for the outworld population and, hence, had to have rudimentary knowledge. *Why didn't I pay more attention in that damn class?* She summoned her vague memories of the lecture on chronic, relapsing fevers, including bhengola. "Caused by a parasite. Symptoms include fever, chills…"

"Convulsions—it's an ugly disease, all right," Wilson said. "The bhengola parasite dies off in the human body after the first cycle of infection, but enough of its loose genetic material remains in the lymphatic system to do the recurrent damage. That's what makes it incurable." Having found the medinject he was searching for, he held it to the sunlight. "Last one. And one is *not* goin' to be enough."

He's right. Bhengola requires around-the-clock drugs to get safely through an incident. Closing her eyes for a second, Andi tried to remember the pertinent section of the Loxton medical-training material. The few facts that came to mind weren't reassuring.

"He'll need careful nursing to survive, do you agree?" Rahuna's head was tilted as he regarded the sergeant. Stroking his chin, the cleric seemed thoughtful.

"Yes." Wilson jabbed the second injectable into the captain's upper arm, rubbing the spot to work the medication into the muscle. "This buys us some time." Rolling Tom's sleeve down, he sat back on his heels, hands resting on his knees. Watching his patient relax under the drug's influence, the sergeant's face remained set in grim lines. "Better but temporary. He won't regain consciousness until the entire bhengola cycle is over."

"How long?" Andi was unable to remember the exact course of the symptoms. *A week? Two weeks?*

"Could be three or four days, ma'am. Maybe longer, with no quine."

"Have you the map handy?" Rahuna held out one hand. "We can't care for him in the open elements, Sergeant. I believe there may be a safe haven we can reach by morning, if we walk through the night, and if Sanenre chooses to smile on this effort. Captain Deverane is a good man, and Zulaire has need of him. I must see the map." Rahuna's insistence spurred the sergeant into action.

Wilson sent Latvik running to retrieve his pack. When it was brought to the front of the column, the sergeant searched through the contents until he found the map readout token, which he keyed into a full view for Rahuna. Muttering under his breath, His Serene Holiness took a minute to orient himself to the representation of the surrounding area. Studying first one segment of the map then another, Rahuna returned to the first quadrant.

Holding one of Tom's limp hands curled in her own, Andi sat cross-legged in the grass, hoping Rahuna would find what he sought.

"Yes, here." The priest stabbed a thick finger at a spot close to the route they'd been following. "We can obtain help here, I believe."

"That's in the damn mountains, sir." Putting his hands on his hips, Wilson studied the surrounding area on the holographic map.

Andi came to look at the map herself. She had trouble reading the shimmering, translucent image, hanging in thin air as it did, then she realized what Rahuna was talking about. "The Monastery of the Clouds?"

He nodded. "The monks there can assist us in nursing the captain. Or at least making him comfortable while he fights off this fever you speak of."

Uncertainty made her anxious. "Isn't the monastery a myth?" *How much faith do I dare put into such a destination? Should we risk Tom's life on a decision to go there?*

Rahuna jabbed at the colorful dot pulsing on the map. "Not a myth, I assure you." He stood, arms akimbo, eyebrows raised as if he was amazed they didn't believe him.

"What if we carry him all the way there and find it abandoned?" Andi made a small gesture at the red dot. "We can't afford to waste time."

Wilson took Tom's pulse, counting the beats with a furrowed brow. "Pulse is racin'." He stared at Andi and Rahuna. "You know the territory and I don't, so I'm open to suggestions."

"We won't find the cloister abandoned." With a wave of his hand, Rahuna refuted Andi's worry. "The Monastery of the Clouds is a venerated shrine of Sanenre. There are always those who choose to serve and meditate in a place close to Heaven, far from the rest of the world."

Wilson stood up, dusted off his pants and walked over to stand right in front of Andi. "What do you think, ma'am?"

Taking a deep breath, Andi shifted her eyes from his, looking down at Tom. "If there are monks still at the monastery, then His Serene Holiness has a point. We know there's no other help closer than the capital. We can't carry Tom all the way there in his condition. I say we go for it." She brought her gaze back to Wilson's face.

Nodding, he swiveled to address the other soldiers. "All right. Latvik, get Abukawal. The three of us will have to make a litter and lash the captain to it. Then we'll take turns carryin' him. Any chance of a comlink at this place?"

The old priest shook his head at the sergeant's question. "Sorry, no. The monks shun all aspects of modern life as part of their discipline. It is meant to be a secluded, private place, remaining unchanged through the millennia."

"Too much to expect, I guess. Our luck has been flat busted this trip." Wilson kicked at a rock. "Damn. Well, then, Miss Markriss, if you'd stay here and keep an eye on the captain for a few minutes? He should be fine for a while, after the inject I gave him, but call me if you see any real change."

"I'll tend to Lady Lysanda and the child," Rahuna said. "Keep them amused, so that Abukawal can be free to help you."

Andi sat beside the unconscious captain for the next half hour, alternating between staring anxiously at him and watching Wilson with his two designated assistants cut branches and lace together a crude litter. They shifted Tom's tremor-racked body onto the litter and restrained him. Rahuna led them out of the valley and up a faint path into the higher peaks.

***

Hours passed in a blur for Andi.

This is the most grueling march we've done yet. Her knees throbbed, her shoulders ached and her head was pounding. Staring at the dry ration bar in her hand, Andi was tempted to toss it over the nearest cliff. She kept herself walking and forced herself to chew and swallow. *I can rest the next time Wilson calls a halt to rotate litter bearers. We must be due for that soon. Thank the Lords for Zulaire's two moons. Between them and the hand lamps, I might manage to stay on the trail and avoid falling off the mountain.*

During the night, Andi marveled more than once at the superb physical conditioning of the soldiers. The men kept climbing at a steady pace, even carrying the litter and their packs. She'd always regarded herself as being in good shape but had increasing difficulty keeping up. The higher altitude caused her shortness of breath and a nagging headache behind her eyes that threatened to become a full-fledged migraine before the night was over.

Sadu fell asleep in his carrier on Abukawal's back. Head bobbing with the warrior's every step, the toddler slumped over. Lysanda walked without complaint, although eventually she lagged behind the rearguard.

The column halted. Lysanda had collapsed by the side of the trail, her eyes closed.

Sighing, Andi trudged back to see what she could do.

Abukawal was already crouched beside the princess. "We'll rest awhile then come along after you. I can carry her, too, as well as the child, if need be." He made shooing motions at Andi with his hands. "You go on."

"I promised the captain I'd look after them both," Andi said. "He made it a condition for bringing them. They're actually my responsibility—"

"And seeing the demands on you, I've gladly made them mine," the warrior answered. "This is a duty I can handle very well, Miss Markriss. I have younger brothers Sadu's age at home. And the lady trusts me. I won't violate her faith in me."

Tempted, Andi looked over her shoulder at Tom, unconscious on the crude litter. Concern for him was foremost in her mind. "He needs me—"

"He does." Abukawal nodded, giving her a gentle push. "Divided loyalties are no good in our current situation. I take the Tonkilns as my first priority now. You go with the captain, care for him with your outworlder knowledge."

Wilson rolled his shoulders. His words were terse, to the point. "I can't leave anyone back here with you, Abukawal. I need Rogers and Latvik to help carry the captain."

"I understand. I have the blaster you lent to me. The Serene One says we are getting very close to our destination. If you find the monastery, then you can send help to us." Abukawal pointed at Tom, moaning and thrashing in ever-more-violent convulsions. "I think we don't have much more time to get him to shelter, do you?"

Wilson wiped at his forehead. "He's slippin' into the most severe part of the bhengola fever cycle. Even if I had the right medication, his survival would be touch and go. Sure hope these monks have something to help."

We're wasting time. Andi came back to the litter and touched Wilson's arm. "Rahuna says it can't be far now. Shouldn't we move out?"

Wilson's shoulders slumped for a brief moment. The movement was the only outward sign of stress Andi had seen him display. Resolutely, he straightened, turning back toward the lit-ter. "All right, Latvik, I'll spell you."

"Good luck," Abukawal called as the litter bearers trudged onward in the predawn grayness.

"Take good care of her, okay?" Andi took a last look at Lysanda, feeling a certain amount of guilt at prioritizing Tom over the royal's needs. *Has he really come to mean that much to me in such a brief time?* The cold dread rushing through her at the idea of losing the captain to the fever was her answer.

Taking a deep breath, Andi turned away, choice made.

Even the stoic Sectors soldiers were reaching the limits of their endurance. Sheer willpower was keeping them all going. Finally, Wilson called a halt. "Rogers, scout ahead and don't come back until you find the damn place, all right? We have to know how much farther. Don't fall off a cliff in the dark, soldier."

Jogging slowly away, Rogers gave them a tired half smile and a wave in return.

Wilson stretched full-length on the hard-packed dirt of the trail, sighed and laid his head on the lumpy pack. "Can you put a fresh cold compress on the captain's forehead for me?"

"Of course." Andi ignored her own aches and sore muscles to tend Tom. They wouldn't let her carry a corner of the litter, although she'd offered more than once. She was happy to do anything to help Wilson with his care.

Tom remained unconscious, muttering under his breath. Sweat poured down his face, and when Andi laid a hand on his forehead, she jerked it back. The captain was burning hot. "Can't you give him something else for this fever?"

"If I do, it sends him into the chills. Those are by far the worst, ma'am. Better he run the fever as long as possible and stave off the chills. See if you can get him to take a little water. Dehydration's a big risk at this stage." Wilson stayed where he'd flung himself, close to the litter.

Without much success, Andi tried to dribble a few drops of lukewarm water from the canteen between Tom's cracked, bleeding lips. After a minute, the captain jerked his head away fretfully.

Wilson took a catnap.

"How much chance does he have?" Andi pitched her voice low. She didn't want anyone but the sergeant to hear her.

With a groan and obvious effort, he sat up, stretching from side to side, trying to unkink the knots in his back muscles, avoiding Andi's gaze.

Leaning across the litter, she put a hand on his arm, waited till he met her inquiring gaze. "I want to know what to expect, to be prepared. I care about him, too, you know."

"I plain don't know, ma'am. He's always beaten the bug off before."

Offering him the unstoppered canteen, Andi frowned. "But you had the, what did you call it? Quine?"

"Right. And this time we don't." The sergeant took a long drink.

Pointing up the mountainside, Rahuna left the rock he'd chosen as a resting place. "I think your man is returning."

Rogers was indeed coming back down, running at a breakneck pace. "The monastery is right around the bend. But you aren't going to believe this—the place is built right into some kind of a mountain peak, as if it was floating on anti-grav lifters. There's one hell of a rickety bridge going across."

"Anyone home?" Wilson asked, closing the canteen and handing it back to Andi.

Rogers shook his head. "I didn't stop to see, Sarge. There's some kind of gong thing right at the edge of the bridge. I figured the priest here would have more luck talking to whoever answers the gong than I would."

"Very wise, young man." Rahuna nodded, turning to address the sergeant. "The Monastery of the Clouds has its defenses against the unknown. Let us proceed. Sanctuary is at hand."

Staring at him with narrowed eyes for a minute, Wilson shrugged. "Yeah, okay. Latvik, you and I have the duty. Rogers, lead the way." He glanced at Andi. "Can you make it a little farther, ma'am, or do you need a longer break?"

I'll make it to the monastery or else. Hands on her hips, tapping the toe of one foot, she said, "Let's just go."

The sergeant leaned over to speak quietly to Andi as he walked past her to take up the litter again. "I wish I felt as sure as you do that there's actually help to be had at this place."

She stared after him. *There has to be help or the captain is going to die.*

CHAPTER FIVE

As Andi rounded the last bend in the mountain trail, Zulaire's huge red sun peeked over the far horizon. A shaft of crystalline morning light flowing between two peaks like a river of molten fire struck the small monastery.

"Amazin'." Wilson stopped in his tracks to stare. "How did anyone construct such a big building on a mountaintop without anti-grav?"

"It's breathtaking." Andi came to stand next to him. Shading her eyes with one hand, she gazed across the spectacular vista. "I once read an old account of a visit here by one of the earliest traders, but his diaries did *not* do this place justice."

The precariously located monastery was designed in the shape of two joined pentagons, the smaller in front, facing them about a quarter of a mile away across the cloud-filled gorge. The white stone walls reflected the golden-reddish beams from the sun, till the entire building glowed. Andi half closed her eyes against the scarlet-tinged glare. Tiled in red, the roof was broken by small chimneys here and there. A massive archway provided entry from the bridge stairs into a circular courtyard. Another steep set of stairs led to a doorway at the second-story level. The conjoined building towered behind, rising another two stories into the sky.

Facing them were blank walls—no windows, doors, or decoration of any kind. The structure filled every inch of space on the rocky pinnacle. The mountain fell away to the canyon floor many thousands of feet below.

As for the suspension bridge—Andi swallowed hard. The bridge was unsupported, except for colossal pilings at either end. Carved stone steps led down from where she now stood, slightly above the level of the monastery. Then came the wooden, hanging part of the bridge, which was by far the longest section. Narrow, without guard rails, the span didn't even have ropes to hang onto. Leading to the immense archway on the other side was a steep set of stairs carved into the rock.

Rogers stepped past her to the beginning of the descending staircase. "The gong is over here."

"All right, Your Holiness, sir, if you could try to get someone's attention," Wilson said, "We'll make sure the captain is secured tight to this litter. One bad convulsion in the middle of the bridge, and bhengola fever will be the least of his worries. And ours." One eyebrow cocked, he assessed Andi. "Can you handle this, ma'am? You're kinda pale."

She let impatience show in her curt tone of voice. "Let's just get this over with."

Picking up an elaborately carved mallet hanging on a hook beside the gong, Rahuna gave the inlaid bronze disk a powerful stroke. The result was a clear, bell-like tone, not the crashing discord Andi had expected. Echoing from the mountains around them, the single note repeated endlessly.

Wilson, Latvik and Rogers cursed.

The sergeant shot out one hand to still the quivering gong. "Lords of Space, if anyone is followin' us, they'll sure as hell hear that."

Andi sucked in a deep breath of the too-thin air. "Loud enough to wake the dead."

"It can't be helped." Rahuna looped the mallet handle's rawhide thong back over the hook. "Now we wait."

Fortunately for Andi's jangled nerves, the delay wasn't protracted. From across the canyon came a crashing boom as the heavy door on the monastery's second story banged open. The crystal morning air magnified every sound, even the soldiers' labored breathing behind Andi. Assaulted by a wave of vertigo, she shook her head to clear it, which did nothing to relieve her pernicious high-altitude migraine.

Across the divide, three figures emerged from the doorway.

"Should we signal again somehow?" Shifting from foot to foot with impatience, Andi stared across the chasm. "What if they stay over there and shut the door without asking what we want? *Look*, two of them are going back inside already."

"Allow me." Moving with judicious care, Rahuna descended the steep stairs and walked onto the bridge. Fearing the morning dew had made the wooden span slick, Andi decided not to watch Rahuna's progress. She focussed on a monk in flowing, orange-red robes, waiting for the priest at the arch. From the moment he arrived safely on the other side, His Holiness talked to the man with great animation, gesturing across the gorge. *I wish I could read lips.*

She grabbed Wilson's arm and pointed. "Here comes Rahuna. The monk's tagging along with him. That's a good sign, right?"

"Considerin' we're all at the end of our endurance. I'm camping right here for the day if we aren't allowed into the monastery. Pursuit or no pursuit." His voice was tired and grim.

As Rahuna came closer on the treacherous bridge, his smile made it clear such dire measures would be unnecessary. Stopping at the foot of the stairs, he called to them, "All is well. The monks welcome our party and will attempt to aid the captain. Can you bring him? I'm too tired to climb up there again."

"No problem, sir," Wilson shouted back. "Can the monk help carry our gear? I'd rather handle the litter ourselves."

"Of course." Rahuna gave rapid orders to the strapping monk following him. Nodding his assent, the man came to their level, moving with a speed and energy Andi envied. Picking up all the packs and bags as if the total weight was nothing, he headed across the skinny, slick bridge nonchalantly.

"Miss Markriss, you and I can help each other across the bridge." Rahuna beckoned to her. "It isn't too bad, a bit slippery. With the cloud cover so low, it's like taking a stroll on a footbridge across a foaming creek."

The analogy seemed far-fetched to Andi. Smiling, she shook her finger at

Rahuna. "Now you're getting carried away with the poetic similes, sir. You almost had me convinced until that last image." Working her way down the mossy steps, she took Rahuna's hand. His fingers clasped hers with surprising strength, giving her renewed energy and confidence. Rahuna tugged her onward, allowing her no chance to hesitate. Together, they took the first step onto the bridge.

"It's a test of faith for the monks, you know." Staying in the center of the boards, Rahuna strolled casually. He took quick glances off to the sides, up into the sky and once peering into the void below.

Determined not to give in to her phobia, Andi kept her eyes on her sandaled feet. "Then they should have a normal bridge for those of us who *aren't* monks." Thankfully, the bridge was wider than it had appeared from the ridge. A stiff breeze chilled her skin, but the span didn't sway as much as she'd expected. She tightened her grip around Rahuna's hand.

He looked back at her with a frown. "Trust my faith to lead us to safety."

"Deal." *If anyone has enough faith, it would be Rahuna.*

No sooner had she said that than a sudden wind gust buffeted them. She knelt, scrabbling with her free hand to grip the rope linking the boards. She hunkered into the smallest ball she could.

After a minute or two that seemed like an hour, the wind stopped gusting. Andi continued clutching Rahuna's hand. He knelt down, nose to nose with her, repeating her name hypnotically. As soon as she opened her eyes, he reached to take her other hand off the rope. "Come on, you can do it, stand up and let's finish our stroll before the next puff of wind tests us."

"My head's kind of spinning right now." Rising to her feet under the pressure of his hands, she kept her eyes closed tight against the vertigo.

He hugged her. "We're going to walk, one step at a time. You must open your eyes, but focus on me. Don't look down."

She forced herself to nod. "Okay."

He tugged, and she took one step.

Okay, I didn't die. I'll try another step. How many steps can it take to get across this damn thing anyway? Andi glanced ahead, over Rahuna's shoulder. *Oh, Lords, bad idea, it must be a* mile *across.*

When the next breeze assaulted them, Rahuna looked over his shoulder at her. "Just count the steps to yourself. Let yourself stop thinking. I'll guide you safely, I swear it."

"Just…keep walking," she said through gritted teeth, wanting the ordeal to end.

The minute she was on the solid staircase below the monastery, she sank onto the mossy stone, breathing deeply. "I hope there's another way out of this place. I'd hate to tempt fate on that bridge twice."

As the soldiers attempted the same crossing with Tom's litter, Rahuna laid a calming hand on her shoulder. "It'll be all right. Sanenre favors us this morning. They won't fall, nor will they drop him."

Wilson and Rogers came down the steep staircase, balancing the litter, then started across the bridge, the sergeant in the lead.

Andi sympathized with their slow pace. *I had such a hard time keeping my balance, and I wasn't carrying anything.* "The men are so tired. I hope they don't slip."

"It'll be fine. See, they're halfway across already. We must move up the stairs to give them room." Rahuna prodded her into motion, getting her to progress three or four more steps toward the monastery.

Andi kept turning to check Wilson and Rogers's progress behind her. "Where's Latvik?"

Face drawn in lines of strain, the sergeant seemed about at the end of his endurance, breathing hard. "Sent him to retrieve Abukawal and the Tonkilns." Wilson had to suck in air before finishing his thought. "He volunteered to go."

"Let the good sergeant save his strength, child," Rahuna chided her. "Come to the courtyard and meet our hosts."

As she walked under the archway, weathered carvings caught her momentary attention. The entire entrance was shaped from a block of some translucent, pink stone unfamiliar to her. Huffing and puffing, Wilson and Rogers toiled behind her with their burden. Rahuna urged her onward. A solid wall two yards high, finished with a layer of darker stone, surrounded the courtyard at the top of the stairs. The pavement underfoot was the same vivid red as the roof tiles. Spiky plants were growing in ornate clay pots around the circumference of the courtyard.

Huge white blossoms unfolded, opening to the sun. Andi breathed in the intoxicating perfume wafting across to her on the slight morning breeze. "How beautiful. I've never seen this flower before."

"Heart of Sanenre." Rahuna sneezed. "One of the rarest of blooms. The monks dry the petals to create incense for rituals. Come, the chief monk will be waiting for us inside the entry chamber." Wilson and Rogers arrived inside the courtyard with the litter. "Gentlemen, you must carry your captain into the monastery, and then your labors will be done for now. The monks will take charge of the patient once he's within their sanctuary."

Wilson exchanged weary glances with Rogers. "Guess we can manage one last set of stairs, sir, if you promise no more after that. Lead the way."

Rahuna hiked up first, followed by Andi. The straining litter-bearers brought up the rear. She gawked at how the surroundings were so calm, clean and pristine. *I need a bath. The soldiers are probably just as grimy and sweaty as I am. We're wildly out of place here. But the only thing that matters is whether the monks can help Tom.*

Standing alone in a column of light, an old monk waited for them. A skylight set in the ceiling above bathed his long, flowing, orange-red robe in illumination, making the monk resemble a living flame. Andi supposed he was meant to represent the embodiment of Sanenre, who dwelt in the fires of the sun. *He really staged this appearance for maximum dramatic effect.* The monk's pale, oval face above the glowing robe was kind, wrinkled, his twinkling black eyes deep-set under snowy-white brows. White hair surrounded his pate, with a gleaming bald spot in the middle. As he extended his arms to welcome them, Andi couldn't help but stare at the bracelets of huge, rough-cut Zulaire rubies on either wrist. Each stone by itself would have been worth an Obati lord's ransom. Elaborate red tattoos adorned the backs of his wizened hands, the details of the patterns now all but obliterated by age and wrinkles.

Hovering nearby as Wilson and Rogers set the litter down, Andi worried. Tom was so pale and so still. She knelt so she could put one hand on his chest to reassure herself he was still breathing. *How much ceremony and discussion must there be before we know if they can help him? And we can't rush through any of it or the monks will be offended. Patience, Markriss.* Negotiation was one of the required skills for her job, and she was very good at it, but the social niceties required before the real discussion could commence were hard for her at the best of times. The stakes were unbearably high today, with Tom's life in the balance.

Not leaving his spot in the dramatic rays of sunlight, the elderly monk addressed them in a deep baritone voice. "I am Tleer, chief monk of the Monastery of the Clouds. I welcome you to our sanctuary in the name of Sanenre. I pray your petition will be regarded with grace and favor."

Preparing to make her own plea, Andi stood up, but Rahuna stepped forward immediately, already talking. "One of our party—a brave and worthy soldier—is ill. We ask sanctuary to tend him and to rest before continuing our journey. The winds of storm swirl in Zulaire, Tleer, my brother. It is laid upon us to do our part to disperse these storm clouds. The light of Sanenre must shine forth once more."

"There may be some risk to you," Andi said. *I can't let him give us shelter without warning him.* "Rebel troops may be following us."

Tleer bowed to her. "It is well intentioned of you to mention this, my daughter, but unnecessary. This shrine exists to serve those who do Sanenre's will. It likewise has powerful weapons to repel those who create shadows on the peace of Sanenre's light."

"There are a few more people in our group," Wilson said. "Another soldier, a local warrior, a girl—"

"And a baby? An Obati baby? Is the warrior Shenti, from the far mountains of Abuzan?" As he fired questions at them, Tleer's wizened face became animated.

"How did you know?" Wilson shot the monk a suspicious look.

"There are foretellings." Rubbing his hands together, Tleer beamed at them, nodding at each person in turn as if conferring a blessing. "But we never know when Sanenre will set prophesied events into motion. We'll watch for your other companions and welcome them."

Moaning, Tom thrashed against the bindings on the litter. *Niceties be damned.* "Please, he's extremely ill," Andi said. "We spent a long time climbing up here, and he's been getting worse by the hour."

Tleer crossed the room to a gong on a giant stand and gave a single tap to the disk. Four monks flocked into the foyer from the unseen hallway beyond, garbed in robes of a more subdued shade than Tleer's.

"My brethren will take charge of the sick man." Tleer motioned toward yet another corridor. "If the rest of you will follow me, we can get you lodged and fed."

"Sir, I'd rather stay with the captain." Resting one hand on the butt of his blaster, Wilson took up a stance between the approaching monks and the litter.

"I'm staying with him, too." Andi frowned at Wilson, in case he planned to object. "You need my help, Sergeant, as sick as he is and as exhausted as you are. Don't even think about arguing. Just tell me what to do."

"As you choose." Serene and calm, Tleer apparently didn't care if his guests fell in with his suggested agenda. He escorted Rahuna and Rogers down one corridor, while Andi and Wilson followed the four monks carrying Tom's litter in another direction.

The monks led them into a bright, eight-sided room. One whole wall was transparent, with a breathtaking view of the canyon and the mountain across the way. A soft, orange rug covered the stone floor. Tapestries of pastoral scenes hung on the walls, the largest depicting a herd of Sanenre's sacred urabu gamboling beside a lake.

Centered below this tapestry sat a bed constructed of dark-veined wood. The center of the headboard was a cunningly carved rendering of an arched urabu's head. The side slats were depicted as much-exaggerated antlers, rising to a point at the foot. Linen sheets covered the mattress, with quilts and furs piled on a nearby stool. Tossed against the headboard was an inviting stack of fringed and tasseled pillows.

Taking in the room's appointments with one quick glance, Andi was satisfied that the accommodations would be comfortable for Tom, sick as he was. *I could sleep for a week. I bet Wilson is thinking the same thing. Look at those lines on his face and shadows under his eyes.*

Producing a stubby knife, one of the monks slashed through the bindings keeping Tom more or less still on the litter. Freed from restraint, the captain thrashed as convulsions racked his body. Standing out of the way, Andi wrapped her arms around herself. Her eyes prickled, her throat grew tight with unshed tears, as she watched him go through so much agony. Meanwhile, the monks worked together as a team, transferring the captain to the waiting bed.

"Let me give him a shot." Wilson stepped to the bedside, medinject in hand.

All four monks stopped, staring at the sergeant.

Hastily, Andi translated for the monks, who didn't appear to understand Basic.

One stepped forward while his three companions ranged themselves between Andi and the bed. "What will this do?" asked the one in charge, speaking a Zulairian subdialect.

Glaring at the monks, Wilson clenched his hand on the butt of his blaster as he addressed Andi in a tense voice. "Are they planning to interfere with me?"

I hope not. "No, I don't think so," she said in a soothing voice. "The monks just want to help, to understand."

"Tell them I'm goin' to stop him from convulsing for a few minutes, so we can get him undressed, sponge him off. We need to reduce the fever." Lowering his voice, Wilson looked at Andi, worry lines bracketing his mouth. "I flat-out hate the next stage of bhengola, the chills, but he has to pass through them to get over this attack, ma'am. Ask what they can do for bonebreakin' shivers."

Andi and the monk engaged in a rapid discussion, covering what Deverane was suffering from and how the next stage of the disease would be violent convulsions.

"We'll bring you a potion within the hour which may be effective." Bowing, the monk glided unhurriedly from the room.

Wilson gave his captain the medication while the remaining monks stood in a line by the window and watched. In less than a minute, the drug had taken effect, Andi was relieved to see.

For the first time in hours, Deverane was relatively quiscient, although he continued to roll his head from side to side, as if seeking escape from the pain. Holding the empty inject, Wilson studied the implement as if it was solid gold. Grimacing, he looked at Andi. "I can't administer this drug too often during any one attack. Has a powerful effect on the heart. Not good for the liver, either. Ma'am, would you excuse us while we make him a bit more comfortable?"

She had her argument ready. *I'm not leaving Tom's side tonight.* "Look, the monks are speaking a Naranti sub-Clan dialect, and you weren't hypnotrained in anything but basic Naranti, right?"

Puzzled, the sergeant shook his head.

"So I'll stay, thank you. You need a translator. I'll just sit in this chair, facing the window, and translate as necessary." Sinking into the cushions, Andi curled up like a cat. "Well, better get on with making Tom comfortable." She waved one hand in a small shooing motion.

Wilson shrugged and turned back to the three monks. "I could probably get by with gestures," he said defiantly over his shoulder.

"You were ready to draw your blaster at least twice already since we got here," Andi reminded him softly. "We can't afford to offend these people, not if we want their help for Tom."

Wilson worked with the monks, unfastening Tom's clothing. Ands translated as needed while keeping her eyes averted, to soothe the sergeant's concern for the proprieties. When Wilson gave the all-clear, she left the chair, to see Tom's limp, unresisting body garbed in loose blue pajamas, topped with a plain brown monk's robe.

The monks streamed from the room in single file, almost marching, taking the battered litter with them, as well as the crumpled uniform.

Making no sound, the last man closed the door behind him.

"I guess now we wait." *Which is always the hardest thing for me to do.* Andi crossed to the bed where Tom lay. Cupping his cheek with her hand, she recoiled in horror. "His skin feels like ice." She grabbed two of the quilts from the chair and spread them over the captain. "How can the fever change to chills so fast?"

"Just one of the many terrifying aspects of bhengola. A lot of people never survive their first attack." Wilson tucked the quilts in further. Shoving his hands in his pockets, he rocked back and forth, face careworn. "He's been fightin' this damn thing for five years."

"But the disease is winning, isn't it?" Andi said. "Even as strong and stubborn as he is. Five years is an eternity to battle bhengola. He can't have much immune-system reserve left to fight it anymore."

Fixedly, Wilson stared at the urabu carving on the headboard and made no reply.

A quick knock heralded the return of their hosts. Opening the door, a monk brought a bowl of clear, steaming liquid to the bedside.

"That smells too good to be medicine." Andi sniffed the air appreciatively as he carried the wooden tray bearing the bowl past her.

Wilson moved to stop the monk from feeding Tom. "Ask him what's in that mixture, ma'am, would you? And what it's supposed to do."

Andi translated as much as she could of the monk's response, but some of the details were beyond even her knowledge of the sub-Clan dialect. Eventually, the sergeant sat on the edge of the bed and spooned the stuff into Tom's mouth himself, while Andi cradled the bowl and the monk kept the captain's head still on the pillows.

Heading for the door, the monk took the tray and the empty bowl. "I'll have one of our brotherhood sit with him while the two of you go and eat some dinner, and perhaps rest."

Exchanging wary glances, Andi and Wilson spoke at the same time.

"I don't want to leave him—"

"I think one of us should stay—"

Andi beat Wilson to the punch. "Go have lunch, sergeant. Take a nap. You carried the litter all night, so you need rest more than me. I can have the monks find you if there's any change. All right?"

"What about you? You hiked all night, too, ma'am."

I'm not setting foot out of this room right now. She glanced at Tom's gaunt, trembling form, her heart clenched with worry. *And I wouldn't be able to sleep anyway.* "I'll get them to bring me a tray. Then I can lounge in this terrific chair, maybe drowse, while I'm keeping an eye on him. Won't the inject keep him quiet for a few hours?"

Nodding, Wilson stifled a yawn.

With an effort, Andi kept herself from yawning as well. "So you'll need your strength to be rested and ready for duty when that time is up. I can't manage him in a full-out seizure."

"Makes sense." The sergeant rubbed the back of his neck with one hand. "You'll have them fetch me if there's any change?"

"Of course. Go on, we'll be fine." Her gaze slid back to Tom, her gut churning with anxiety. *Please, Lords of Space, let him be fine. Let him pull through this attack.*

***

"Come on, Tom, that's it; take another sip of this tea for me. You'll feel better." For at least the twentieth time over the past few hours, Andi held the cup of herbal tea to the captain's parched lips. He responded to her voice as he had before, swallowing obediently, although his eyes stayed closed.

Too tired to walk back to the chair, Andi set the cup on the floor beside her. She sat cross-legged next to the low bed, resting her head on the mattress, using her arms as a pillow. *I hope the worst of the crisis is over.*

Studying Tom's face, lined now with pain, it was hard to believe she'd only met him a few days ago. His body stayed perpetually braced, tense against the bhengola's assault. He'd seemed uncomfortable with the robe, pulling at it restlessly, so she'd ease the garment off, leaving him clad in the pajamas. Andi massaged his shoulders for a few minutes, working the knots out of the muscles. *The man was hard muscle everywhere.* A wistful sadness stirring in her heart, she ghosted her fingernail over the sword and comet tattoo on his bicep. *Some Special Forces thing, I bet. I'll have to ask him about it when this is over.*

Sighing, she pulled the covers up over him again. *I hope I get that chance.*

Remembering their moonlit conversation at the camp beside the lake, Andi stroked his cheek tenderly, leaning closer to him. "You try to be so uptight and military. Disciplined. But inside you're one sensitive guy, Tom Deverane. Your parents would be proud of you." She bathed his forehead and readjusted the quilts to make him more comfortable. Every time she touched him, his muscles visibly relaxed, which pleased her and seemed like a good sign.

As sunset colored the sky outside the mysterious window, someone knocked. Andi opened the door to an anxious Wilson.

She surveyed him from head to toe. His face seemed more rested, the big shadows under his eyes gone. "Wow, you look like a changed man," she said approvingly. "A meal and a few hours' sleep did you wonders." She leaned on him for a moment, one hand on his shoulder, shaking her foot, which was all tingly and numb. "Did Lysanda and Abukawal get here?"

"Hours ago. Rahuna woke me to tranquilize her before they could get her across the bridge." Wilson took Andi's place at the bedside, reaching to check the captain's pulse.

"I'm not surprised to hear that. She's a total baby about heights. Won't even take an aircar anywhere," she said. "I think Rahuna hypnotized me to get me across."

"No sign of any pursuit so far, by the way." Wilson adjusted the quilts over Tom's shoulders.

"That's a relief," Andi said. "The whole time we were in that village and slogging through the jungle, the back of my neck tingled, like we were being watched. Maybe they just don't know or care that we got away in one piece?"

"Maybe. I'm not letting my guard down until we get back to the capital. You shouldn't either." Shaking a finger at her, Wilson frowned. "Even this monastery isn't safe from attack. So he's been quiet? Is that why you're in such a good mood, I hope?" The sergeant picked up the little tea pot and shook it, raising his eyebrows. "You got him to drink some of this?"

Nodding, she yawned. "I think he might marginally improved, yes, though there's been no change in his temperature. Will I find a guide outside? I need a real bed and sleep."

"Monk's outside waitin' to escort you." Wilson stared at the floor, then the ceiling and finally at her. "I want to thank you, ma'am, for all you've done to try to help the captain."

Andi gave him an impulsive hug, which he awkwardly returned. "He saved my life at least twice, you know. I'll be back to spell you this evening, after I've had some sleep."

As she left the room, Wilson started humming one of his endless repertoire of wordless tunes.

Smiling softly to herself, Andi felt her heart swelling with hope. *Maybe Tom's fought through this bhengola attack after all.*

***

To her dismay, when she reported back to the sickroom in the late evening after a refreshing nap, Tom was in the throes of powerful convulsions. The whole bed shook with the force as he thrashed, muttering incomprehensibly.

"How long has he been like this?" Andi picked the quilts up off the floor and tried to rearrange them over Tom.

Wiping his brow, Wilson stepped out of her way. "Started about half an hour ago. I knew you'd be coming soon, so I didn't send the monk to find you."

"What can we do?" She tucked the quilt around the captain's feet again. "He's going to break a rib or something if this continues."

Shouldering her out of the way as another set of convulsions began, the sergeant locked his arms around Tom to keep him from falling onto the floor. "There's nothing." Wilson's voice was flat and final. "I don't have *anything* in the medkit to stop this. Quine is the only remedy." Jaw set, teeth clenched, he struggled with Tom, blocking her attempt to help. "Stay back, ma'am. I can ward off the blows better than you can."

Tears burning in her eyes, she bit her lips and looked away from the bed rather than watch Tom go through another series of the torturous convulsions. A hoarse groan from their patient, followed by a sharp curse from Wilson, made her turn back. She wiped the moisture from her cheeks. "No. I won't give up. Rahuna said the monks could help him, and it's way past time for them to come up with something better than soup and herbal tea." Shaking her head, she yanked the door open and issued curt orders in fluent Naranti to the waiting monk. He'd seated himself cross-legged on the floor, leaning back against the wall. Jumping up as soon as Andi stuck her head outside the sickroom, the man barely listened to her message before sprinting down the corridor, orange robes flying.

Tleer and Rahuna, both sleepy-eyed and wrapped in hastily donned clothing, came hurrying into the sickroom a few minutes later. Taking one look at Tom, Rahuna stopped on the threshold, jaw dropping. Tleer ran right into him, putting them both off balance for a moment.

"Do the monks have anything, anything at all, that could help control these seizures?" Andi asked Rahuna, grabbing his sleeve and pulling him into the room.

Tleer shook his head, staring at Tom with wide eyes. "We don't. I've never seen such an illness." Tilting his head, he rubbed his bald pate. "We've searched in the histories."

Andi swallowed hard. *Now is not the time to lose my temper.* "Then we need to come up with something, anything."

"Ma'am, can you ask them to hold him still for a minute? I need to run a diagnostic." The sergeant's request cut across the rapid exchange of Naranti.

Shaking the entire bed again, Tom suffered through a tremendous convulsion before collapsing bonelessly onto the mattress.

"*Wilson, is he*—" Andi flew across the room to the bedside.

Wilson slumped over, leaning on the headboard, one hand to his eyes. "No, not dead. Not yet. He might have lapsed into a coma." Straightening, he squared his shoulders, taking a deep breath. He went to his pack against the wall under the window, searching through the contents. "Let me do the diagnostic."

Andi stood beside the bed, her gaze never leaving Tom's pain-racked face. Even in the coma state, his forehead bore deep wrinkles, showing the physical torment his body endured. She stroked his arm, wrapping her fingers around his icy hand. A tear trickled down her cheek. *Please don't die. Please don't leave me. I just found you. I can't lose you now.* "You have to keep fighting," she whispered.

Tleer and Rahuna had been conferring near the door. Now His Serene Holiness came to Andi's side, putting an arm around her shoulder to hug her while she watched Tom.

Wilson ran his diagnostic scanner, starting at the top of Tom's head and working down to the toes. He checked the readout and repeated the scan, lingering over the captain's abdomen. When he finally spoke, Wilson's voice was tight and a muscle twitched in his cheek. It took him two tries to find his voice. "His kidneys and liver are shuttin' down. I give him till morning maybe. Less if his heart wasn't so damn strong." The sergeant's voice vibrated with frustration. Now he looked at Andi, moisture glinting in his eyes. "All we can do is make his last hours more comfortable, ma'am. I have the drugs to accomplish that."

The room spun around her, a roaring in her ears as the edges of her vision went black. Bringing her hands to the center of her chest, she pressed hard, trying to ease the constriction in her lungs, fighting the tears. Rahuna guided her to the chair by the window, making her sit.

The cleric knelt beside her, gently smoothing her hair off her face. "How familiar are you with the canon of Sanenre?"

Lords of Space, I know he means well but... Raising her head, she patted his hand. "Sir, thank you, but this is *not* the time—"

"You misunderstand me. There may be something in the traditions of Sanenre that can help him," Rahuna said. "Something concrete, something as real as the chair you sit on." He thumped the arm of the chair for emphasis.

"What—what are you talking about?" Andi shoved her hair back, staring at Rahuna.

"Sanenre and his people possessed sacred devices with which they performed miracles."

"I've heard the legends. Are you saying the ancient devices are *real*? That there's one *here*?" Andi gestured at the room around her. *Those legends said Sanenre could do just about any kind of miracle. But how can I put my faith in some magical prehistoric contraption?*

Wilson paced over to the chair from the bed, touching Andi's shoulder to get her attention. "Ma'am, I'm only gettin' one word in ten here, since no one's speaking Basic. What are they talking about?"

"I don't know, sergeant. Let me get some more details." She glanced across at Tom, lying so still and pale. *I'm ready to grasp at any straw right now.* Andi turned back to Rahuna. "Please, go on, sir."

"When the time came for Sanenre to return to the sun's flames, he left his miracle devices in certain sacred places, such as this monastery." Rahuna smiled a bit apologetically. "The knowledge is quite closely held within the priesthood, as you can imagine. These devices can be used in cases of dire emergency."

"Does this device heal the sick?" Andi swallowed hard. Rahuna nodded, Tleer nodding like a mirror image.

Shielding her eyes with her hand, she fell back against the chair cushions, a thousand questions hammering at her mind even as her nerves tingled with sudden hope. "Are you offering to let us try to save Tom with Sanenre's gift?"

Hands together in a prayerlike gesture, Rahuna inclined his head. "Tleer and I have been reading the sacred texts and casting omens all day. I believe Captain Deverane stands at the center of the work to save Zulaire. The flames of planetary warfare would consume us all no matter which Clan has lit the fuse. Only our little band of travelers knows the truth about the Naranti. *I* am the only one who can accept the Tablets of Authority from the Obati to sidetrack this Clan war. I'd be lying dead in the ditch right now if your captain hadn't intervened on my behalf, so it's my place to save his life in turn. I was hoping it could be done without revealing our secret to you, without invoking the sacred device, but I bow to the will of Sanenre."

Oh, thank the Lords. Andi wiped the tear tracks from her face with an impatient backhanded swipe. Leaning around Rahuna, Tleer offered her a square of cloth to blow her nose. The prosaic little gesture made her smile.

After giving Wilson a rapid translation, she said, "Are you okay with this?" She studied his stern visage. He *had* to agree to this proposal, or he and his blaster would be an impossible obstacle to anything the Zulairians might do.

Wilson shifted his gaze to Rahuna and Tleer as they waited for his decision, then stared at his unconscious captain. The muscle started to twitch in his cheek again. "All right. As long as he isn't going to suffer anymore pain. He'll be dead by mornin' no matter what we do, so we might as well give this thing a try."

Rahuna sprang into action, throwing the door open to reveal four waiting monks and the litter. Habits rustling across the soft rug, the men padded into the room on bare feet. With Wilson's help, Tom was shifted off the bed and onto the litter. Andi tucked the trailing edges of the quilts around him. Just hang on a little longer. *Keep fighting. Please.*

The monks carried him out of the room, Tleer following. Rahuna stopped Andi before she could enter the corridor. Wilson came back to stand next to her.

Rahuna stared at Andi for a long moment. Puzzled, she gazed back. *Why the delay? Now what?*

The elderly man transferred his gaze to Wilson. The sergeant shifted into a parade-rest stance, hands behind his back. Rahuna nodded. "You must both agree not to ever discuss this with anyone except the captain himself, impressing upon him the need for total discretion. Sanenre's gifts must remain secret."

Andi nodded, as did the sergeant.

"Forgive me," Rahuna continued, "but I know how fascinated the Sectors authorities are with anything of this nature. You'll understand my caution once you've seen more."

"We'll keep the secret." Placing one hand over her heart, Andi spoke in a solemn tone. "Tom's life means more to me than anything."

Wilson came to attention, hands at his sides, staring above Rahuna's head. "I swear by the Soldier's Oath, on my honor, sir, never to reveal anything to do with what I may see or learn tonight."

Rahuna shook Andi's hand, then the sergeant's. "I believe you both. The captain should be honored to have such loyalty from his friends."

Wilson jerked his chin toward the procession ahead of them. "Hadn't we better catch up to Tleer and his monks?"

After a trip through twisting hallways, Tleer and the litter-bearers stopped before a massive door set into the inner wall of the corridor.

Fashioned from the same translucent, pinkish stone as the outer arch, the portal had a small herd of urabu carved inside the stone, clustered around a spreading tamaril tree. Translucent though the stone was, Andi couldn't get so much as a glimpse of what lay beyond.

Turning suddenly to face them, one hand raised, Tleer put his back against the portal. "Behold the door to Sanenre's sanctuary, his private rooms at this abode. It's forbidden to disturb the sanctuary without dire need or direct invitation."

Andi moved to stand beside the litter. Stomach knotting with sudden fear, she raised her head at this comment from Tleer. *I hope he's not having second thoughts.*

Apparently, Rahuna shared her misgivings, pushing forward. "Dire need will have to suffice," he said. "It's been many a century since Sanenre issued invitations."

As Tleer nodded, Andi exhaled. *His Serene Holiness must have done even more persuading than he admitted to gain this favor for Tom.*

Fumbling in the pocket of his habit, Tleer located a tiny carving of an urabu buck. The chief monk pressed the translucent stone figurine into a matching indentation in the doorway.

A chime sounded three times, the notes coming from the air around them. The miniature urabu appeared to leap from the door into Tleer's shaky, outstretched hand. Parting in the center along an invisible seam, the halves of the door slid into the walls.

Tleer crossed the threshold first, tucking the urabu key in his vast pocket. The litter-bearers followed. Rahuna gestured for Andi and Wilson to precede him, then stepped nimbly across himself, right before the two panels slid together again.

Ahead, the featureless corridor seemed as if it was a part of some building other than the rough stone monastery. Here the floor was bright red, made from the same shiny tiles protecting the monastery's roof. Diffused light allowed Andi to walk safely, although she puzzled over where the light emanated from, springing up in front of the group and traveling with them, impenetrable gloom behind.

The corridor slanted downward at a subtle angle, going on forever as far as Andi could determine. When she eventually reached the end of the hall, a massive black stone door barred the way. *I've sure never seen anything like this on Zulaire.* The surface was burnished to a mirrorlike finish. Goose bumps rose on her arms. Shivering, she stepped closer to the sergeant, whose hand went to his blaster as she bumped into him. *Guess I'm not the only one whose nerves are on edge.*

Rahuna ran his hand across an incised legend on the door's left side. Closing his eyes, he chanted, repeating a long phrase over and over with subtle variations in tone each time. Tleer and the four monks joined in with a harmonizing tune.

Andi chuckled when she realized Wilson was humming along but poked him in the ribs. If this door was set to recognize an aural key, it wasn't going to accept his burring baritone, which wobbled at just the wrong moments. Musicality wasn't one of his stronger points.

She gave him a small smile then closed her eyes for a minute, memory taking her to her intimate late-night conversation with Tom by the lake. *I hope we get another chance to sit in the moonlight together.* Glancing at the litter, where the captain lay with his eyes closed, as if paralyzed, Andi felt regret clotting her throat. *I never even kissed him.*

With a whoosh of displaced air, the black stone door, which had to weigh several tons, disappeared. Nerves jangling, Andi flinched, hand over her mouth to keep from swearing. *Lords of Space, this place just keeps getting spookier.*

Rahuna dragged her across the threshold, close on the heels of the litter-bearers, with Wilson right behind, treading on her heel. One of the monks stumbled, and the sergeant dove forward to catch the end of the litter, preventing Tom's limp body from pitching onto the stone floor.

A rush of air shoved her forward, stumbling. Hand on the wall to keep her balance, Andi pressed a hand over her heart as it trip-hammered like a drumbeat. The portal had sealed them in as mysteriously as it had opened a few moments earlier.

"Not far now." Rahuna took her elbow, turning her to continue on with him.

The walls, floor and ceiling in this new corridor were a glaring white that hurt her eyes. After a few steps, as the passageway curved to the left, they emerged into a small, pentagon-shaped room with a sunken center. She and Rahuna stood at the edge of a flight of shallow steps leading into the main portion of the room.

"Tell me I'm not seeing this." Wilson paused on the threshold, apparently transfixed by whatever waited in the chamber.

Taking a step to see for herself, Andi gawked, her mouth falling open. The monks transferred Tom from the litter to the exact center of a table made from solid emerald. *That stone is the size of a groundcar.* One man took the quilts, while two others picked up the litter. Bowing to Rahuna, the quartet departed, back the way they'd come, apparently to wait by the door.

"Unnecessary witnesses are forbidden." Tleer stood at the end of the emerald. "Come forward, don't dawdle." He beckoned with outstretched arms. "I fear we've no time to waste. Your captain is far gone toward the next life. He leaves this world soon."

Eyes brimming with unshed tears, Andi rushed down the stairs, Wilson hard on her heels. "Show us then," she said. "What do we do?"

"Stand on either side. Observe, there are marked areas for the supplicants." Rahuna pointed at an octagon of opal set into the floor at the monstrous emerald's midpoint.

The iridescent colors in the opal whirled, making her dizzy. Blinking the sensation away, she took her place in the center. Kicking off her sandals because it felt wrong to her to sully the gemstone with shoes, Andi stood barefoot on the stone, wiggling her toes. Wilson walked around the other side to take his assigned place, while Rahuna took up a position at the foot of the emerald.

Huge, unfaceted Zulairian rubies had been set in alternating bands with smaller emeralds and carved disks of opal on the walls. "It's like being inside a giant's jewelry box," Andi said.

"Don't seek to examine the workings of Sanenre." Rahuna waggled his finger at her.

"And don't touch the device," Tleer warned even before Rahuna had finished speaking. "Only the one to be healed can endure direct contact with the energies the stone will pour forth during the ceremony. Anyone else who touches the emerald of Sanenre before the ritual is completed will die."

Frowning, Wilson shifted his stance. "So, what do we do? Stand here with our hands at our sides? I could've done that in the sickroom. What does it take to activate this baby? Tom doesn't have time for us to chitchat."

Rahuna nodded. "Standing with your hands in your pockets is a hard thing for a man of action, I realize, Sergeant. But necessary, I'm afraid. Tleer will chant the words of invocation. When—*if* the device is activated, you'll be moved by the power of Sanenre to do what's needed." He ruined the positive impact of the last pronouncement with his next, half-heard mutter. "According to the old records, at any rate."

Squinting against the rainbow glints arcing off the facets under the lights, Andi eyed the emerald. *But where's the machinery? What's going to turn on?* All her fear and anxiety channeled into her twitchy hands as she pleated and unpleated the sides of her dress in a gesture she was unable to control. *What if this is all mere legend?* Her chest hurt at the thought. *What if the device doesn't work?* "When was the last time this thing was used?"

"One thousand twelve years ago, when the Obati High Lord was wasting away from an unknown ailment. He was the direct ancestor of our present-day High Lord Tonkiln." Rahuna's voice was calm and even.

Somewhat reassured at this matter-of-fact answer, although concerned at the span of time since the device was last utilized, Andi reached out to touch Tom's hand. *I hope he knows I'm here, that he's not going through all this pain alone. And I hope all this astoundingly beautiful, gem-based technology still works!*

"We begin." Tleer cleared his throat twice, adjusted his robes, stood up straighter and swallowed hard.

Andi leaned in Rahuna's direction. "If this room hasn't been used in over a thousand years, how do you know what to do to activate it?"

Evidently possessing keen hearing despite his age, Tleer glared at her, the fierce expression at odds with his benign, wrinkled face. "I spent the afternoon poring over the crumbling records, practicing the required syllables with the oldest monk in the brotherhood." Now he hummed a note to calibrate himself before chanting in a dialect unfamiliar to Andi, the sound echoing around the room.

Glowing brighter and brighter, until she found it hard to look at, the emerald captured her attention. A low-pitched hum seeped from the gems set into the walls. The sound built, vibrating in her ears first, then thrumming in her bones. Stuttering, her heart beat irregularly. A wave of vertigo assaulted her.

The other lighting dimmed, giving way to the bright-green illumination generated by the glowing emerald. Flickers of green flame curled up from the corners of the stone. Seeing all this activity gave Andi hope. *Maybe Tom does have a chance.*

No sooner had the reassuring thought crossed her mind than the humming began dying, while the light emanating from the emerald's heart flickered and dimmed. Panicky knots in her stomach, Andi looked around the room. Gemstones all over the walls were going dark. Lump in her throat, she pleaded with Rahuna. "*Do* something. *Please.*"

Leaving his assigned spot, the cleric hurried to stand next to Tleer. Rahuna spoke to the chief monk in a voice too low for Andi to catch the words, making sweeping gestures as he talked, pointing at her and at Tom. Tleer continued to chant half heartedly while Rahuna harangued him, although the old man's voice shook and he stumbled over the syllables. After a long minute, the emerald glowed with renewed inner light. The hum restarted, pulsing in time with Tleer's words.

"Ah, a test of our faith perhaps." Rahuna patted Tleer on the back and returned to his post at the end of the emerald. "Pray continue your efforts, my brother."

Enough with the damn tests. Time for results. Andi studied Tom, relieved to see his chest rising and falling slightly.

A voice spoke from overhead, deep, melodious. She peered across the green glow at Wilson, but he shook his head. Overriding Tleer's chant, the voice spoke again.

Tom's body suddenly lifted from the surface of the emerald, floating about five inches above the stone. Instinctively, Andi reached to touch him, to keep him safe, before yanking her hand back as she remembered Tleer's stringent warning. A gentle, green luminescence flowed in the gap between Tom's spine and the gem. His body revolved to the right, still supported by nothing but air. Lancing in from an invisible source, short bursts of thin, green light attached themselves to Tom, writhing around his neck and face like vines while his body slowly spun. As the lights homed in on his forehead, the captain's eyes opened.

Andi was startled. *Is he awake? Look over, look at me, give me a sign.* After a minute, Tom's lids lowered again, eyelashes sweeping his cheeks. The green lights abandoned their exploration of his face, concentrating now on his chest and abdomen. The voice from the ceiling uttered periodic remarks. *I don't care what language this is, that tone suggests someone making a report. But is it good news or bad?*

Like a recording running down, Tleer stopped chanting. The machine's hum continued, apparently sufficiently launched into its cycle not to require further human prodding.

Elevated by a cushion of light, Tom's body stopped its slow rotation and held steady.

One of the intense, green beams uncoiled from a spot above his heart. Turning in midair, the foot-long bar of light flew at Andi like an arrow or a snake. Instinctively, she flinched, crossing her hands in front of her face as a shield. The light stopped short, emitting its own buzzing hum, and hovering. Cautiously, she peeked between her fingers, then lowered her hands to her sides. Like bejeweled smoke, an opalescent haze rose around her, rising from the octagon at her feet. *This is Tom's only chance to live. I can damn well stand here and endure whatever Sanenre's device throws at me.*

"It's all right." Andi didn't know if she was trying to reassure herself or Tom. She was sure he'd have been more courageous if their positions had been reversed.

Moving in a lazy S curve, the green beam played over her face as Andi screwed her eyes shut. A faint, prickling sensation spread through her nerve endings, followed by intense cold, uncomfortable but not painful. For a minute, her nose and her ears were plugged. Choking back a gasp, she felt tingling on her tongue and lips, going down her throat, spreading through her sinus cavities. Andi gagged and coughed while the feelings ebbed. The nagging migraine headache was gone for the first time since she'd climbed into the foothills on the way to the monastery. Raising a hand to her cheek, she was half afraid to find herself scarred or bleeding, but there was no damage to the skin.

The voice spoke again, right in her ear, like someone standing beside her. The phrase had the lilt of a question.

What does it want? What am I supposed to do? In answer to her silent appeal, Rahuna was no help, raising his shoulders in a silent shrug. Andi cleared her throat, licked her lips with the tip of her half-numb tongue. *Pretend I'm talking to a doctor maybe?* "Your patient has what we humans call bhengola fever. A deadly disease from another planet, not from Zulaire. Chills, convulsions, organs shutting down. He's dying." Reciting the symptoms and inevitable progression of the disease was more than she could bear and her voice broke on a sob.

Wilson nodded encouragement at her from across the width of the emerald. Swallowing against the tears overwhelming her voice, Andi spoke again. "Please help him—Zulaire needs him."

And so do I. One tear ran down her cheek, splashing onto the smooth surface of the emerald, where the liquid vaporized in a burst of rainbow steam.

Opalescent light now enclosed her on three sides, playing along her arms and around her head like a miniature aurora borealis. Careful to avoid the potentially fatal contact with the emerald, Andi leaned forward to take Tom's hand in both of hers. To her delighted surprise, his skin was warm, but not feverish and certainly no longer ice cold. His fingers curled around hers. *No tremors. He's been shaking nonstop since the attack began.* Glancing at Wilson she saw he had a grip on Tom's other hand, similar illumination outlining the sergeant as well.

The three of them were linked by clasped hands and a cocoon of light. *How long have we been here?* The air was damp, slightly metallic-tasting as she breathed. *Could be days for all I know.*

Tom stirred, kicking his feet. Encouraged, she leaned closer.

Blinking, he opened his bleary eyes, pupils contracting as he focussed on her face. "I was dreaming of you," he said, curving his cracked lips in a smile. "But this is still the dream, isn't it?"

"Don't worry. Go back to sleep, everything'll be fine in the morning." She squeezed his hand tight.

Nodding, Tom shut his eyes.

The hum stopped. The voice spoke two short words. Finality was unmistakable, even in the unknown language. For the length of a heartbeat a musical chiming note played from deep inside the emerald. As the green light thinned and ebbed below him, Tom drifted back to the surface of the emerald. Andi let go of his hand as Wilson did the same on the other side. The opal light blazed around them one last time before dissipating. She staggered, bracing both hands on the emerald to steady herself.

Too late, she remembered how her tear had vaporized the instant it had touched this same surface during the healing process. The glow was dying away deep inside the immense gemstone, however, and there was nothing but a mild, burning tingle in her fingertips.

Tom snored.

The prosaic, normal sound made her laugh.

Rahuna moved to Andi's side, wrapping a quilt around her shoulders. Tleer did the same for Wilson. "You'll be tired." His Serene Holiness bent to retrieve her discarded sandals, sliding them onto her feet. "Try to fight the exhaustion until we get out of Sanenre's corridors."

Tugging, pushing and prodding, Rahuna and Tleer managed to coax Andi and Wilson from the healing chamber, through the two mystical portals.

CHAPTER SIX

Deep into the middle of the next afternoon, Tom finally stirred, kicking the quilts half off the bed and muttering as he dreamed. Andi woke, uncurling from the comfort of the large chair where she'd been napping since lunchtime. The encounter with Sanenre's healing device had left her exhausted. Since *she* was so lethargic, she wasn't worried when Tom didn't awaken as the day wore on. Wilson's diagnostics also confirmed reversal of the captain's condition. His liver, kidneys and other systems functioned now within the norms in all respects.

As Tom continued to show signs of regaining consciousness, Andi smoothed out the wrinkles in the simple peasant dress she'd taken from the village. Pulling her hair back, she crossed to the bed. His forehead felt normal to her touch. She rubbed his bare shoulders, massaging the well-defined muscles. Half naked, he wore no shirt because he'd kept pulling at the fabric in his sleep, finally taking the robe and pajama top off without ever fully wakening. Mitch and the monks had given him a bath and a fresh change of clothing after the healing ceremony, while Andi changed the sheets.

She stared at his chest, lightly dusted with hair. A line of darker hair ran from his belly button down below the waist of the pajama pants. Andi realized she was following that enticing line with her eyes—*again. Well, I can't help it. He's got the sexiest body I've ever seen.* Tom shifted on the pillows, and Andi lifted her fingers from his skin. A drowsy sigh escaped his lips, and he blinked a few times before focussing on her face.

"So, you *are* here. Not a dream?" His voice sounded raspy. "A good dream."

"Not a dream." She smiled, happiness warming her. "Let me get you some juice."

With surprising strength he clasped her wrist, detaining her at the bedside. "Wait." Tom rose on one elbow. "Don't leave."

Regretfully but gently, she peeled his fingers from her wrist. Walking to the table, Andi spoke to him over her shoulder. "Mitch said you'd need liquids when you woke. He stressed the point. I have the juice pitcher right over here, cooling in a bowl of ice from the mountain. Let me get you a drink, rearrange those pillows. *Then* we can talk. A little. You're still pretty weak."

"Where are we? I've never seen anything like this on Zulaire." He glanced at the tapestries and the view out the window.

Andi poured juice into a large mug. "It's the Monastery of the Clouds, in the upper ridges of the eastern mountain range. I think we're safe enough here. For now. And, no, you're right, this isn't a typical Zulairian facility." Returning to the bedside, she leaned over to help him prop up while he drank from the glazed green ceramic cup. "Take it slow."

"Tastes good." He licked his lips and grinned. "Tangy. Is there more?"

"A whole pitcher full." She got him a refill. He'd been drinking it for the past few days, but obviously didn't remember those earlier, half-awake encounters.

Taking the mug from her, he sank into the pillows without further protest after she fluffed them as much as she could. He'd apparently lost interest in the history of the building for the time being. "A bhengola attack?"

"Yes. You passed out on the trail, a few hours after we rescued Rahuna. Remember?" Andi sat cross-legged beside the bed, so he wouldn't have to keep looking up at her. She clasped her hands in her lap against the nearly irresistible urge to touch him.

"How long..." He frowned, apparently trying to remember the onset of the attack.

"Four days now," Andi said. "Mitch told me you've had this for years, taking some black-market medicine to keep it in check. How can you still be on active duty with a chronic condition like this?"

" 'Mitch,' huh? You and my sergeant got to first-name basis while I was out of it? Should I be jealous?" Raising one eyebrow, he gave her a teasing smile before taking another swig of the juice. He tipped the last drops onto his tongue, then handed her the mug. "Command didn't have to know I had bhengola. The condition never affected my ability to do the job."

"That's hard to believe. How could it not?" She set the cup on the floor. "I'm not trying to be judgmental. It's none of my business. Mitch explained about how Command would have just kicked you out if they knew the truth. But weren't you risking your life every time you went on another mission?"

Reaching out, he took her hand, twining his fingers through hers, stroking his thumb across her skin. Andi stilled at his touch. Electricity ran through her nerves, and she shivered ever so slightly.

Wordlessly Tom urged her to sit on the edge of the bed, moving over so she had enough room but maintaining the contact between their bodies. His expression was serious, his gaze steady on her face. "The first attack came while I was on Panamilla 2, after we secured our objective but before scheduled evac. Aliquinalone is easy to get there, of course, so Mitch dosed me through it with liberal quantities. The attacks weren't too frequent. Doesn't show on the medscanners for some reason unless I'm having an attack. I made sure never to be available for the annual fitness-for-duty certification if I had symptoms."

"I'm sure you had your reasons to hide it." Andi looked away. *Who am I to judge what he did or why he did it?*

"This assignment was unusual, having a squad under my command. Mitch and I work alone ninety percent of the time." Tom reached out with his other hand to gently turn her face back toward him, cupping her chin. "Hey, I would *never* put my guys at risk. I get about a week's warning before an attack comes on, which gives me time to lie low."

"What kind of warning?"

Green eyes intent on her, he stroked her cheek softly with his hand. "The whole visible spectrum of colors shifts on me, enough so nothing looks normal. Like an aura. And for sure nothing smells or tastes right. I know an attack is coming and I know what I have to do. The first bhengola symptoms started the day the orders changed, which was another reason I wasn't too pleased to be diverted to the Obati summer compound. I thought we'd have time to get back to the capital anyway. I wasn't counting on all hell breaking loose." Releasing her, Tom stretched, yawning. His joints and tendons popped as the kinetic stress in his body released. "Can I get some real food?"

"The monks offered to prepare special broth for you, and bread made of *healing* herbs." Raising her eyebrows, she winked.

"Lords of Space, stuff probably tastes like sawdust. I'd rather have something more substantial." Tom stretched again, frowning. "That's odd. I always feel like I've been worked over by five guys with clubs the day a bhengola attack ends."

"Not this time?"

"No. And I'm not complaining." He laughed.

She rose to adjust the quilts, shifted one pillow to better support his back against the urabu headboard.

"I have to say you're a definite improvement as a nurse. Mitch never fluffs the pillows." Tom watched her efforts with a broad smile. "The attacks have been getting more severe the last few years, although not more frequent. But he always hangs in there for me."

"We've been trading off the nursing duty," Andi said. "He's devoted to you."

"Been through a lot together." He reached out to her. "Sit down? Please?"

As soon as she perched on the edge of the bed he wrapped one arm around her waist, gently drawing her closer. Andi could feel his semierect cock against her lower back. Delicious heat pooled in her most-intimate parts, reacting to his nearness. *But he just woke up, we can't get carried away until he's fully recovered.* Shifting a few inches, she nervously moistened her lips. "Mitch said—he said you were dying. Your kidneys and liver had shut down."

Toying with her hair, Tom asked, "Then why am I still here? I assumed he'd found one or two more injects of quine at the bottom of the medkit."

Andi shook her head. Those frightening minutes before Rahuna and Tleer had escorted them to the healing chamber were going to be fresh in her mind for quite a while. "No, all out of quine. Even Mitch lost hope."

"What aren't you telling me?" Tom took her hand, watching her face, his voice softening. "It's all right. Whatever you and Mitch did for me worked. I'd just like to know."

Stroking his arm at her waist, she sighed. *This explanation isn't going to be easy.* "Rahuna and Tleer offered to treat you...their way."

He frowned. "What do you mean 'their way'?"

"The god Sanenre, or whoever built this place, left a few ancient devices running, reserved for planetary emergencies. Rahuna convinced Tleer to save *you.* He believes we'll never reach the capital unless you lead us there. He thinks your survival is essential to ending the inter-Clan war." She smiled. "Mitch and I weren't about to argue."

Tom exhaled in a quick whistle, shaking his head. "I've a lot to live up to then. Have to justify his faith in me...although I'm at a loss. My part in what's happening on Zulaire is pretty small. I'm just a soldier trying to get his squad back to base."

"You're being too modest." Andi fell silent for a minute, toying with the green mug, making it twirl around on the rug with her big toe. *Here comes the hard part.* "Before I explain the rest, you have to promise me something. Rahuna had one mandatory condition before he would help you. Mitch and I already agreed."

"I can't violate my Soldier's Oath to the Sectors." Tom's gaze was level, his lips set in a straight line. "Although it would be hard to refuse Rahuna anything."

She shook her head a little. "Mitch didn't think it was a problem." Keeping her gaze locked on his eyes, she said, "You can't talk about what happened here, not ever. Rahuna doesn't want the Sectors authorities to learn about Zulaire's ancient sites and devices."

"No problem." His response was prompt and firm as he relaxed against the pillows. "I *have* no memory of anything."

Andi drew up her knees in front of her and clasped her hands around them, lowering her head to rest on her arms. Looking at him sideways, she said, "Mitch believes the healing device did more than stop this one attack. The indications are that the treatment eradicated the whole bhengola syndrome."

Closing his eyes for a moment, he was obviously thinking through the ramifications of the revelation. "So *I* may be cured, which would be a terrific thing for me. But the millions of other bhengola sufferers in the Sectors can't come to Zulaire for treatment. There's probably no way for anyone to duplicate the device used. Therefore, no one is harmed by my silence. End of subject. Agreed?" He held out his hand.

Andi uncurled and shook on the meeting of the minds, not surprised to note that his grip was firm. *The old Tom is definitely coming back again.*

He studied her face, his eyebrows drawn together in a frown. "You look tired. Tell me you aren't sitting in the chair all night. I'll have to reprimand Mitch for letting you pull hard duty."

"I'm fine. I insisted on helping. Neither of us wanted to leave the monks in charge because we didn't want you waking up with only a stranger in the room." Andi put her hands on the mattress, bracing herself on the bed, ready to stand up. "In fact, you should probably try to get some more sleep."

"I've *slept* enough." His voice was deep, caressing. He leaned toward her, his eyes moving down her body then back up to her face.

Every nerve inside her thrummed. There was an intimacy about being so close to him now that he was over the illness, a sense of possibilities in his body touching hers, even casually.

"Thank you for taking care of me." He rested his hand on her thigh, laced their fingers together.

"You're welcome." She wanted to touch him, settled for stroking down the length of the tattoo on his bicep with her forefinger. "I like this. Special Forces?"

"Yes. I have a couple more in other, more interesting places." He shifted his hips on the bed, and his increasing arousal became even more apparent.

"I know, I've seen them." She blushed and stammered a bit. "Mitch and the monks did most of the—well, the personal nursing care for you. But I—I helped. Well, you were sick."

"I'm not sick now." He studied her face. His hand left hers, to massage her upper thigh through the tights, stroking in circles that moved ever higher toward the vee between her legs.

"No, you're not." Meeting his eyes, she shook her head, wet her lips with the tip of her tongue.

Holding her gaze with his, he cupped her and rubbed his hand against the fabric barrier. His eyes flicked to the door for a second. "Are we likely to be interrupted?"

"Not for several hours, until Mitch comes back to take over."

"Good." Slowly, he tugged the tights down, past her knees then rolled them off her toes with exquisite care. He dropped the garment on the floor and slid his hands firmly, slowly up her legs, massaging the sensitive nerve endings. Pushing her legs further apart, he stroked the sensitive skin of her upper thighs. His fingers reached under the edge of her silk thong, to touch her soft curls and slide over her most intimate parts. When he brought his hand away, Tom licked his fingers, slowly, one at a time, as if savoring a rare treat, always watching her face.

I'm creaming for him. No other man ever had that effect on me, but he's just so hot, so sexy. Andi blushed.

His hands were on her shoulders, tugging her closer. Her lips met his. It was a soft kiss at first, but after a minute, he coaxed her lips apart with his tongue, exploring her mouth, persuading her to kiss him back. *He tastes so good, tangy, like the juice.* She twined her tongue around his more aggressively and felt his cock jump against her. Tom groaned, deepening the kiss. She made little sounds of pleasure, trying to tell him how much she wanted this, how wonderful he made her feel. Andi settled onto the bed, locking herself against his body, curling one leg around his, trying to hold them tightly together. His musky scent rose, enticing, filling her nostrils and further arousing her senses.

He threw back the quilt with an impatient toss, scooting over to provide enough room for her on the mattress and held her close, blanketing her body with his. His fully aroused cock, long and hard, pressed into her belly. Rocking his hips, Tom made sure she felt every inch of his penis, straining to find a way to penetrate the cloth barrier between them. She stroked the well-defined muscles of his abdomen, then slid her hand down that fascinating hairline, following it past the waistband of his pajamas. Finding what she sought, Andi gripped the impressive girth of his manhood, working her hands along the length, cupping his heavy sac, curling her fingers around the weight, gently massaging. She traced the ridge in the center of the sac with a coy fingertip, applying slight pressure. Murmuring his pleasure against her lips, Tom reached down to urge her to explore further. Andi pushed his fingers out of her way, encircling his cock with her hand so she could stroke from base to tip in a slow, firm, figure-eight motion. Sliding her hands to the base of his throbbing manhood, she tightened her fingers into a ring for a minute. He was hard steel under hot velvet, definitely ready for her.

Groaning, Tom nibbled at her lips, then kissed his way down her neck, alternating caresses with tiny bites, which left Andi squirming in waves of pleasure. She kept one hand wrapped around his cock, using the other to tease at his nipple, stroking for a moment before taking the sensitive nub gently in her teeth, laving it with her tongue. Throwing his head back, Tom arched his body against hers, grinding against her pelvis.

He cupped one breast through her tunic, thumb rubbing the nipple until it was hard and aching for more. The fabric intensified the sensations, and she twisted her body as waves of arousal spread through her.

When she rubbed her thumb across the plum-shaped tip of his cock, spreading the droplets of first arousal, his hips bucked. Raising her head, now it was her turn to bring her fingers to her mouth and lick the precum off them with dainty flicks of her tongue.

Tom pulled back for a minute, looking into her eyes. "Are you sure?" he asked. "I want you, I've wanted to make love to you practically since we first met. I'll never forget that dress you had on at the dance, especially after you got it wet. But—"

Andi feathered kisses along his jaw. "Having come so close to losing you this week, I swore that if you survived I was going to show you exactly how I feel. So, yeah, I'm sure."

"Good," he said with masculine satisfaction.

Wasting no more precious time in talk, he lifted her dress over her head, balling it up and throwing it in the general direction of the chair. The clasp on her lacy bra took him a moment to undo and then he took in every detail of her body with hungry appreciation, eyes lingering on her chest. "Perfect. Just the right size, and so soft." Andi took a deep breath, putting her hands under her breasts, lifting them for his attention. He bent his head to the closest nipple, suckling the bud till it pebbled and then blowing across the damp surface to make her shiver with pleasure. Laughing in delight at her response, he paid homage to the other nipple in much the same way. Then he stared down her half-naked body and back up to her face. "You still have way too many clothes on."

"Do something about it then," she dared him, arching her hips.

With carefully calculated and controlled strength, he ripped off her filmy silk thong. He rolled her naked body under him, his heavy arousal resting in the cradle of her thighs. Heat spread through her as he moved in shallow strokes along her sensitive folds. "You're so beautiful," he murmured, lowering his head to suckle at her breast. His hand stroked her sides and stomach, then sliding back to tug and tease her nipples.

Andi arched under him, rubbing his shaft with her needy body. Kissing the small tattoo over his heart, she could feel his heartbeat. With her tongue she caressed the spot where his neck met his shoulders, then applied pressure with her teeth, not a full bite, but his cock surged against her as she bore down. She skimmed her palm over one flat nipple before teasing it with her tongue, using a swirling motion as if she was licking an ice cream cone. Carefully, she raked her nails across the other, until it was hard. He shivered, and his cock twitched again.

Already so wet, aroused to the point of delicious, aching pain, she was desperate to have him inside. But Tom was in no hurry apparently, continuing to explore, stroking, caressing, until he slid his fingers through the curls at the vee of her thighs. He murmured in appreciation, moving his fingers purposefully until he found her clit. Rolling the sensitive nub between his fingers, he worked to heighten her arousal even further. Clenching her muscles around him, Andi sighed with pleasure. They kissed again while his fingers stroked pushed deeper inside her, bringing her to a climax.

As she finished, he broke off the kiss, taking a second to pull off the soft trousers he was wearing. She kept her hands on his body, caressing, rubbing, not wanting to be without skin contact for even a minute. When he settled back over her, she cupped his heavy balls, tucked up tight against his body, then unable to resist the temptation to wrap her hand around his engorged shaft again, loving the feeling of caging all that masculine power for a moment.

Tom returned to his expert stimulation of her most private places. Taking her hand off his cock, he transferred her hold to the muscles of his ass, before positioning himself to glide deep inside her with one thrust. The weight of his sac bumped against her as he moved in and out with deliberation.

Andi stroked his back with her thumbs, up and down beside the spine, holding him close as he moved inside her, his hips pistoning in a slow rhythm that tantalized. His girth filled her channel as no other man had ever done, each thrust causing delicious tingling through her entire pelvic area. "Kiss me?"

Obliging with a hot, steamy kiss, tongue thrusting deep into her mouth, Tom took possession with enthusiasm and skill. His hands caressed her body while she clenched her core muscles around his cock, massaging him in the age old, intimate rhythm of pressure and release. Trying to merge them into one, she held him tightly, arms around him as far as she could reach.

"You feel so good." He wrapped his big hands under her butt to tilt it so he could go deeper. "You're so tight, it makes me crazy."

She locked her legs around his back. He shivered, holding himself still, then thrusting deeper when she loosened the pressure. Andi reveled in the way every move of his built upon her pleasure, and tried to reciprocate, using everything she knew to intensify the experience for him as well. Judging by the rapt expression on his face above her and the way his hips pumped harder, driving them both toward climax, her efforts were effective and appreciated. Andi lost herself in the sensations, every thrust of her lover's hot penis building inexorably toward the moment of release. Deeper and deeper, touching sensitive places no other man had ever reached for her, Tom's strokes were smooth, forceful. All her senses concentrated on the fullness and enticing pressure his cock applied to the delicious ache inside her. The pleasure was overwhelming. Andi screamed his name as she tipped over the edge into ecstasy. He matched her passion, going deep on the last driving thrust, his own release shuddering, powerful. He held still as the fading convulsions of her climax milked every drop of his seed.

Holding her close as the tremors faded, Tom murmured sweet things, smoothed back her tousled hair, nipped at her ear lobe, kissed her forehead. "Next time we're going slower, I promise." His hand cupped her breast, gently massaged the nipple. He lowered his head to lap at the still pebbled bud lazily, like a big, contented cat sipping cream.

"I don't know if I can survive a second round." She hugged him and laughed. "But I'm willing to try."

"I may not be up to that today," Tom said regretfully. "I guess the bhengola took something of a toll on me."

"Not from my vantage point." Andi kissed his cheek.

They lay together, Tom carefully taking most of his weight on his elbows, his softening cock still nestled inside her body. He kissed her lips tenderly. "You're one very special lady."

He rolled over onto his back. Andi sighed a wordless protest as his cock slipped out of her. Drawing her close against him, Tom pillowed her head on his shoulder, keeping possession of her hand. "I just remembered you said we're in a monastery, didn't you?"

"Yes, as a matter of fact, we're surrounded by monks." Andi chuckled. "But *we* didn't take any vows of celibacy."

"Good thing. That's one vow I couldn't keep, not around you." He kissed the tip of her nose. "It was hard enough to keep my hands off you when we were dancing. Did I mention that dress you had on made it very hard to concentrate? I could barely remember what I was really there for."

"Glad you noticed." She snuggled in closer to his warmth.

"I said so at the time, as I recall." Reaching to the foot of the bed, Tom tugged the furs and comforters around both of them, holding her tightly. "That guy was a fool."

"Guy?" Andi tilted her head as she tried to follow his thought.

"Whoever you said you were waiting for that night. That guy. He was a fool to stand you up."

"Oh. Him. Let me explain—" Andi tried to turn in his arms so she could see his face.

He pressed her head onto his shoulder, dropping a kiss on her curls. "Shh, he's not important now. Time enough for that subject later. Today is about *us*, you and me. No one else." He yawned.

"I should let you sleep." She made a move to shift away, getting ready to stand.

"Where do you think you're going?" He drew her back, curled around her. "I'll sleep just fine, as long as you're here with me." One big hand moved to cup her breast again.

She relaxed into his embrace, drowsy herself and very content. She dozed off briefly, and a few minutes later, when she wakened, she could tell by the rhythm of his breathing and the relaxation in his body against hers that he'd fallen asleep.

Gently she disengaged his hand and turned to see his face. She touched his cheek, feathered a kiss over his lips. *He's an amazing lover.* He'd survived a near-death experience with her help, of course he was grateful. *Is there more to it than just gratitude? Some of what he'd said seemed to imply that maybe his feelings ran deeper.* She'd known he'd been attracted to her since the night of their dance. Andi sighed. *After we get back to the capital in one piece,* then *I can see what comes next between us.*

Lords, keep him from getting orders to ship out offworld to another assignment any time soon. Or me getting transferred by Loxton!

***

When Mitch came to assume the duties of caretaker several hours later, Andi was demurely curled in the big armchair, no evidence of her interlude with Tom to be found. No telltale signs there for the sergeant's sharp eyes. Still, her cheeks flamed in a small flush as she slipped away to her room for real rest.

Returning to the sickroom later in the morning after a good sleep and a hearty breakfast, she found Tom sitting in bed working his way through an overflowing breakfast tray. Mitch leaned one elbow on the large chair, sipping at a cup of coffee, glancing out the window from time to time. Both had the air of men at peace with the world.

"Good morning, ma'am." Mitch smiled, waving his mug carefully at her. "I saved you a cup of coffee, if you'd care for some."

"*Would* I?" Andi helped herself to the coffee waiting on the slender table. She sipped at the steaming brew as she strolled to the bed. "How are you feeling this morning?"

"Like my old self." Tom stretched out a hand, palm up. When she put her hand in his, he drew her closer, planting a kiss on her cheek. "Amazing what a good night's sleep and a decent meal will do for a guy." Winking at her, he let her go.

Mitch watched the byplay with raised eyebrows and a serious face. Glancing from Andi to Tom, he cleared his throat. "I'm, ah, glad you don't kiss all your nurses, Captain."

"Just the beautiful ones." Grinning, Tom took another drink of his coffee. "Which leaves you *out*, Mitch."

Andi's cheeks felt hot. She kept her head down and backed away from the bed, moving toward the refuge of the chair. Taking a sip of the coffee to lubricate her dry throat, she tried a casually teasing tone. "What? No gratitude for the high-quality nursing he provided? And here poor Mitch and I stayed up all night, the last three nights in a row, no less, listening to you snore. And you do snore, don't try to deny it."

The door crashed open, startling the room's occupants. Andi jumped, her coffee sloshing as Mitch drew his blaster. Tom threw the covers aside to get out of bed.

Corporal Rogers ran into the room, followed by Rahuna and one of the elder monks. "We're under attack, Sarge," Rogers reported. His salute for Tom was belated, amazement on the soldier's freckled face. "You're better, sir? Sorry I forgot to knock, sir."

"What do you mean 'under attack'?" Tom planted his feet firmly on the floor. "*Situation report, corporal.*"

Rogers went to attention, eyes straight ahead, hands at his sides. His voice was clipped. "A force of approximately thirty men tried to come across the bridge at dawn a few minutes ago. Latvik and one of the monks standing guard sounded the alarm. We've repelled the first attack, but it took a lot of firepower. The hostiles are massed across the ravine."

Swaying somewhat in the attempt, Tom stood. Andi and Mitch collided as each came to help him.

"Take it easy."

"Don't rush it, sir."

Glaring at both of them, Tom waved them off. He grabbed his neatly folded uniform lying at the foot of the bed.

"The monastery defenses are holding for now." Rahuna spoke for the first time.

"What kind of defenses exactly?" *I know they mentioned this before but really, what kind of shields or weapons would a monastery have?* Remembering the complicated, highly advanced mechanisms in the healing chamber, Andi wondered if there might be a similarly powerful set up for guarding the monks' privacy and security.

Rahuna nodded, showing every bit of his age this morning, cherubic face lined and unhappy. "Yes, when the monastery was built, the Ancients installed devices to prevent attack across the ravine, but the power seems to be failing. The monks say it hasn't been used since the last Clan war, four hundred years ago."

"Maybe we drained it too much yesterday when we—" Mitch abruptly snapped his mouth closed on the secret of the healing chamber as Andi made a chopping motion with her hand.

"Whatever kind of protective field this place has, it's fading in and out, like the power source is running ragged." Corporal Rogers's eyes remained focused on Tom, oblivious to the byplay between the sergeant and Andi. He stepped toward the bed, leaned forward, expression intense. "And, Captain, the attackers have a blast cannon, sounds like Mark 80 at least, and they're using it nonstop on this force field."

Tom fastened his uniform shirt. "Where in the hell did insurgents get that? Not ours from the APC?"

Rogers shook his head. "No, ours slagged when it was sabotaged in the garage. Whatever their weapon is, it's adding to the stress on the monastery's defenses. I don't like the looks of things, sir."

"Tleer has declared it's time for you to leave. He sends his apologies for not giving you the message in person, but he's busy preparing the exit for you." The elder monk made his presence felt in the room, giving Rahuna a slight bow.

Stomach churning with anxiety, Andi jumped from the chair to confront the monk. "You're not thinking of handing us over to *them*, are you? Do you know what they've been doing in the villages and at the Obati nobles' summer compound?"

But the monk was shaking his head, long braid flying about his shoulders. "No one is talking about surrendering you to the rebels. There's another way to leave the monastery, but it takes much time, requiring you to start now."

"What other way?" Hands on his hips, nostrils flared, Mitch looked askance at the monk. "It's a sheer drop on all sides of this place—no mountaineer, no matter how expert, could handle the descent, let alone the party we've got. Might as well jump out the window here and get it over with." He turned to Tom. "You haven't seen the pinnacle this place sits on, sir. In my opinion, it would be impossible to descend without anti-grav, which we don't have."

The monk bowed his head. Apparently, his calm wasn't the least bit impaired by Mitch's impromptu situation report. "Of course we don't mean to hand you ropes and suggest you climb down the cliff wall."

Andi noted the monk's placid face and the way he kept his hands linked. *Sounds like he's explaining something elementary to a roomful of children. Backward children.*

In the same faintly lecturing tone, the monk offered a bit more detail. "Those who built the monastery hollowed out a passage in the plateau, to the base of the mountain at the river level below. Your path to escape lies there. We waste time."

How can we descend a staircase two miles high? A pulse of vertigo making her nauseated, Andi glanced at Tom. From the expression on his face, he must have been thinking along the same lines. She raised her eyebrows and shook a cautionary finger at him. "You're nowhere near well enough to attempt it."

"No choice. Good thing I'm better today." He picked up his uniform pants and paused. "I want one minute of privacy to put my trousers on, and then you're going to take Sergeant Wilson and me to see the situation for ourselves, Corporal."

Andi allowed herself to be ushered out of the sickroom by Rahuna and the officious monk. Once in the corridor, the deep rumbling coursing through the stones of the building, including the floor's flagstones, became more pronounced. Her heart pounded in rhythm, and she swayed, steadying herself by bracing against the wall.

No, it wasn't her imagination—the stones were vibrating with the power of whatever ancient device provided their defense at the moment. A piece of white mortar crumbled out from between two of the ancient slabs and fell at her feet. *Things are going from bad to worse if the building is starting to shake itself apart.* Andi looked over at the monk accompanying them. "What will you do?"

He stared at the fragments of mortar, the corners of his mouth turned down as if displeased or bored. His voice was flat. "We'll gather at the hidden entrance to the shaft and chant you on your way. Then we'll withdraw further into the innermost chambers to wait. After the first alarm, we cut the wooden footbridge, so the renegades can't cross easily. Should they somehow reach the monastery, they won't be able to locate us." He raised his head to gaze at Andi from narrowed eyes. "And you'll be long gone. Once the invaders have seen the monastery, they, too, will leave. There's nothing here for the likes of them. Rebel fighters don't care about us."

They weren't indifferent to the poor priest at the Shenti temple. "I'm sorry we brought this trouble to you," she said.

The monk's shrug was nonchalant. "Don't worry. The prophecies said the monastery was to offer hospitality to those holding the fate of our world in their hands. We've enacted the role faithfully for you. Don't you agree?" He stared pointedly at Rahuna.

His Serene Holiness nodded. "It shall be as Sanenre wills. The monastery defenses have never failed in all of recorded history."

"All right, people. Let's move it." Tom and Mitch stepped into the corridor. Touching Andi's elbow gently, Tom gave her a small smile as he passed. "Lead the way, sir, if you please," he told the monk.

"The exit shaft to the river passage is in this direction." Standing aside, the man made a sweeping gesture with his arm.

Tom caught at the monk's sleeve before he took more than a step. "No, I need to see what kind of weaponry they're using against us first." He shook his head, hand on the blaster at his side. "I have to know so I can make a full report. There's got to be time for me to look outside. But you can escort Miss Markriss and His Serene Holiness to the safety of the exit for me."

"I'm going with you," Andi said. "I've seen everything else on this trip. I want to see this, too. I'm a witness." *And I feel much safer when you're around.*

"All right, I'm not wasting time arguing. Just keep back, behind Mitch and me." Tom frowned at her but motioned to the waiting monk. "Let's go."

Rogers, having gone ahead while the others were waiting for Tom to get dressed, greeted the group at the monastery's entrance. The rumbling of the defensive devices was pronounced here, causing Andi to clap her hands over her ears.

Reaching out, Tom cautiously tapped Rogers on the shoulder. The corporal looked around. "Sir, the hostiles have stopped firing for the last few minutes. I think maybe they're getting ready to make some kind of demand."

Tom took Rogers' place at the edge of the doorway and risked a quick glance, then another. Whistling, he glanced at Mitch. "Now I'm getting the picture of what it must have been like for you to carry me to the monastery."

"Going over that bridge was awful." Andi grimaced. "I don't know how Mitch and the soldiers managed it."

"All in a day's work," Mitch said cheerfully. He pointed above their heads with his blaster. "What's that green light? Is that the shield, Rogers?"

Craning her neck, Andi saw a wall of translucent, green light above her, extending about thirty feet out from where she crouched. Projected from the arch in some unknown fashion, the shield extended below the bridge and far above their heads.

Tom tilted his head back to study the luminescence, too. "Does it go all the way around the monastery?"

Before anyone had time to answer his question, the reassuring wall of light flickered, thinning to a pale green. Andi could barely see the shield against the increasing sunlight. An opportunistic, sizzling blast from the enemy's weapon penetrated the now-insubstantial defense, striking the edge of the great arch above their heads. Stone chips flew in all directions. People scattered, ducked. Tom pushed Andi behind him, shielding her with his own body. One shard of stone struck her cheek, stinging like an insect bite. She slapped her hand over the spot, and there was blood on her palm when she checked. Tilting her face with his big hand, eyeing the injury, Tom wiped the blood away with his thumb. He rubbed his hand on his pants leg.

He gave her a reassuring pat on the shoulder. "Just a graze. Might not even scar. Stay further back, okay?"

Andi sighed in relief. "No problem." Leaning on the wall because her legs were rubbery, she moved away from the entrance as ordered.

"Shield's back," Rogers said. "I've seen the same fluctuation several times since the attack began."

Andi stared at the soldier next to her. *Rogers sounds a whole lot calmer than I am right now.*

"I fear we may not have much time before this ancient safeguard falls." Rahuna withdrew into the safety of the corridor, stopping next to her.

"*Incoming.*" Mitch yanked Tom flat against the inner wall as a second bolt of pure energy sizzled against the stones of the monastery. More rock crumbled under this next assault. Gasping, Andi scooted further back, her hand locked on Rahuna's elbow, dragging him with her.

"Not a Sectors cannon." Tom crouched well inside the entry. "Mitch, what do you think?"

Risking another quick look around the edge of the arch to check the status of their green defensive shield, the sergeant considered. "You're going to think I'm crazy, sir, but it whines and spits like…*Mawreg* armament. Blast beam's the right color."

"Precisely what I was thinking." Tom's fist clenched on the butt of his blaster. "Wish we had the viewers handy. I'd like to make sure."

Mawreg? Andi's stomach lurched at the idea of the dreaded, sadistic enemy. *But the Mawreg are nowhere near this sector. And the Seventh Star Guard Fleet is between us and them. Tom and Mitch have to be wrong.*

"It's locals using the thing, sir, not Mawreg." Rogers added another piece of information to the puzzle. "Latvik and I shot at least a dozen guys in the first attack, before the green light shield came on. Where would the Naranti get a Mawreg weapon? And how would they know what to do with it? Every briefing I've ever had indicated those alien bastards don't work with indigenous planetary residents. Once the Mawreg pull out the high-powered ordnance, the local populace is fodder."

Or the locals commit mass suicide to avoid what the Mawreg would do to them. Like on Halarikon 3. Andi's stomach heaved again. She swallowed hard. *Wish I hadn't eaten breakfast.*

Tom came to offer her his hand, pulling her upright while scanning her face. "You okay?"

She nodded. "I'll manage."

I never doubted it." Warm smile lighting his face, Tom kept his light hold on her hand, pulling her into the shelter of his free arm.

He makes me feel so protected, so safe. But if there are Mawreg out there, nothing and no one can save us. Andi shivered.

Tom eyed the force shield. "I don't like the way the light flickers on and off. Time to escape may be even shorter than we anticipated. Where's Latvik?"

"Sent him with another monk to gather the gear," Rogers said. "We'll meet wherever the entrance to this river passage is."

"Well done."

Rogers drew himself up to his full height at the compliment, grinning.

"Do you think the rebels can bridge the center gap?" Andi asked. "It's quite a space to cross. Maybe we *are* safe to stay here."

Tom's assessment was unflinching. "I could get across the gap, given the time and manpower, both of which the Naranti have in ample quantities. What do you think, Mitch?"

"Yes, sir, I'd say so."

Andi gave the sergeant a wry glance, pursing her lips. "Gee, that's so reassuring. You could have lied to me, made me feel better."

"And even if they never get across, they still win if we stay bottled up here." Tom addressed Andi and Rahuna. "We've got to get our information back to the capital before this war gets any bigger. At some point, the momentum of events will be unstoppable, no matter who started it. Time's running out for restoring peace on Zulaire."

"This place may be bristling with unusual stuff all right, but it's lacking in the one thing we need now, which is a simple comlink." Mitch sounded resigned.

The monk had remained a few yards back, in the relative safety of the main hallway, hands folded inside the sleeves of his red robe, waiting for the outworlders to finish their discussion. Tom walked to him now, towing Andi with him. "All right, if you'd lead the way to this passage, we're ready."

Saying nothing, the monk wheeled, moving at a rapid pace through the corridors, past the door to Tom's sickroom then leading them toward the center of the plateau. The constant vibration in the walls and under her feet reassured Andi that the Ancients' safeguard was still holding. Once the shield failed, the mob would waste no time constructing a temporary bridge, crossing the ravine, seeking them out in the monastery. *At least the mysterious corridors might confuse them as much as the maze of twisting hallways confused Mitch and me last night.*

A minute later, their guide stopped in the middle of a hallway that kept spiraling onward endlessly away from them, around the core of the building.

Pacing back and forth in front of a carved wall frieze, Tleer was impatiently waiting. As soon as he saw Andi, he fumbled in his deep pockets, first one then the other. Finding what he sought, he raised the little translucent urabu carving. Chanting in the long-dead language of Sanenre, the chief monk inserted the odd key into the wall, placing it like a puzzle piece into the depiction of yet another herd of playful urabu. Stepping back, still chanting, Tleer peered nearsightedly at the door.

Nothing.

Lords of Space, not another test of faith. I wouldn't have the patience to be a monk. Andi sidled closer to the mural.

"Sir, we better have a backup plan." Mitch shifted his stance, checking his blaster's charge level, then looking the way they'd just come.

Tom waved him off.

A burst of mechanical whining from inside the walls took Andi by surprise, assaulting her ears and vibrating through all the bones in her face. When the sound stopped, a section of the wall in front of her had ceased to exist, like the black door had done the other night when they went to the healing chamber. Tleer gestured for Andi to hurry through the opening, stepping across the threshold himself, turning to extend a hand to her. As she walked in front of him, Andi could have sworn she saw the little stone urabu leap into his palm. Closing his hand into a fist, Tleer jammed the key into his pocket before she could be sure.

With a SNAP the wall reappeared behind them.

"Doors? Or illusions? This place could drive a person crazy," Andi said.

"Thank the Lords of Space, you're here, sir." Cradling his blaster, Latvik emerged from the crowd of silent monks.

Andi counted off the rest of their party gathered in this circular room, along with monks of all ages. The chamber was crowded, hot and airless. Sadu cooed at her, happy in his backpack on Abukawal's broad shoulders. The Shenti warrior held Lysanda within the curve of his arms. She looked as blank-faced as ever, locked in her own self protective shell, willing to go wherever he asked.

Latvik distributed gear to Tom and the others. Taking the pack he offered her, Andi shouldered it with a muttered curse. *I sure didn't miss hauling this burden around.*

"Are you ready?" Tleer was as serene as ever. Any tension he'd been projecting had ebbed away as soon as the last door had slammed shut behind them.

Impatience written in every tense line of his face, Tom narrowed his eyes as he studied the room. "Where's the passage?"

Examining the chamber as well, Andi couldn't see any obvious exits.

"You're standing on it." Tleer pointed at the floor.

Taking a reflexive step backward, Andi stared. The floor under her feet, the entire center of the room, was a single circular disk of stone. The perimeter of the chamber's flooring was a two-yard-wide band of variegated rock tile into which the central black stone had been set.

The monks were already moving away from them, taking positions pressed against the walls, standing shoulder to shoulder on the tiled band.

"How does this work?" Tom took a few impatient steps to his left then back to his original location, apparently anxious to get on with their escape. Andi sympathized.

"You must push this." Tleer indicated, but didn't touch, a small carving in the exact center of the floor. "You'll descend through the passage to the base of the mountain and can escape to the river."

Tom offered the chief monk his hand. "I can't thank you enough for taking us in, for treating my fever—"

"It was foretold. You've given us the joy of prophecy fulfilled in our lifetimes. We must thank you." Tleer shook his hand, bowing. "Now, be on your way, for our walls can no longer offer you sanctuary." Walking off the black disk, the old monk joined his comrades, who scooted closer to each other along the wall to make room for him.

Andi glanced around at the ring of monks, an impassive yet excited audience. Some of the younger ones quivered with anticipation, apparently eager to witness the miracle of the escape device being utilized after sitting untouched for millennia. Even the more disciplined elder monks had an air of repressed excitement about the coming activation of one of Sanenre's miraculous machines.

She was wrenched from her reverie as Tom gave crisp orders in his command voice. "All right, spread out everyone, and stay away from the edge."

Leaning closer to the carving in the center of the floor, Andi had a flash of recognition. "It's the Heart of Sanenre flower."

"Nice to know, but how does it *work*?" Squatting beside her, Tom examined the metal flower from all angles. He tried moving it from side to side. No luck. The monks offered no suggestions. The entire congregation was chanting in a hypnotic rhythm. *I wish they'd stop that.* Andi fanned herself ineffectually with her hand. *There's no air moving in here at all.*

Experimentally, Tom pushed on the top of the flower, increasing the pressure as it gave under his hand, until there was a decisive click. The flower blossom, folded, retracted into the carved stem, then the stem itself receded into the disk in one continuous motion. A small panel slid closed, concealing the flower.

Nothing else happened. Andi shut her eyes and bit her lip.

"These devices do have something of a delayed reaction." Rahuna's voice was tentative.

"You're not responsible for whether it works or not, sir," Andi said. Her pulse seemed to throb in time with the vibration in the outer walls again. Taking off her pack, she sat on the floor. Tom opened his mouth, but his words were lost in a sudden cracking, a great tearing noise. Andi scrambled to her feet again, pack hanging from one hand.

There was now a noticeable disconnect between the edge of the disk and the mosaic flooring around it. The gap grew an inch at a time.

"Not too dramatic an escape so far, is it?" Tom stood next to Andi. Bending over, he spoke next to her ear. "At this rate we'll still be here when the enemy breaks in."

"Captain, I think the descent is accelerating," Mitch said in the next instant.

"Right." Looking around, Tom gestured with his blaster. "Sit in the center and hang on to each other. It's a long way down and no telling how fast we'll fall."

Andi swallowed. "Or how hard we'll *land*. I wish there was something to hang onto." As if her desire had been a command, small metal flowers shot up around the disk, leaves arranged to provide handholds for the passengers. Tom sat down behind her, caging her in his arms as he took a grip on the nearest sculpture. Gratefully, she leaned against his reassuring warmth and bulk.

The disk started falling faster and faster, straight into a fetid black hole in the plateau. Soon the platform was descending so fast Andi found it hard to breathe, despite the air rushing past the edges of the disk in a shrieking updraft. Tom kept her secure in his embrace. Wailing, Sadu indicated he'd had enough of this new experience, near strangling Abukawal in his distress.

"Maybe halfway by now." Tom shouted his estimate. "Brace yourselves for landing."

"*Hang on.*" Yelling, Tom curled one arm around Andi's waist so tightly she felt cut in half. She turned around and clung to him with all her strength, grabbing his uniform shirt in clawed hands, getting an unbreakable grip ducking her head against his chest.

The disk came to a violent halt, knocking Andi flat, sprawling on top of Tom. Drifting like a petal the last two yards, their platform came to rest on the floor at the base of the passage. Other than water dripping incessantly somewhere, there was silence. Andi peeked at her surroundings, illuminated by dim light from some source off to the left. The passage they'd just fallen through had widened out into a vast cavern. *I'm no structural engineer, but how can the mountain top support its own weight and the monastery, with such a void at the center? More ancient mysteries?*

"Sir, I think my arm is broken." Latvik sat wedged at an awkward angle. Trying to stand, he subsided with a grunt of pain. "Sorry, sir."

"Rogers, you know how to immobilize a broken arm, take care of it. We'll have to set the bone for you later, Latvik. Try not to make it worse, okay, soldier?" The young private answered Tom with a weak nod as the captain moved on to the next challenge. "Mitch, I need you to do a recon, on the double."

The sergeant stood, staggering like someone who'd been on a boat in a rolling sea. Unholstering his blaster, he jumped off the disk into the clear space beyond. He shone his hand lamp around, revealing the mouth of a tunnel. "I hear fast movin' water out there, sir."

"The river, I hope. Check it out and report back." As Mitch moved off into the gloom, Tom helped Andi to her feet. "All right, people, I see nowhere else to go except out to the river, so let's get ready to move. For all we know, this disk is going to take a return trip to the top any second now."

The mere suggestion was motivation enough for Andi to get herself and her gear onto firm ground. Then she turned to help Lysanda and Sadu make the transition off the disk.

"Where the hell is Mitch?" Peering in the direction the sergeant had gone, Tom drew his blaster.

"Here, sir!" Stepping into their small area, returning from the mouth of the tunnel, Mitch aimed his hand lamp at the ground. "It's a short walk to the riverbank. Maybe a few yards."

"What shall we do when we reach the river, Captain?" Rahuna asked. "The waters run deep and fast in the mountains, with sheer canyon walls on all sides. We can't ford it, nor swim to safety."

"It's a bit late to be thinking about topography." Andi knew she sounded grumpy.

"The monks didn't give us much time to consider what this escape route might involve, did they?" Tom sounded thoughtful. "Maybe we overstayed our welcome."

"The tunnel ends about six feet above a tiny beach. It's a big, nasty river with the cliff face on both sides, just as His Holiness describes." Mitch's terse report was disappointing.

"Remember we have flotation devices in our emergency gear." The captain pointed at the pack by Andi's feet.

"Well, now I'm certainly happier about hauling this heavy damn pack all over hell and gone." Andi lifted it up and set it down again, laughing. "What other surprises have we carted around?"

The ground under her feet rolled and pitched. Ominous rumblings came from the passage as rocks fell. Taking a few hesitant steps toward the daylight, Andi balanced carefully while the tremors continued.

"Into the tunnel—*quick*." Tom shoved her in the direction he wanted her to go. Grabbing at Lysanda's hand, checking over her shoulder to see that Abukawal had Sadu and was running behind them, Andi fled.

The captain and the injured Latvik were the last to reach the dubious safety of the underground passage, as a large chunk of rock came crashing from above, shattering the disk they'd descended on into a million pieces. Fragments of the black stone flew everywhere. A large piece exploded on the cavern wall near Andi, raining smaller shards on the floor. More boulders plunged down the shaft, driving the refugees into a headlong run through the passageway to the river, dust expanding into the space after them.

"Keep going. We've got to get outside," Tom yelled.

Coughing, Andi needed no encouragement to run as fast as she could, Lysanda stumbling after her. First to exit the cavern, Andi was confronted by the massive

Chikeeri River. As Mitch had promised, a small expanse of rocky beach lay below the lip of the tunnel, the river lapping against the sand. Deceptively calm water flowed past, but a few yards out, a violent torrent boiled and foamed. Releasing Lysanda's hand, Andi half slithered, half jumped down to the beach. Turning, she encouraged the princess to make the descent.

"Don't get too close to the lower part of the beach yet," Tom said as he jumped, landing close to Andi. "Might be unstable, or slippery. Abukawal, keep a close eye on the baby."

Another rolling quake shuddered through the beach under their feet. Dust exploded from the tunnel behind them.

"What do we have to do to make these boats of yours a reality?" Andi smothered a cough as the thick cloud swirled around them. "I'd like to get out of here before the whole mountain collapses on top of us."

Holstering his blaster, Tom rubbed the back of his neck and tugged at his collar. "Well, not exactly boats. More like elaborate rafts."

"Meant for night ops, for crossin' a lake or something similar." Mitch took the pack from Abukawal and dumped out the contents.

"Rafts?" Andi put one hand on her hip and pointed at the river with the other. "You want us to go onto that raging torrent on a *raft*?" She eyed the boisterous Chikeeri River, boiling and heaving its way to the far-off ocean.

"I don't see any choices." Tom indicated the dust-choked tunnel entrance. "We can't go back to the monastery, and even if we could, sitting with the monks isn't an option for the success of our mutual mission, you agree?"

"No choices. We must keep going forward and risking all." Rahuna threw a small rock into the river. Raising his hands in a calming gesture, he turned to Andi. "Sanenre is deciding for us so Fortune will favor us."

Sitting on her pack, Andi gave an unladylike snort. "Somehow I don't find that reassuring at this stage."

"We've managed so far," Tom said. "All right, we have to lighten the load or the rafts'll sink the minute they hit the water. These craft are rated for two fully kitted Special Forces operators, and we're going to try transporting eight adults and a child, plus gear. Discard any-thing not essential to survival." He turned back to confer with Mitch. "How's it coming?"

"About ready to trigger the canisters, sir." Setting two military-issue, black cylinders on the ground three yards apart, the sergeant made sure they were well balanced on the sloping rock beach. "I suggest you step back, ladies and gentlemen."

He waited while Andi and the others got out of the danger zone, then pushed a button on the hand controller.

The transformation from cylinder to raft wasn't dramatic, but it was *fast*. Andi watched closely as the two canisters morphed, section by section, into matching black rafts, high-sided, with bluntly V-shaped prows. *All right, that does look like a sturdy design.* Surely boats made for the Special Forces could take more punishment than a normal raft would ever be expected to endure. *Military operators get the best gear available. Everyone knows that.*

At the stern of each raft was a small, glossy black rectangle. Curious, she went to examine one more closely.

"Propulsion unit," Mitch said when he noticed Andi eyeing the box. "The latest in mili-tary miniaturization of the standard ground vehicle power source. Top secret."

"We need plenty of power to steer away from rocks and keep our way in the rapids." Reassured, she breathed a sigh of relief.

"They have limited capacity. I hope we hit a smoother stretch of river soon." Shading his eyes with one hand, Tom stared downriver. "Are there waterfalls?"

"Falls, no," Andi said. "High potential for whitewater boating, yes. The Chikeeri was ranked as one of the most dangerous rivers in the Sector."

The beach under her feet heaved in a series of moderate quakes. Andi struggled to stay upright on the slippery rocks. Abandoning the raft, Tom grabbed her. Gratefully, Andi clung to him while thunderous crashes echoed from the tunnel.

"Time to do this, people," Tom said, releasing her. "I swear the whole place is self-destructing. All right—boat assignments. I'll drive one. Mitch, you skipper the other. You'll launch first. We'll load Abukawal, Lysanda, Sadu and Rogers in with you."

"At least the Chikeeri flows in the direction of the capital." Andi made her voice light and happy in case anyone needed encouragement. "A boat trip saves us a lot of walking."

"Yeah, that's a positive, although I'm still hoping to find some transport." Eyebrows knitted in a frown, Tom looked over his ragtag group. "Is Latvik's broken arm set?"

Andi turned and saw the hapless soldier sitting against the embankment, white-faced and biting his lip. His broken arm was now encased in a protective cast, camouflage-colored to match his uniform. Giving his comrade a hand, Rogers reported, "He's good to go, sir."

"I'll make it, sir, no worries." Latvik's face was set in grim lines, but he cradled his blaster in his good arm, ready for action.

"All right, then. No help for it," Tom said. "We need to get going or starve to death on this beach. The most important thing to remember is pure and simple—*hang on.*" He stared over the foaming water. "The river's going to try to drown us. Mitch and I'll do our best to keep that from happening, but if you fall in, there's not a whole hell of a lot we can do for you. You can't fight the current, so if you do fall in, try to surf it."

Andi watched the rushing river. There was quite a possibility of the boats coming to grief, particularly since they weren't designed for whitewater. "What if the boat flips over?"

Tom grunted. He exchanged glances with Mitch, and both men shrugged. "Pray the boat doesn't turn over, okay?" The captain bent to pick up one boat by the bow, Mitch moving to take the stern. As they trudged toward the river. Tom spoke over his shoulder. "All right, briefing finished. Let's go."

If Latvik can do it with a broken arm, I can do it. Andi nodded firmly to herself, walking after the men toward her assigned boat.

Getting the first raft into the river and holding it steady was a tricky chore. She stayed at a safe distance, biting her tongue against offering unnecessary advice. The current, even this close to shore, sucked at the boat. Mitch came close to falling into the river without the raft at one point, Tom jerking him to safety.

Abukawal took Sadu and, working with the sergeant, managed to lash the toddler in his carrier in the center of the heaving raft. Popping his thumb in his mouth, Sadu gazed around with wide-eyed interest, seeming undismayed by this new experience. Lysanda was next. She entered the raft without much protest, Abukawal addressing her in the sweetest of tones, coaxing her to sit next to Sadu as if this was some special treat arranged just for her today.

As soon as the first raft was loaded, Latvik slashed the sturdy tether keeping the boat snubbed to the beach. Eyes narrowed, holding her breath, hands clenched on the straps of her backpack, Andi observed the process, trying to figure out how to ride safely in her boat, when it was launched into the wild river.

To her surprise, watching Mitch's raft, the ride was deceptively slow at first, until the current grabbed hold and jerked the boat toward the main channel, bobbing and bouncing in the swirling waters. From her vantage point still safely on the beach, Andi saw Mitch straining to remain in control of his craft. Then the boat was gone, swept out of sight around the next bend in the river.

This is going to be a wild ride. Andi took deep, calming breaths. Her stomach churned as she thought about being whirled helplessly in the midst of the turbulent river.

She jumped as Tom touched her shoulder, saying, "No help for it—let's get our boat launched. Don't want to get too far behind the others." He had his eyes focused on the center of the torrent.

It was a struggle for Tom and Rahuna to maneuver the raft into the water. Andi helped as best she could, holding onto one of the ropes and struggling not to let the current rip the hawser away from her. The ground still trembled, with occasional violent spasms. Andi and Tom exchanged glances after one loud rumble. Unnerved by the bobbing of the raft, she clutched at him when he helped her step over the side. He kept his grip on her arm but pointed to the seat he wanted her to occupy. "Take the middle position. It'll be safer."

She looked over at Latvik, still on shore. "He's got the broken arm. Let him have the center."

"Now is not the time to argue with me. Get in the center seat." Tom's voice was low and sharp, his face set in grim lines.

She sat where ordered, clutching at the sides of the narrow raft for dear life. Latvik clambered aboard, followed by Rahuna. Working as a team, Andi and the cleric lashed gear Tom had decided was essential into place. When he'd seen the last item securely stowed, the captain stepped into the boat, slicing his combat knife through the tether in one smooth motion. He half fell into place in the stern, against the propulsion unit, as the current grabbed the raft and sent it twirling on its way.

Stark terror assaulted Andi as their boat left the beach. Despite Tom's best efforts with the motor to keep the boat pointing ahead in the center of the river, the raft kept spinning like a top. Vertigo swept over Andi.

The river pushed the boat into crazy detours, catching it in rip currents and eddies before throwing it back to the main channel. Tom had to make split-second judgments about which side of the river to take and where to attack each set of rapids. During several stretches, their speed increased dramatically, and the boat flew above the river, before crashing into the water, drenching them. Each time, the jolt of cold water across Andi's body came as a shock, like a slap.

Once in a while she caught a glimpse of the other boat, way ahead of them on the Chikeeri. Gut twisting with worry, Andi tried to count the heads in the bobbing, plunging raft.

For the most part, she concentrated on hanging onto the boat and shaking the water out of her eyes after each wave.

The sound of the river was immense, deafening. Fifteen-foot waves reared up in spots, crashing against boulders too massive for the river to tear loose. Then came another of those terrifying, out of control slides down a chute, the raft turning sideways despite Tom's frantic efforts to steer.

"*Rocks, watch out!*" Latvik yelled from his vantage point more toward the bow.

His voice was the last thing she heard before Andi flew through the air. Gasping reflexively at the shock as she landed in the frigid river, she took an inadvertent, choking gulp of water. Going all the way under, Andi panicked, thrashing, unable to tell which way was up in the churning water, unable to move her arms, her feet. *I can't breathe.* Everything she tried was useless. Like any other piece of flotsam, the current controlled her.

As she was pulled through the calmer waters after the end of the slide, Andi managed to surface for one huge breath of air, before she was shunted into some rocks. The painful collision stunned her, knocking most of the air out of her lungs. Grasping at the boulders with enough desperation to tear her nails, Andi could only win a moment's freedom from the river's plans for her. Rocks covered with a slimy funguslike growth defeated her attempts to find handholds. The pain in her hands was a distant thing, not important as she fought to live. *Can't hang on, nothing to grab.*

Slipping down the side of the boulders, she was on her way again, bobbing in the freezing water for a minute or two, then spinning around, dragged under, held, released to grab a precious breath, pummeled by branches and other debris caught in the river's inexorable grip. Andi heard shouts behind her. *But there's nothing anyone can do to help. He'd said so.*

Smoother water over a sandbar gave her hope for a second, but her legs were too weak to hold against the current. She spun violently into an eddy, and a submerged brush dragged her under, wrapping itself around her body. Andi fought to kick her way clear, holding her breath as long as she could.

At the last second, as her lungs were ready to burst from her chest, the patch of brush tore loose from its roots. Andi shot to the surface. *Air, thank the Lords.*

Her arms were slabs of stone, impossible to lift. *So cold. So freezing cold.* Her vision in the brief seconds above the waves dimmed. She'd swallowed a lot of the icy water, trying to breathe in the few chances she'd gotten. But the cruel currents always dragged her under again. *Damn it. The river isn't giving me a fair chance—not any chance—to fight back and survive.* Blinding pain burst in her head as she struck something submerged in the river. *Tom, I love you. I wish we'd had more time—*

CHAPTER SEVEN

Sand, gritty, cold, damp under her left cheek. Voices saying angry things above her head. Hands pulling and poking at her.

Leave me alone, she tried to say, but her voice was a husky rasp with no power to communicate.

As she was sinking back into unconsciousness, a cascade of cold water crashed over her. *Am I still in the river?* Panicking, struggling to rise, she screamed, a hoarse croaking voice all she had. Coarse, male laughter sounded all around her. *Am I hallucinating?*

Hands grabbed at her arms, bringing her to her feet, holding her upright as her legs buckled. She leaned over and vomited up a great gush of river water. Cursing, disgusted, the men let her fall to the sand while she retched. When there was no more water left in her stomach, Andi curled into a fetal position, protecting her aching guts. "Please, just leave me alone. Let me die in peace."

"The river spirits dropped you on our beach alive, outworlder bitch. Therefore, you're to be used for our purposes." The harshly exulting stranger spoke the Naranti dialect. "Get her up. Keep her on her feet this time."

Rough hands seized her elbows and shoulders, hauling Andi to a standing position as she swayed, weak in the knees. She realized she was barefoot, sandals lost in the river.

Exerting supreme effort, she opened her eyes to find a Naranti man standing right in front of her. Two other men held her, and a group of six more surrounded her on a strip of silvery beach at a bend in the river.

"Let me go, *please*." Andi blinked, shook her head to clear the fog. Her vision was going dark again at the periphery. "I need help…"

"You need help all right." The Naranti rebel facing her spat into the sand by her feet. "You and all your outworlder kind. We'll take Zulaire back and throw you and the Obati into the fires of the sacrificial cauldrons. We'll enslave the Shenti and force them to do what we command."

I was better off drowning in the damn river than being captured by the rebels. The realization sent fear knifing through her body, dispelling the faintness.

"Enough conversation, bitch." The man walked away, calling over his shoulder, "Bring her. Our leader will be pleased at what the river has given us today."

After Andi had gone about three steps, wobbling like a drunken trooper, one of her captors scooped her up with a curse and carried her, slung over his shoulder like a sack of zinbital leaves. He trudged up a small hill from the tiny beach. Andi checked as best she could from her awkward vantage point, but there was no sign of anyone else from her party having washed up on the sand with her. *I'm on my own, but at least no one else is going to be a prisoner.*

After crossing the hill's summit, her captors made good time on a dusty trail, soon reaching a small village. The man set Andi on her feet at the edge of the dwellings, telling her to walk now or else. Exerting all her willpower, Andi managed to keep up with the men on either side of her.

The village lay deserted except for a sizable throng of armed Naranti. The fighters crowded around, bumping into her, calling out lewd suggestions, asking questions of the patrol that had captured her. The leader of her little procession ignored all distractions, heading straight for a house at the far edge of the town.

Taking quick glances, Andi realized this settlement had suffered something similar to the fate of the one she'd been in on their first day after the massacre.

A number of the houses were burned. There were no bodies, so she hoped the residents of this place had received warning in time to escape.

Leading her to the porch of the most imposing house, the squad leader grabbed Andi's wrist to pull her after him. "Wait here," he instructed his companions over his shoulder. The other rebels stayed in the street, amusing themselves with more ribald suggestions for Andi's eventual fate. *Don't listen to them, don't hear the words, can't let it affect me the way the men want it to. I've got to stay calm. If I'm going to get out of this alive, I have to be able to think.*

Dragging Andi across the porch, stumbling as she went, he flung open the door so he could make a grand entrance with his prisoner. "See what the spirits have cast up from the river, my leader."

A crowd of men turned to stare at her with varying degrees of annoyance, surprise, and disdain. She stood as straight and tall as she could, but her knees were still rubbery. *Breathe, just concentrate on breathing right now.*

"See what I've brought." Perhaps unsatisfied with his comrades' lukewarm reaction, her captor yanked her forward another few steps, toward the heavy wooden table dominating the center of the room.

The crowd shuffled apart. His back to them, a man was studying a sheaf of papers and maps laid out on the table. After a long minute, he directed his attention to her in a disinterested fashion.

Iraku.

Trying not to throw up again, Andi swayed and closed her eyes for a moment.

Taking a moment to stack his files neatly, the Naranti elder left the table and swaggered over to her. He still had the insolent manner she remembered so well from her days at the Tonkiln estate.

"Miss Markriss." Iraku drew the syllables of her name out, obviously savoring the fact that she was his captive. "You survived the fire."

Anger burned through her dazed wits. "Too bad you found a way out, Iraku. You deserved to roast in the four hells for what you did to those poor, defenseless people."

Betraying absolutely no emotion, Iraku slapped Andi across the face, rocking her head back. She sank to her knees on the uneven wooden floor, cheek numb, eye socket aching from the force of the blow. Eyes watering, she tasted blood on her lips.

Iraku seized her by the shoulders, leaning down to put his face level with hers as he shouted, "You know *nothing* of what I did, of what I am doing, for the good of Zulaire, for the honor of the Naranti Clan. Do not speak your ignorant outworlder thoughts to me, do you understand?" His long fingers dug into her upper arms so hard his nails broke her skin.

Straightening as best she could, Andi kept her eyes lowered and nodded even as her skin crawled at his repulsive touch. *Arguing with him right now isn't going to keep me alive to fight another day.*

Releasing her, Iraku threw his arms out wide, inviting the others to share his good mood. He laughed and spun around in an impromptu dance. The crowd joined in his mirth, probably not comprehending what pleased their leader so much about a bedraggled outworlder female. "This, *this* is excellent. The prisoner will provide another key piece in the puzzle we weave for the stupid Shenti, arrogant Obati and their outworlder allies. You've done well, men. Tie her up and put her on the couch in the next room. Post a guard." Iraku walked back to the table. Almost as an afterthought, he said, "Gag her. Outworlders can be most persuasive, and this one talks entirely too much."

The men hauled her to her feet and tied her hands behind her back before taking her to the designated couch jammed into an alcove at the rear of the room. Forcing her to lie down, the guard made a mocking ceremony of adjusting a pillow under her head while Andi glared at him, cursing him and his descendants for the next ten generations in fluent Zulairian. The rebel—whom she recognized now as one of the servants from the Tonkiln household—took his belt off to bind her ankles tight before forcing his rolled-up bandanna into her mouth to serve as the gag. The taste and feel of the cloth made her retch. She struggled not to throw up, afraid of choking.

Taking a position at the end of the couch, the former servant ignored her while he strained to hear the conversation going on at the big table.

Andi lay on the stinking couch, trembling, ignoring her aches and pains. *I have to figure out how to escape.* Iraku obviously had some kind of plan for her. *And I doubt I'm going to like it.* To test the restraints, she flexed her arms. No slack, no chance she could get her hands free.

The house filled with still more Naranti warriors. Weapons lay everywhere. Some men puffed on thin, rolled zinbital leaves. The intoxicating smoke filled the poorly ventilated room. Iraku remained the center of attention. Bits and pieces of the planning reached Andi, all about attacking more villages. From what she heard, the crowd seemed to be waiting expectantly for something or someone.

Overcome by the zinbital smoke and exhausted from her ordeal in the river, she dozed off.

When she jerked back to wakefulness, her chest was tight, every breath a challenge. Behind the gag her mouth had gone bone dry, and she'd lost the feeling in her hands. Her efforts to get more comfortable attracted the lax guard's attention. Cursing, he checked her bonds, no doubt adding to her bruises in the process.

Satisfied, he rolled her over onto her back again and returned to his post.

At the roar of arriving vehicles, all the rebels in the room went quiet, glancing toward the door, shuffling their feet. The crowd moved back from the table at the center of the room. Only Iraku appeared unaffected by whatever was about to happen. The door crashed open and three or four new rebels swaggered in, followed by an offworld being. The latter glided across the floor in a sinuous series of moves. The upper half of its body was some hard, chitinous substance, adorned with inlaid symbols in gleaming gold. Protruding from its body at intervals, skinny brownish-red tentacles waved constantly in the air, expanding and contracting, turning this way and that. *Sampling the scents? Listening, maybe?* As a Loxton agent, Andi was used to working with nonhuman sentients and comfortable doing so, but this being was repellent. As she watched the newcomer move, she realized her visceral reaction was as if she faced a venomous snake.

Closing her eyes, Andi turned her head for a minute before deciding she'd be better off observing the situation. *Lords of Space, that thing's ugly. I've never seen anything like that, certainly not on Zulaire. Not even when I was offplanet at Loxton Academy. But if it's not from the Sectors, can it be a Mawreg ally?* Her heart skipped a beat. *Or even a Mawreg itself?*

Andi stared in amazement as all the armed Naranti rebels in the room knelt, heads bowed, chanting something in a Clan dialect she didn't recognize. She kept catching a muttered name—*Kuzura*. She'd seen representations of the ancestral spirits known as Kuzura on the ancient tablets in the capital city museum. But this thing was *not* Kuzura. *I don't think it can be a Mawreg, though. Humans aren't supposed to be able to look directly at them without going into seizures.*

Short, wriggling red stalks grew like hair from the top of the creature's body. All of the head tentacles turned as the being greeted Iraku in fluent Naranti. "You've done well, my son, succeeded beyond measure. The foolish ones went to ground in their capital city, afraid to venture out. The Obati and Shenti no longer trust each other. The strength of both Clans is sapped by mourning for those your forces killed."

Iraku didn't kneel to the newcomer but stood with bowed head. "They beg my Clan to come and mediate, as we've always done before. A few more such raids, a few more mysterious slaughters, and the Naranti Clan will be given the powers over all, to solve their problems as we see fit." Iraku's excitement was so intense he actually spit as he gloated. "And this time we'll *never* hand back the Tablets of Authority."

Moving independently, like a nest of baby snakes, the stubby, red tentacles leaned toward Iraku.

Maybe that's what it's using to project its voice? Hard on the heels of Andi's speculation, the being asked another question. "What of Rahuna?"

Andi tensed at the mention of His Serene Holiness. She hoped the boat carrying him had made its way safely down the Chikeeri River. *Maybe he's telling Lord Tonkiln and Sectors Command what he knows right now.*

Rolling up a map, Iraku shrugged. "No news. We believe he was killed in the ambush along with his staff and my entire squad." The report sounded bitter to Andi. "I lost a lot of good men there. Who would have thought priests would—or could—fight?"

How little you really know, you arrogant old fool. Thank goodness Rahuna's going to thwart your plans. A little thrill of pleasure at Iraku's coming defeat warmed her from the inside, although she still took care not to let her vengeful thoughts show on her face.

With a sinuous motion, the alien moved back and forth. "I've brought you more reinforcements, plus additional armaments. My people have said a special blessing over these weapons. Use them, and you can't be defeated. I give you the word of Kuzura."

"And we're grateful." Iraku inclined his head and spread his arms wide.

The being shifted its upper body. More of the wriggling protuberances atop its misshapen head dipped into view. Andi shuddered but kept her gaze on the enemy. Quivering obscenely, the stubby, red tentacles turned one by one in her direction.

Oh, Lords, it just realized I was here. She recoiled into the hard couch cushions as the "Kuzura" came toward her, Iraku trailing in its wake.

You see me as I am, do you not? She heard a raspy, guttural voice inside her head. The alien stopped next to the couch, extruding long waving tentacles.

Andi stared at the golden ornamentation on the upper carapace. *If that thing touches me with those tentacles—ugh, they have suckers on the underside.*

Next moment the being had wrapped a tentacle around her arm, the sinuous tip exploring her body invasively as Andi squirmed. She felt suckers clamping onto the skin of her arm.

These others see the picture I wish them to, but you…

A metallic buzzing steadily grew louder in Andi's head. The room swam before her eyes, a massive weight pressing on her from all directions. She couldn't breathe, nor move. She feared her heart would stop beating from the immense pressure. Searing pain flared above and behind her eyes, like hot metal rods being driven into her skull. The alien flickered in and out of her vision. Her eyes hurt so much she couldn't keep them open. *It's willing me to die.* Straining against the crushing sensation, Andi fought the restraints with terrified desperation.

The attack ended, the pressure receding, leaving her feeling as if she'd been trapped deep underwater until the tide turned. Andi went limp, gasping for breath around the gag in her mouth. Her whole body ached as if she'd come down with benghola fever in the last two minutes.

"This one must be killed without delay." Trailing its cold tentacles over her as it went, the alien moved from one end of the couch to the other. Shrinking back, Andi tried to minimize the contact with her bare flesh.

Grinning, Iraku pulled out a curved dagger, toying with it suggestively, looking at Andi. "I've decided to stage her death as a ruse. There's an outlawed fertility ritual among the Shenti peasants. Hot blood spilled in the fields. I'll revive the ritual tonight, with her. When her people find her drained body, the stupid outworlders will believe the Shenti are guilty. The Sectors will be eager to support my Clan taking power if they fear both the Obati and the Shenti Clans have gone rogue." Iraku puffed his chest out with pride over his gruesomely imaginative plot.

Andi had read accounts of the ancient ritual, practiced before the god Sanenre had arrived. The earliest days of primitive civilization on Zulaire had been savage, cruel. She suppressed a mental picture created by Iraku's plans. Andi's hearing was still fading in and out but at least her vision was coming back, interrupted by flashes of light and dark patches at the periphery. *He's insane enough to carry out his plan. I've got to be ready for any chance I might get to escape.*

"An unnecessary subterfuge." The alien's contemptuous tone suggested it wasn't pleased with Iraku's idea. "Others have tried to enmesh the outworlders on Zulaire to no avail. A few casualties mean nothing to them. Kill her now and be done. She's heard too much here."

Andi opened her eyes long enough to see Iraku frowning. She recognized the angry expression as one the servants at the compound had dreaded. When upset, he was at his most tyrannical and unreasonable.

He didn't appear to appreciate criticism of his plans, not even from a fabled Kuzura. Arms crossed, lips compressed, nostrils flared, Iraku stood taller. "I disagree, great one. If the outworlders think themselves at risk, they'll pressure Lord Tonkiln to step aside, to hand over the Tablets of Authority. *She* is of great importance to the outworlders. They sent troops to escort her to safety."

"It's a waste of time, my son." The alien now used a softer, more conciliatory tone, long, skinny tentacles whipping around its body in agitation. "Better to kill her now." Andi shivered. "There must be no chance for her to escape and tell of what she's seen here. Have your men throw the body in the field. We need to be on our way to the highlands."

Iraku appeared reluctant to concede even a small portion of the scheme. "She must be *killed* in the field, great one. The hot blood must be spread in a circle—"

He's certainly taking a sick pleasure in planning this hideous faux sacrifice. How can these other Naranti follow someone so twisted? Appalled, Andi tried to catch the eye of the Naranti nearest to her, to look for someone sympathetic, but there was no one.

"All right, do as you please on this matter, so long as it doesn't cause delay." The alien aimed its red sensory organs at Andi. Afraid of another painful assault on her senses, she pressed her body into the couch cushions, scrunching her eyes shut as the tip of one long tentacle touched her cheek. Her mind became fuzzy, her thoughts disjointed. Andi jerked her head away. The audience of Zulairians guffawed. The contact ceased.

She opened her eyes to see the false Kuzura gliding toward the door, tentacles neatly coiled against the shell-like upper body. "Join us at the rally point in the western hill country as soon as you have finished here," it said.

Iraku bowed his head. "I'll be there before the dawn, great one." He wrapped his fist in Andi's hair to hold her still and put his face right down next to hers. "You die at sunset." Cackling, he strode off to supervise the distribution of weapons.

She closed her eyes. Hot tears prickled behind the lids then slid down her cheeks. *Maybe it would have been better to have died in the explosion back at the summer colony. I fought so hard across so much of Zulaire to escape. And now I'm going to be killed in some horrific way by Iraku?*

No. She squared her shoulders as she made her resolution. *I'm not dead yet. I won't be an easy victim for him. I'll fight and try to make him pay for the deaths of so many innocents. Somehow…*

***

The Naranti came to get her at sunset, as promised. The guards ripped the gag from her mouth and removed the belt restraining her ankles but left her hands bound. Supporting her by the elbows, the men got her to her feet. After having been in one position for hours on the couch, she had trouble walking the first few steps. Her back ached, and her muscles cramped.

Andi tried to keep the tiny flame of anger and courage deep within alive while trudging across the porch and down the two steps. The evening breeze lifted loose strands of her hair as she walked from the house between her two guards. Iraku strutted ahead of them. *My favorite time of day. How ironic. And now it's the time I'm going to die.*

She refused to give Iraku the satisfaction of seeing her fear. *I'm not begging him for my life. Even if I wanted to, he's in some exalted state, unreachable. Maybe he's envisioning himself sitting on the Planetary Lord's throne.* Every instinct clamored at her to run, to make a try for freedom, but she knew it would be a futile attempt. Ready to block any escape attempt, the thugs kept their hands on her, tight enough to bruise.

She reached the big land vehicle. Without looking back, Iraku climbed into the driver's seat. The man on her right opened the passenger door and grabbed Andi by the elbow. His grip made the ropes bite into her already lacerated wrists, and she winced, crying out. Manhandling her into the backseat, the guards placed her between them.

Leaning against the vehicle's cracked cushions, she tried to marshal her thoughts. *I can't let myself be paralyzed by terror. I may have some tiny chance to get away from them, so I have to stay alert.* Tom's face filled her mind's eye. But he was miles away by now. *I'm on my own with the madman and his fanatical followers.*

Well, all right, what harm can one last appeal to reason do?

As the truck bounced over the rutted track, she leaned toward the driver's seat. "Iraku, I'm sure the Sectors authorities would pay ransom for me. My family is important offworld—"

Lifting a hand off the wheel, her enemy made a fist. His voice grated harshly over the whine of the engine. "Silence her."

The guard on the left slapped Andi openhanded across her bruised face, and she felt her lower lip split.

Iraku hit the brakes so hard a cloud of dust blew all around the truck while it shuddered to a halt. Glaring at Andi, veins in his neck throbbing with angry emotion, he said, "Don't try to bribe me. Don't sully the purity of our cause with talk of money."

I couldn't possibly sully anything as horrible and sadistic as your cause. Why won't he listen to reason? Taking a risk, she pushed the topic of ransom. "I'm only trying to tell you the Sectors authorities aren't going to react to you murdering me the way you're hoping."

"If you utter one more word..." Iraku said in a flat, lethal tone, using Sectors Basic, probably so his henchmen would not understand, "...I'll tell them that having their way with you will increase the potency of their manhood because you're an alien bitch. Maybe I'll assure them that the longer they take with you, the louder you scream and beg for mercy, the stronger their manhood will rise. Do you understand me? One word, yes or no."

Licking blood from her lip, she had to swallow twice to unlock her jaw enough to speak. "Yes."

"Then be silent, and I'll let you die unmolested, which is more than you deserve." He waited a second. Then, apparently satisfied Andi wasn't going to provoke him further, Iraku set the vehicle in motion once more.

She stared past the guard to watch the landscape flowing by, trying to make plans, but ideas tumbled one after the other in her mind, useless fragments. The prospect of dying like some old-time sacrifice was too terrifying for her mind to hold. Andi felt herself detach from reality as Iraku brought the vehicle to a smooth stop beside a partially harvested field of grain. She had the sensation of watching someone else yanked from the vehicle and dragged across the rough ground. That woman twisted, struggled and screamed curses at her captors in four different languages, but Andi remained safe in her quiet cocoon of unreality.

This is not happening to me.

Everything will be all right.

Somehow.

At the center of the field the guards yanked her to a halt, forcing Andi to kneel. Small pebbles and jutting roots dug into her lower legs and knees, the pain snapping her back into harsh reality—this *was* happening to her, and it was all too real.

As the men held her in the kneeling position, Iraku clutched his long hunting knife in his right hand. A wave of cold determination gave her renewed strength. *No, he's not doing that to me. I won't make my death easy for him.*

Fueled by adrenaline, Andi fought to stand, surprising her captors and actually breaking loose for a second or two.

All too soon, the two Naranti men shoved her into the sacrificial position again. As she knelt on the harsh roots, stones and packed dirt, her shoulders ached, nearly dislocated in the desperate struggle.

Chuckling as he shook his head, Iraku appeared to find her efforts amusing. He patted her cheek. "You outworlders never give up, do you?"

Andi jerked her head away from him. "Don't *touch* me, you bastard."

"Defiant to the end." Iraku examined his knife, running a careful finger along the edge, revealing yellowed teeth in a big smile. "We won't take the time to utter the superstitious twaddle of the Shenti peasants. Maybe the offering of your blood will please the harvest spirits anyway. The crop next year might improve. What do you think?"

She spat at him. "I think you're insane. Go to hell."

Throwing the knife in the air, Iraku guffawed, catching the weapon by the leather-wrapped hilt. One guard got a good grip on Andi's hair close to her scalp, yanking her head back to expose her throat. Blood pulsed hard through her jugular vein, the strain on the blood vessel accentuated by the cruel angle.

"*Tom*," she whispered, closing her eyes, trying to blot out these horrible moments. She breathed a prayer to the Lords of Space. *Please, let my last thoughts be of the man I love.*

The harsh whine of a blaster cut through the night.

Flaring heat rushed past her. Screaming, the guard holding her hair crumpled in slow motion, cut nearly in half by the beam. As he fell, he dragged Andi, still on her knees, with him. Sprawled sideways in the dirt, she kicked, trying to work her body into a position where she could stand. *This is my chance.* The other man released his grip on her shoulder to seek the source of the attack just as a second blast came. His body fell across Andi and the first dying Naranti, the dead weight pinning her down.

From somewhere in the field, Tom yelled, "Andi, get out of there!"

She squirmed frantically to get out from under the second guard's body. Kicking the corpse out of the way, Iraku reached out with his free hand and dragged her upright to shield him.

"Don't hurt her, you son of a bitch." Eyes narrowed, Tom moved closer, focussed on Iraku,, blaster trained on the rebel leader, poised to counter anything he might try.

Iraku circled to the side, away from the threat. Putting the knife to Andi's rib cage, he pressed inward. Pain made her gasp as the point jabbed through her clothing, breaking her skin. "The woman dies if you come one step closer," the rebel leader said.

Andi, dragged along with the Naranti as he moved, yanked her arm against his grasp. "*Tom.*" Iraku held the blade to her throat, silencing her.

Tom glanced her way over his leveled blaster for one searing second. All his love and fear for her lay in the tormented expression on his face. He shifted his gaze back to Iraku. "You won't get away. Give it up. *Just let her go.* Let her go, and I let you go. Simple."

"Simple indeed." Iraku held Andi closer to him, arm wrapped around her waist. He stood so tall and strong, he clutched her like a rag doll, her feet barely touching the dirt. "And, of course, you'll let me go back to my people, go on with my business?"

"Your business is no concern of mine. She is." Tom sounded so calm, his voice level, matter of fact.

"Even if my *business* is disrupting the entire planet and taking control of Zulaire for my Clan?" Iraku's voice sounded harsh, sneering. Andi couldn't see his face, but she could imagine the way his lips would be pursed and his eyes would gleam. She'd seen that expression all too many times. He was savoring his power, the way he'd enjoyed humiliating the lesser servants at every opportunity. "I find it hard to believe you don't care about Zulaire and my holy war, Captain Deverane. What about your superior officers?"

"The Sectors doesn't give a damn what your three Clans do to each other. If you kill her, though, you'll bring a firestorm down. Once you force the Sectors to get involved, no power on Zulaire can stop us from obliterating the Naranti. We'll crush your people and turn the planet into a wasteland." His voice was hard, making a promise not a threat. Tom's eyes were narrowed, jaw clenched.

"If she's so important, she goes with me as my safeguard." Iraku backed up a few more feet, dragging Andi with him. The sharp edge of the knife scored her skin, and she flinched, biting her chapped, split lip.

"Like hell she goes with you. So you can kill her at your leisure later? I'm not some dumb trooper fresh off the first transport, pal." Tom centered the blaster's aim at Iraku's head.

Her captor's grip on the knife at her throat never slackened. Andi fought to get her breathing under control. *Be ready, don't panic.* Tom would help her find a way to break free, to save herself.

Tom permitted himself one more rapid, anguished look at her. His hold on the blaster wavered, the barrel dipping for a second. *Lords of Space, he does love me.*

It's all there in his eyes. Andi felt warmth flow over her, loosening her tight muscles, calming her racing thoughts.

Iraku's arm tensed around her waist. "Throw down your weapon, Captain. I'll walk with Miss Markriss to my vehicle, slow and easy. You'll follow us but keep your hands visible at all times. I'll release her and drive away unmolested. Agreed? After all, your only desire is her life, right?"

Iraku must really feel in control of this entire situation, if he's using such a mocking tone to Tom with a blaster aimed at his head.

Iraku exerted a fraction more pressure on the knife, the edge digging into her skin painfully until warm blood trickled down her neck. "I'm not ready to be a martyr. I do my people and my cause no good if I sacrifice my life for the pleasure of killing this worthless woman."

Straightening out of his stance, Tom clicked the safety on his blaster and dropped it to the parched ground by his feet. Bouncing once, the weapon came to rest against a clump of stalks. He put his hands up, palms facing Iraku.

No, no. What is he doing? Andi moaned wordlessly in protest.

Iraku glanced at the blaster, then back at Tom. He nodded approval. "Good. So sensible, you outworlders. Now we walk." He adjusted his arm upward, to encircle Andi's chest.

Locked in this insane dance, she stumbled across the field, returning to the road. *Maybe Tom has some backup plan. He must have something in mind.* Tom shadowed them at a two-yard distance. Iraku's knife never wavered from its position pressed against her throat. At the roadside, the rebel leader paused.

Iraku isn't going to let me live. The minute he feels safe enough, he'll slit my throat. But he'd have to let go of her chest in order to reach for the vehicle's door latch.

Andi braced herself. The minute Iraku started to shift, she jerked backward, taking her adversary unaware, knocking him off balance. As she'd hoped, he released Andi to save himself from falling. Throwing herself to the side, the knife slicing into the underside of her chin, she fell at Iraku's feet. Ignoring the pain of the fresh wound, she scrabbled to put distance between her and her captor.

Grabbing her ankle, Iraku wrapped his hand around it like a steel manacle, trying to drag her back to him. She rolled over and kicked at his face with her other foot, taking great satisfaction in the impact as she landed a glancing blow on his cheekbone, jarring him enough to dislodge his clawlike grasp on her ankle.

Tom launched himself at Iraku, lashing out in a lightning-fast move that broke the Naranti's already faltering hold on Andi. Iraku shrieked as his arm bones cracked. Knocking the knife from Iraku's hand with another swift, deadly kick, Tom followed with a roundhouse blow to the head. Iraku reeled, unable to get his balance, stumbling along the length of the vehicle under the force of Tom's attack.

Ignoring Iraku, dropping to his knees in the dust next to Andi, Tom cradled her in his arms. Throat tight, all her muscles clenched, she was still in fight-or-flight mode. He tried to stanch her bleeding neck wound with the tail of his uniform shirt. "Shh, don't cry, it's all right now. I've got you." He wrapped her in his arms.

Andi sobbed, burying her head against his chest. "I thought I was going to die."

Iraku scrambled in the dust behind them, staggering away.

"Drop him, Mitch!" Tom yelled.

The sergeant stepped around the vehicle where he'd apparently been hiding and cut Iraku down with a fusillade of blaster fire.

It's over. Black dots danced in her vision.

"Andi, *Andi*." Tom's embrace tightened around her, his voice tensing with panic. He gave her a little shake.

"I love you." She stared into his eyes, her heart so full of emotion she could hardly get the words out, but he had to know what he meant to her. "You were all I could think about when I thought I was about to die."

He gathered her close for an intensely demanding kiss. Andi responded with equal urgency. When she pulled away, he hugged her again. "I love you, too."

She laughed, savoring the words and the feeling he put into them.

Tom lowered his head to stare into her eyes. "Don't you ever scare me like this again, you hear?"

Pain in her neck from the knife wound brought her up short when she tried to nod. "No problem."

He helped her lean against the side of the vehicle and worked to untie her wrists. "Mitch, medkit on the double. Her neck is bleeding. There's a blaster proximity sear on her left side. These wrists look pretty raw, too."

"I'm a mess." Andi rested her head against the truck, all her various pains throbbing and aching and burning in turn, low-level nausea lurking in her gut. She wiped away the tears on her cheeks with the back of one hand.

"Let's get her into the vehicle, sir." Mitch returned from the edge of the field, where he'd dragged Iraku's corpse. "Be easier to work on her there, more comfortable for her, too."

"Right." Picking her up as if she weighed nothing, Tom placed her with loving care on the cushions in the passenger compartment. Cupping her cheek, he said, "Stay with us, sweetheart. Not a good time to go to sleep."

He crouched by her side as the sergeant made fast work of applying field dressings. Mitch obviously tried to be as gentle as possible, but it hurt every time he touched her. Andi gritted her teeth against the pain but still whimpered once or twice and flinched away.

"The knife wound is a long scratch, ma'am. Messy but superficial." Mitch finished with her neck wound, switching to an examination of her wrists. "Give me a minute to dress these rope burns. The blaster proximity sear isn't too bad, either. You *are* goin' to need a quick session in the rejuve resonator when we get back to the capital, though. Blaster sears tend to fester down through the layers of the skin if left untreated." He went looking for something else in his medkit.

"Iraku was going to kill me in another minute. I could feel him getting ready to do it. I knew I had to try something." Andi shuddered at the memory, still too raw and recent to bear much thinking about.

Tom hugged her. "You did the right thing. I knew you'd make a break, give us a clear shot at Iraku. You're a fighter. Right, Mitch?"

The sergeant nodded. "Be proud to serve with you any time, ma'am, and that's a fact. Now hold still, I need to give you a couple of injects here. Antibiotic mixed with a sedative and a painkiller." Jabbing her arm with a device from the medkit, Mitch rubbed the skin to work the medicinal cocktail into her bloodstream. "Didn't hurt, now did it?" Andi shook her head. There wasn't any pain aside from a mild tingling.

Tom's clasp on her hand tightened. "You never should have had to go through all this. It's my fault."

"It's not your fault." Staring at him, she tried to comprehend his comment.

"I should have gone in the river after you."

Softly, she laid her hand on his cheek. "And maybe then you'd have drowned, while I was captured. Don't torture yourself. You had all the rest of the group to worry about back there on the river, not just me."

"When we couldn't find you, I thought I'd go crazy. To have come so far only to lose you—"

"I'm fine, thanks to you and Mitch." *He's tearing himself up over this.* She kissed Tom on the lips. "What happened after I got knocked out of the boat?" she asked. "All I know is, I woke up on a beach at the river bend, with Iraku's thugs all around me."

Tom pulled her into his lap. Leaning her head against his strong shoulder, she wrapped one arm around his back. As he talked, she could feel the vibrations of his deep voice against her ear. "Our boat got hung up on a nest of three huge boulders. I think the collision with them is what sent you flying. Eventually we reached calmer water, landed about half a mile above the village. We headed downriver, in the direction of the capital, until we found where you'd come ashore and knew you'd been captured."

Andi frowned. "How could you tell?"

"The tracks." Mitch pointed at her feet. "I read them as one barefoot woman crawlin' out of the river, surrounded by big men with big feet in boots. Lost your shoes again, ma'am?" He grinned.

"I was afraid we wouldn't be in time to stop whatever those bastards had in mind," Tom said, clearing his throat.

Andi pulled him closer to kiss him. "Stop being hard on yourself. It's over now."

"We need to be goin', sir. Are we taking the vehicle?" Mitch thumped the side panel of the truck next to them. "The initiator is still in the control panel. No need to hotwire it."

"Yes. Someone'll come to find out what's keeping Iraku, and we'd better not be here." Tom helped Andi stand up, Mitch also putting out a hand to steady her. The captain pointed at him. "You'll drive. Just let me get my blaster first."

"Yes, sir."

Andi grimaced. "I lost mine in the river. I think."

"Good thing you're a civilian then—no reports to fill out." Before heading into the field, Tom kissed her again, long and leisurely.

"Where are the others?" Andi glanced around as if Rahuna and the rest were going to come walking out of the field, too.

"We're supposed to rendezvous with them tonight at a rest stop complex by the transportway." Mitch strolled around the truck, opened the door and threw his medkit inside on the bench, before helping her climb into the backseat.

"South Amri?" The caravan had stopped there on her trip out from the capital three weeks ago with the ill-fated Tonkiln family. The younger children had needed the facilities before the last leg of the journey to the summer compound. Lady Tonkiln had refused to set foot in the place, requiring her servants to bring her an assortment of refreshments from the restaurant. "Are we so close?" Andi asked.

Mitch nodded. "We hope the place'll be deserted, given the state of unrest on Zulaire."

Blaster in hand, Tom jogged into the circle of illumination from the truck's headlights and cab. "Let's move."

A few moments later, Mitch set the vehicle in motion, increasing the speed as he got used to the controls. Andi reclined on the cushions in the back, curled against Tom's reassuringly solid chest. His blaster was close by in case of need.

Settling against his shoulder, she sighed in contentment. "If I was a cat, I'd purr. You generate so much warmth."

He gave her a gentle hug. "You should try to grab some shut-eye while we're driving."

"Sleep sounds divine." Andi yawned, stretching gingerly. She had so many aches and pains now, despite Mitch's painkillers, that any movement was an ordeal. *Maybe the drugs haven't kicked in yet. I can hope.*

Tom chuckled. "Well, then, stop talking. We can debrief later. You need to rest."

"No, there's something you need to know. I should have told you sooner." Andi smacked her forehead lightly. "There are alien beings, maybe even Mawreg here, *on* Zulaire. They're behind this entire Clan war."

The truck swerved, skidding on the dirt road, as Mitch reacted to her dramatic announcement. Desperately, Andi grabbed at Tom to keep from being flung against the door.

Mitch straightened the truck with a violent jerk on the controls.

Tom hauled her back across the padded bench seat. "Are you sure? How do you know?"

"There was an alien with Iraku, giving him orders about what to do next. It brought him weapons of some kind, too." Remembering the creature's touch, she shivered.

Mitch and Tom exchanged glances in the rearview mirror before he turned back to her, frowning. "Can you describe the alien?"

"Tall, thin, some visible exoskeleton. Carapace heavily ornamented with inlaid gold. Red stalk things growing where eyes should be. Fleshy tentacles with suckers instead of arms. I guess it was surprised I could see its true form. It told me the Naranti see it as one of their ancestral spirit figures. But I've seen the murals of the Kuzura, the spirits. This thing was *nothing* like a Kuzura," she said, rubbing her arm where the tentacles had rested.

"A Betang. Well, I'll be damned. This is a fucking mess." Leaning against the seat cushion, Tom pinched the bridge of his nose, eyes closed, then rubbed his jaw and sighed. His other hand clenched around the hilt of his blaster.

"Betang?" Andi tilted her head, looking at him for enlightenment.

"A client race of the Mawreg. They often send Betang in to soften up planets they want to invade. Betang can project illusions." Reflexively, Tom checked the charge level on his weapon and slammed it back in the holster. "This is a disaster."

"Remember the blast cannon the rebels had, back at the monastery?" Mitch asked from the front seat. "We were sure it was Mawreg-issue. This confirms it."

"Mitch and I were supposed to be backing up the planetside Sectors forces, do a little digging into oddities puzzling the intel guys. Which you've now resolved with your Betang encounter." Reaching out, Tom took Andi's hand, lacing his fingers with hers.

"Lucky to survive that, ma'am," Mitch said over his shoulder. He whistled. "Very lucky."

She nodded. "It wanted Iraku to kill me at once but backed off when he explained his plan, the mock fertility ritual killing, because he was getting so worked up about it." Struck by a puzzling thought, she looked at Tom. "Why could I see this Betang creature for what it was? The Zulairians couldn't—they'd have run screaming down the road if they could have seen what I was seeing. *I'd* have run if I hadn't been tied up."

"Not all humans can see through a Betang illusion field, which has cost us dearly in a number of situations, I might add. There's a particular genetic drift on the DNA code for sight and depth perception which gives a person immunity, in varying degrees, to the Betangs' powers." Tom feathered a kiss on each of her eyelids. "Those beautiful eyes saw right through its deceptive cloaking."

"It did try to do something to me, to my mind. I thought I was going to have a heart attack on that couch. I guess I owe Iraku for saving my life at *that* point." Andi frowned.

Tom pulled her closer into a tight embrace. "Damn, you were lucky. The Betang can kill humans with their minds once they've sampled the person's DNA." Obviously still edgy about her near miss with the Betang, which seemed to bother her taciturn captain even more than the knife at her throat had, he said, "Maybe the Bet was afraid to go against Iraku at this stage. They do use civilian puppets at first, for a few years, to ensure their foothold on the planet."

"But why are they after *Zulaire*? It's a backwater. Even the Sectors isn't very interested in anything Zulaire has to offer." Andi hastily leaned the other direction as Mitch brought the truck around the next curve in a wide swoop. "Although there are exotic minerals in trace amounts. I was trying to get my company to invest in some exploratory excavation."

"Never try to figure out why something interests the Mawreg." The sergeant met her eyes in the rearview mirror. "But the minerals might be the draw."

Tom nodded his agreement. "Command needs to know this. It's even more critical than the Naranti being behind this sudden Clan war. Mawreg involvement affects the entire Sector."

"We could take this vehicle and hightail it straight down the damn freeway." Even as he made the suggestion, Mitch hit the accelerator.

"Risky. May be our only chance, though." Pounding a clenched fist against his palm, Tom swore. "*Damn.* If the Mawreg penetrate this Sector we're facing catastrophe."

"Is the situation really that bad?" Andi swallowed in sudden fear.

Eyes narrowed, lips compressed, Tom nodded. "The big brass and politicos keep details from civilians to avoid panic. And maybe you don't get much of what they do release to the media, since Zulaire is in such an isolated Sector, but once the Mawreg get entrenched, their presence is like a cancer. We have to make it cost too much for them to stay. Sometimes it takes the destruction of entire planets to eradicate them. Once in a while victory requires the destruction of whole systems."

"What about the people on the planets?" Andi's jaw dropped. *I can't imagine the destruction of an entire solar system.*

Tom turned her chin with one finger so they were gazing at each other. "Sweetheart, the Mawreg don't leave any people alive." His mouth tightened, deepening the wrinkles. "I'd hate to see it happen to Zulaire. Despite the current situation, it's a damn nice planet."

"And it's worth fighting for." Andi squared her shoulders and clenched her jaw. *Mawreg takeover isn't going to happen here. We can't allow that.*

"Hitting the transportway," Mitch said. "Should be a better surface now."

The ride did indeed smooth out. The main road was well kept, as opposed to the ruts and potholes of the village access road. Despite ominous whining from the old engine, the sergeant accelerated to the truck's top speed.

"Shit!" The truck swerved suddenly as Mitch yelled, brakes screeching until the vehicle slewed to a stop sideways. The cranky engine sputtered and died.

"What the *hell* are you doing?" Tom had braced Andi during the sudden stop, and even now the truck had stilled, he maintained his tight hold on her.

Mitch was apologetic, eyes open wide, mouth a thin line. "Vehicle abandoned in the middle of the road, sir. Didn't see it in the dark until I was nearly on top of it. Sorry."

Revving the motor into life again, he prepared to continue on their way, but Tom stopped him. "Wait. Let's check this out. With the size of our party, we could use another vehicle. Keep the engine running."

Climbing out, the men walked back to the abandoned vehicle. Andi waited in the truck for a minute then slid out, not wanting to be left alone in the dark. *I may never want to be alone anywhere ever again.* As she approached them standing by the abandoned car, Tom's hand lamp illuminated the vehicle's front panels, showing an intricate pattern of an urabu dancing in the midst of flames overlaid on a gleaming, yellow undercoat.

Andi stopped, her mouth falling open in a short gasp of recognition. "*Gul.*"

Tom stared at her as she walked up. "You know the owner?"

"Yes, this car belongs to Gul Tonkiln, the older son of the Planetary High Lord. He was supposed to return to the summer compound for his sister's handfasting, but he never showed up." *I can't believe it, but he must be dead.* A pang of sorrow made her heart skip a beat for a moment. Trailing her hand along the embossed panels, Andi walked the length of the car. *Hard to remember back to that day now. He wanted to see if the relationship had a future. I guess I always knew it didn't.*

Raising her head, Andi squinted against the light in Mitch's hand. Hastily, he redirected the beam to the ground.

Tom had an odd expression on his face, eyebrows raised. He looked away from Andi. She sighed. *We're going to have to talk.* Rapping her knuckles on the engine compartment of Gul's car, she said, "I don't see any damage. What do you think happened?"

Mitch walked over to join her, squatting to look more closely at the elaborate Tonkiln insignia. "Ambush most likely. Maybe they staged some kind of fake accident, and he stopped to help."

"Gul wouldn't stop to help," Andi said with a bitter laugh. "He'd only pull over if there was a big obstacle in his way. And then he was lured out of the car somehow." Hard to remember now what she'd ever seen in the arrogant Obati lord, especially with Tom's solid, dependable presence beside her. *But Gul didn't deserve...* She hugged her arms around her waist, suddenly chilled.

"No sign of a body." Mitch darted an uneasy look her way, then glanced down at the road.

Leaning over, Tom tried the door. "Autolocked. Probably why the attackers didn't boost it or blow it up. We could blast it open, but the electronics would be ruined. What I want most from this vehicle is a working comlink."

Unnerved by the hard, shuttered expression on his face, Andi eyed him warily for a moment. Drawing in a deep breath to fortify herself, she said, "I can open it for you."

"You drove his *personal* groundcar?" Tom's voice was flat. She glanced at his face, but he kept it carefully blank. "How close were the two of you?"

Raising an eyebrow, annoyed now, Andi was edging toward offended. *It's really none of his business who I was involved with before I met him.* "I drove it in town occasionally." She triggered the lock with her thumb. Pausing for a moment after the doors opened, not looking at Tom, she elaborated. "Gul Tonkiln and I knew each other well, but it wasn't serious." Her small burst of anger had tired her out, making her aches worse, and she didn't even glance Tom's way before sliding into the driver's seat of the beautiful machine. Automatically, the car adapted itself to her height and reach. Soothing music played as the dim internal lights came on. She caught a faint hint of Gul's aftershave, citrus and wood. A small stab of memory made her eyes prickle as she thought of him, and all the people who'd died in this stupid Clan war.

For a very long moment, Tom didn't budge. Sighing, Andi made the first move, leaning her head out the open doorway. "Didn't you want to use the comlink?"

"I'll stand guard," Mitch volunteered, glancing from Andi to Tom before quickly walking out of earshot.

Tom came around to get in the other side, easily sliding into the passenger seat. "Hey."

She turned her head at his soft greeting. Eyebrows raised, Tom met her gaze steadily, a tentative smile curling his mouth. "If I need to apologize for being an asshole just now, consider it done. The thought of you with any other guy—even before I met you—makes me crazy, Andi."

She kept her frown going for a second longer, then took pity on him and smiled a little. "Apology accepted. We can talk about it later, but…I was never in love with him, Tom. We had fun, we were a couple off and on, attended a lot of business dinners and awards ceremonies together. No man has ever meant anything close to what I feel for you. Okay?"

"Okay. I am sorry it appears he's dead."

She sighed. "Me, too."

He stared at her for a few more seconds and then switched his focus to the com system, pulling out the small earpiece and clipping it to his ear. Examining the dashboard, he flipped the system from music to communication. "Figures he'd have an illegal scanner, but it's our good fortune tonight. He could surf the Sectors' military channels."

Head tilted, he fiddled with the controls. "Zulaire Command, this is Patrol KJ123, declaring an emergency. Need immediate extraction, party of eight military and civilians, highest priority."

A response came almost immediately.

"Identify yourself. You are an unauthorized station intruding on military networks."

"Patrol KJ123, Captain Deverane commanding. I'm declaring an emergency, priority Red Alpha, do you understand?" Tom put more emphasis into his question. Frowning, he gave Andi a sideways glance of pure frustration.

"Current code word?" The male voice on the other end of the link sounded hostile to her, and she didn't understand the man's odd reaction.

Tom didn't seem to like it either, taking a deep breath before he answered. "Soldier, I've been in the field for weeks, out of touch. I don't have the current code word. It was 'pond scum' when we were last briefed."

"Nice try, whoever you are. If you *were* with the good guys, then you'd know the entire planet is under lockdown. No emergency extractions, no evacs, no sorties, *nothing*. Now get off this military link before I do a tracer and have you arrested."

Drawing himself up in the seat until his head nearly touched the roof, Tom's face grew even more grim, a vein throbbing in his neck. "You're addressing a senior Sectors officer declaring a priority Red Alpha. Get me the officer of the watch, on the double."

"Yeah, right. You ain't decoying anymore of *my* guys out there into an ambush like you did to poor Deverane. At least you had part of your story right. Have a nice night, asshole." There was a sharp click. The channel hummed a second, then died.

Andi jumped as Tom punched the dashboard, denting the panel. "Stupid fucking bastard of a ground trooper doesn't know a Red Alpha priority from his ass. *When* we get back to the capital city, I'll find this idiot and guarantee him a posting to the most desolate, Mawreg-infested planet I can identify." He leaned back in the seat and sighed, looking at Andi. "Guess we go back to the original plan."

She stared at him with her mouth open, never having seen him lose control before. "Are you all right? Did you hurt your hand?"

He shook out his fingers, looked them over. "No, just bruised my knuckles. It was a dumb thing to do, I realize, but to finally get my hands on a comlink then not be able to reach someone in authority—" He broke off and sighed. "There's so much at stake right now. Having a known Betang on the planet elevates the situation to the top of the crisis scale."

"What—what was the original plan? I've kind of lost track of that at the moment." Andi looked around at the car's controls blankly.

"We've still got to get ourselves out of this mess on our own," Tom said. "Can you drive with all the stuff Mitch pumped into you back there?"

"I think so. It's not too far now to the station."

"We'd better hightail it. We've been in this one spot far too long already. Especially if the rebels, or the Betang, are monitoring com chatter. I'll go tell Mitch what's up." Tom climbed out of the low-slung sports car with an effort.

Andi laid her head on the wheel. Every cut and bruise hurt. Her wrists ached where the ropes had bitten into them. *I'm tired, and I want this whole ordeal to be* over.

A minute later the car dipped as Tom swung back into the passenger seat. "Follow the truck and leave the lights off. The less attention we get, the better."

Andi cruised down the transportway in the truck's wake. She turned the com on and found soft music. The drugs were kicking in harder now, waves of disorientation sweeping over her every few minutes. The blaster sear on her side stung and throbbed.

"I wish I could drive for you." Tom rubbed her shoulders as best he could. "You look worn out."

"I'll make it," Andi said. "We're getting pretty close to South Amri, right? We Loxtons are tough." She squared her aching shoulders and smiled. *Lucky this car practically steers itself.*

"So you are Loxton's great-granddaughter?" Relaxing into the passenger seat, Tom reached for her free hand and clasped it.

She glanced over at him. "How did you know?"

He pointed, directing her attention back to the truck's taillights ahead of them before answering. "The details were in the background briefing when we came onplanet. I didn't pay much attention. You weren't someone I expected to meet."

"I see." Conversation might keep her more alert, Andi decided, despite the fact it took energy. "The briefing was correct. There are a lot of us in the third generation, though, so the connection doesn't mean all that much. We still have to work our way up through the ranks if we want to go anywhere in the Loxton family business. Which is what I'm doing." Andi rolled her head in a lazy circle, trying to loosen the tension in her shoulders. "Did you think it was my great-grandfather who had you diverted to rescue me?"

"Not exactly," he said.

"What does that mean?"

Tom sat in silence for a minute. She glanced over and saw he was rubbing his forehead, eyes narrowed in a pained expression. Jaw clenched, he met her gaze. "You have to admit it was pretty odd for us to be pulled away from our primary mission to extract one lost Sectors citizen. When we got our pre-Zulaire briefing, the officer had suggested you dating Gul was a cover, that you were actually his *father's* mistress. I told you before, changing my orders required someone with a lot of pull. The Planetary High Lord was the obvious answer. I'd forgotten the Loxton connection. I'd forgotten all of that until my orders were changed."

The miles ticked away on the readout.

She bit her lip and shot him a small, uncertain glance, her heart clenching. "Tom, what if I *had* been the Planetary High Lord's mistress?"

"Meeting you was like—like a gift, Andi, like the Lords of Space reached out and showed me a taste of heaven." His voice was choked with emotion, and his brilliant green eyes locked on her face. "I love you. I've never said those words to any other woman. I never will. You're it for me. Unless you had a husband, I'd have done my damnedest to convince you to give me a chance." Now he ran his hands through his hair in frustration. "I'm not saying this right. I'm not the best with words, but *I* know what you mean to me."

She rested her hand on his thigh. "Tom, I know. I feel the same, starting when you showed up at the dance that night."

Wrapping his fingers around hers, he kissed her cheek softly. "When we get out of this mess, when we have downtime, I'll *show* you much I love you. I promise."

A fairy tale…this is like an ancient fairy tale or a legend. I found my knight in shining armor, and he rescued me. How lucky can a person be? Andi laughed, suddenly remembering. "You know, I met the urabu on the afternoon you arrived at the compound. I even touched one."

"Urabu? Like the carvings all over the monastery?" Tom wrinkled his forehead and looked sideways at her. "I thought they didn't exist." Circling her wrist with his fingers, he unromantically checked her pulse. "You're not making much sense right now. Are the tranquilizers affecting you too much? Do you want me to flag Mitch over? We can all ride in the truck. We don't have to keep this vehicle."

"No, I'm fine." She laughed again, tossing her hair. "On Zulaire, there's a legend about the urabu. If they appear to you, you live happily ever after, like in those old children's stories. And the day I met you, I'd just encountered a whole herd of them, out in the glade where I was sitting. It was magical. Once in a lifetime."

"I'm not much on fairy tales." He peered at the badly dented control panel then thumbed the tab that made the windows disappear. Cold night air rushed in at them.

Andi shivered. "What the hell—"

"I think fresh air might clear your head a bit. You know, the ordeals you've gone through since we met aren't my definition of happily ever after."

Andi shook her head. *Hardheaded military man. Well, he can think what he wants, and I'll know what really happened. The urabu were real, I saw them, and they've brought me Tom.*

"Concentrate on the road, woman." He tapped the windshield. "Turn off to the station coming up." The sign was much defaced, but enough of the legend remained to tell her where she was. "Watch for Mitch's lead."

She toggled the switch to make the windows close again. A little touch to the acceleration tab, and she was closing in on the old truck. "You know, I'm overdue to accept another assignment, somewhere other than Zulaire," she said.

"Why have you stayed then?"

She shrugged. "I love this planet. The people are so warm and friendly—ordinarily—and it's a beautiful world. I felt at home from the first day I landed. But I *am* ambitious, and the only way to make planetary agent is to move around. The company will never promote me into the job here. My ultimate goal has always been Sectors vice president for Loxton, and that requires a lot of varied assignments."

He stretched one arm out along the seat back behind her, toying with her earlobe. "I warn you, I like to sleep with the windows open."

"We can handle that issue when we come to it. You're tickling me." Andi jerked her head to dislodge his hand.

Laughing, he left her earlobe alone. "Well, it probably was your family who got us diverted to extract you. Nothing else makes sense. It would take someone with heavy political juice, Sectors-based pull. I don't think anyone on the planet could work it, not even Tonkiln. Once your boss left Zulaire, old man Loxton would have known, trust me. And he'd have found out you were left behind."

"It's nice to think my grandfather cares. I haven't seen him in years." Andi guided the luxury vehicle up the off-ramp close behind the truck. The small convoy hummed along for another half mile before pulling into the rest station's courtyard.

"You can be my chauffeur anytime." Tom kissed the soft spot where her neck met her shoulders, then clambered out of the car to greet the rest of the party, who were coming from the darkened restaurant to meet them.

Releasing the controls, Andi fell back against the soft contours of her seat, exhausted. *I can't go one more step, not even to find a place to lie down or something to eat.* Her body ached, and at the core, she felt weak. Surviving the river, then the incident with the Betang, followed by her near death at Uraku's hands, had worn her out.

The vehicle's door opened, letting in the scent of night-blooming flowers. Lifting her easily with his strong arms, Tom carried her into the restaurant, where a temporary camp had been established. He bumped open the door to the private back office with his hip and laid her on a couch there. Yanking a tablecloth free from a nearby stack, he used the fabric to tuck her in. After making a pillow with another tablecloth, her captain kissed her cheek. "Sleep now, sweetheart. I'll wake you when it's time to move."

She caught at his hand. "Thanks for saving my life."

"My pleasure. Thanks for saving mine."

Arching up from the couch, she pulled him toward her. He met her halfway, kissing her with pent-up hunger. Andi teased at his lips with her tongue, penetrating his warm mouth, exploring. His arms came around her, holding her close as his tongue tangled with hers in a delicious dance. Breaking off, he kissed his way along the side of her neck, nuzzling the soft spot at her shoulder.

Andi resisted when he tried to pull back a moment later. She tugged at his shirt, pulling it loose so she could run her hands underneath the fabric, resting her fingers on his warm back. He sat on the couch beside her. "I thought you were tired?"

"Maybe all of those drugs Mitch gave me have kicked in."

Stroking her hair, combing out tangles as he went, Tom smiled. "Even if the meds are working overtime, you're injured and I need you to rest before we start the last leg of the journey."

Yawning, accepting the truth of his assessment, she curled up carefully on her good side, pillowing her hand under her chin. "You were all I thought about, when Iraku was going to kill me."

"Finding you was the best thing that ever happened to me, lady." He kissed her cheek.

"Likewise."

"Remember what I told you that night by the lake, when we were camped out?" he said. "How I didn't think I could ever settle down in one place?"

"Yes, of course." *A woman doesn't forget a remark like that.*

"Now that I've found you, I know I can stay wherever you are. *You* are everything I need. Nothing else matters." Leaning over, he kissed her, taking exquisite care not to aggravate any of her wounds.

Touched he felt such security with her, Andi returned the kiss with intensity, happy in the knowledge they could have a future together.

With obvious reluctance, he broke the embrace a long moment later. "I hate to say this, but I have to go. We're running out of time." Tucking his shirt in and then readjusting the tablecloth that was to be her makeshift blanket, he kissed her forehead. "Try to sleep, okay?"

As she heard the door shut behind him, Andi closed her eyes with a grateful sigh. No nightmares waiting for her now, only sweet dreams.

CHAPTER EIGHT

When Andi woke, Rahuna was sitting in the chair next to the couch, reading a small book of meditations. When he saw she was awake, he gave her his beautiful full smile. "Good, you've slept yourself out, child." Sliding the book into a pocket, he stood.

"For now." Andi tried to move, but her stiff, sore limbs were aching, her reflexes sluggish. Her left side where the blaster shot had come so close was the worst, aching and burning as if she'd three broken ribs. *It even hurts to breathe. Those drugs of the sergeant's must have worn off.* "What time is it?"

"Still the middle of the night, I fear. Come, I have some food if you're hungry." Rahuna walked over to the couch.

"*Starved.* You must be my guardian angel." *When was the last time I ate?* " Any coffee?"

Rahuna tugged her to her feet with elaborate caution while she clutched at her side. Matching his steps to her halting pace, he supported her as she hobbled out of the office. She picked the closest chair at the first table in the restaurant. Like a waiter at a fancy restaurant, Rahuna pulled the seat out for her with a flourish. "There's coffee. The soldiers said since this was our last stop before the capital, we might as well finish the supply. I saved two cups for you."

Before she could thank him, Rahuna hurried out, returning with a large tray from which he spread a bountiful meal for her, including an omelet, fruit, breads, preserves as well as the promised coffee.

"Where did all this come from?" she asked around a mouthful of fruit.

"South Amri was abandoned by its owners in a great hurry. The power was still on when we arrived. There's a big generator out back, behind the buildings. Corporal Rogers wouldn't let us use many lights when we got here, but we were able to cook. Well, *I* was able to cook."

Andi took a bite of the omelet, which was tasty and, although not hot any longer, still warm enough to eat. "Where is everyone?" Taking some of the toast, she made a sandwich with the omelet in the middle and munched happily.

"Lysanda and the boy are asleep in a small, private dining room over there." Rahuna pointed vaguely to the other side of the restaurant. "She wasn't comfortable to be left alone in this big, open space. Abukawal is on guard on the roof, watching the off-ramp. The soldiers are outside behind the restaurant, working on the truck and the other vehicle you brought in."

"It was Gul Tonkiln's car." *I still can't believe he might be dead.* Assaulted by memories and the pang of sorrow, Andi closed her eyes for a moment. *Yet another person who didn't deserve to die in this insane Clan war.*

"Andi?" Rahuna laid his hand over hers. "Come back from wherever your mind is roaming." He handed her another triangle of toast. "It would seem Lord Tonkiln has lost his firstborn, as well as the others who perished at the summer compound." Voice low and hushed, he said, "Tonkiln's paid a high price for refusing to take the early warnings seriously."

"You don't think there's a chance the rebels might be holding Gul for ransom?" Appetite gone, Andi set the toast down, untouched.

Rahuna shook his head, lips pursed, eyebrows drawn together. "This doesn't seem to be the rebels' pattern. I fear poor Gul has passed to the next world, murdered no doubt. I continue to give thanks to Sanenre your captain intervened on my behalf, to spare me a similar fate."

"Mmm, *my* captain." Andi felt like purring. "Has Tom said what he's planning to do now? How do we get to the capital from here?"

Picking up a ripe fruit and contemplating its bruised skin, Rahuna shook his head. "Not to me. He and his men have been modifying the two vehicles. The captain wouldn't even take time to eat, nor let the sergeant have a break. I brought them food out back, in the garage. The men gulped bites here and there as they worked. So, I believe we're going to take the vehicles." Rahuna bit into the fruit and munched on it, giving a small sigh. "The comlink here at the station was inoperable, by the way. A severe disappointment to the captain. Rogers said several vital parts were missing."

"Tom hoped to call for an air evac." Andi sipped her coffee then devoured the last two bites of her omelet, which now tasted like cardboard. *Doesn't matter what the food tastes like, I need to eat while there's food available. I need my strength.* "You're quite a cook, sir, if I may say so."

"As a young candidate for priesthood, one is set many tasks to learn, you know. I was assigned to cook for the brothers at the south coast monastery. The supplies left here didn't run to much more than tibu eggs and basic spices, so I was unable to be creative." He frowned at the fruit and set it on the platter, fastidiously cleaning his fingers with a cloth napkin.

Andi finished her cup of coffee in one unladylike gulp and pushed her chair away from the table, wincing at the pain in her left side from the hasty move. "Let's go find Tom and see how they're doing. I don't want to linger at South Amri a minute longer than we have to." She took a few steps then stopped, hand pressed tight to the bandages on her side. "I'm so stiff my joints are about paralyzed. Mitch said I'll need a short session in rejuve, but if this gets worse I'll need a week."

"Take your time. Lean on me." Rahuna escorted her out of the restaurant and around the back, supporting her the whole way. The soldiers had rigged a dozen work lamps, now trained on the two vehicles, making the garage area as bright as midday.

Tom stood off to the side of Gul's car, supervising Rogers while he cut a major portion of the roof off. Tools pilfered from the station's garage lay everywhere. As

Rahuna and Andi paced around the corner, arm in arm, Tom made his way to them, yelling "Mitch!" over his shoulder as he did so.

"You shouldn't be strolling the premises." He folded Andi in his arms for a quick kiss. From the corner of her eye, she saw Rogers and Latvik open-mouthed and staring at this affectionate display.

The sergeant ran up behind him. "What's the emergency?"

Tom nodded toward Andi. "See if she's okay, will you? I don't want her to aggravate the blaster sear."

"So considerate," Andi murmured.

"You have to be able to drive when we're ready to roll out of here." He loosened his grip on her waist a bit as she winced.

"You always have an agenda." Andi laughed. She glanced at him, batting her eyelashes flirtatiously. "Must it always be a military objective you need me for?"

"Minx." He kissed her again. "Wait until we get back to the capital, and then we can discuss other objectives I might have in mind."

"If you'd go over there, ma'am, sit down, I'll be one minute." Mitch left, presumably to retrieve his medkit, returning as Rahuna and Tom got Andi settled onto an empty crate off to the side of all the frenetic activity.

"What's the plan for the car?" She stared across the service bay, to where Rogers and Latvik strained to lift the severed portion of the roof off the vehicle's body.

As Mitch did a quick but careful examination of her various injuries, Tom braced her with his arm behind her back. "You'll drive the car—*if* you're strong enough."

"I'm good to go." Putting her shoulders back, she straightened from her slouching position.

Nodding in support of her self-diagnosis, Mitch re-taped the bandages on her side. "She'll do fine, sir. The sear isn't any worse. Does it ache yet, ma'am?"

"*Yes.* I'm also stiff everywhere, like an old lady."

"I have somethin' for the pain, but best to wait til right before you need to drive." Mitch held the inject in his hand but glanced at it with a troubled frown.

"If I administer it too soon, the drug will wear off in the middle of our run for the capital."

"Makes sense. I can wait." Andi pushed his hand back toward the open medkit. The sergeant dropped the inject into its receptacle and shut the lid.

Clapping him affably on the shoulder, Tom said, "All right, thanks. You can get back to the cargo hauler and I'll be there in a minute."

"The rest of the plan?" Andi prompted.

"Sorry—I'm dog tired." Tom ran a hand over his short-cropped hair. "We don't have time to reset the car to allow anyone else to drive it. I'm afraid if we do a rush job, we'll short out the whole system, leaving it useless. So *you* are the designated driver. I'll ride shotgun, and Rogers will be crammed into the back with a piece of heavy-caliber hardware we found in Iraku's truck."

Andi stared at the men working on the beat-up hauler. An impressive pile of munitions had been stacked with military precision off to the side. She pointed at the cache. "Were all those weapons in the truck?"

"Oh, yeah." His eyebrows drew together in a grim frown. "Enough to equip quite an operation. All Betang-made imitations of Sectors hardware, which will serve as confirmation of your story, once we get to the capital. Those damn Naranti hotheads are taking this planet to hell, begging your pardon, sir." Tom nodded respectfully to Rahuna.

Hands in his pockets, Rahuna bowed. "I don't disagree. It saddens me, for my Clan and for all Zulaire. I hope you'll be able to save us from this disaster."

"How many Betang do you think are here already? There was one in the village, which was enough for me." Andi crossed her arms and hunched forward, adrenaline rising as she remembered how terrifying the creature had been.

He rubbed her shoulders carefully for a minute, soothing some of her stress away. "An advance team can be anywhere from one to five agents. Then, if things go their way, the enemy arrives in waves, followed by Mawreg heavy cruisers. The planet's lost then. Fortunately for Zulaire, the advance team usually needs a year or two, Terra Standard, to create enough chaos."

"When do we leave here?" Andi rubbed her arms as the night chill sank in. "This place makes me jumpy. Anxious."

"*Mitch.* How much longer to rig the cargo hauler and the car?" Tom's voice carried across the din of the service area.

Waving a grav wrench, the sergeant didn't even look up. "Two hours max, sir."

"Okay. I want to hit the transportway before dawn, if we can." Not waiting for the sergeant's answering nod, Tom turned back to Andi and Rahuna.

"And we're just driving directly home?" Andi drew a straight line in the air with her hand.

"Right. It's about four hundred miles, so I figure maybe a shade under two hours, if we're lucky and don't run into any roadblocks or renegades. There's no cover between here and the capital—it's pretty much a flat plain. Well, you two know."

"Why not stay here until night falls again and make our run under cover of darkness?" Rahuna asked.

"We're still too close to the village where Andi was held prisoner," Tom said. "Iraku will be missed and once someone goes to look for him and the weapons, it'll be simple to figure out where we went with the cargo hauler. Our obvious destination would have to be the capital. Any commander with any sense at all would check for us here since South Amri is the only rest stop or building along the route."

"And not defensible," Andi clarified, earning a nod from Tom.

Smoothing his robes, Rahuna stood away from the wall. "I'd better get back inside to check on Lysanda and Sadu. She'll be terrified if she awakes alone. Are you coming, Andi?"

She shook her head. Those familiar butterflies were back in her stomach, making her queasy. Being outside in the open, near the soldiers with weapons, soothed her anxiety. The fresh night air was bracing. Proximity to Tom was also high on her list of must-haves. "I'll just sit here out of the way and watch."

Rahuna nodded and strode away, the long skirts of his robe flapping around his legs.

Tom watched the cleric for a moment, then glanced at Andi. "I've got to get back to work—we're running out of time."

"Is there anything I can do to help?" she asked.

He kissed her. "Not even if you were an expert mechanic. I need you rested and ready to drive. But I appreciate the offer." He walked to the cargo hauler, grabbing a load of tools from a cart as he went, then disappeared behind the hulking vehicle.

Jittery, Andi leaned her head against the wall to get more comfortable, closing her eyes against the glare of the work lamps. The clamor of men at work became white noise around her, almost soothing, and she drifted off to sleep.

***

A loud bang startled her awake, to the cold sensation of tendrils drooping over her arms and legs. Andi jumped off the crate, eyes wide open, her fists clenched, heart racing. "*Tom!*" She started frantically rubbing at her arms, even though she could see there were no tentacles grabbing at her.

He sprinted from wherever he'd been, followed by Mitch. Catching her in his arms, Tom captured her hands to halt the desperate arm-rubbing. The sergeant hovered nearby. Rogers slid out from under the cargo hauler, and Latvik leaned around the side, blaster in his good hand, to see what the fuss was about.

"I'm sorry if we woke you. We just sealed the hauler's engine compartment. Was the noise what startled you?" Running his hands up and down her arms, Tom tried to examine her as she cringed, shuddering against him.

Unable to quell the trembling, she buried her face against his chest. "I couldn't breathe," Andi said. "I felt like there were tentacles wrapping around me, squeezing the life out of me. The Betang was invading my mind like at the river village. It has to be somewhere close to us. We've got to get out of here or we'll die."

"Andi, you were asleep, you were probably dreaming—"

Impatiently she shoved away from him. "*No*, this happened after I woke. The Betang's touch is unmistakable. Trust me. *We're out of time.* The enemy knows where I am, and it's on the road to us." Unable to sit still, needing to be in motion, she started pacing back and forth, wringing her hands.

Tom swung into action, raising his voice and snapping out commands. "Okay, we move *now*, people. Rogers, get Rahuna and the others, and don't forget Abukawal on the roof." Turning to Andi, taking her by the elbow, he steered her toward Gul's car. "Come on, let's get you situated. Mitch, she'll need the next medinject so she can drive." He scrutinized her face. "Can you handle driving, sweetheart? Is the Betang touch still there?"

Trying to calm her nerves, Andi breathed in deeply, one hand on her chest. She shook her head. "No."

He beckoned to the sergeant. "Double-time it with that inject, damn it."

As Mitch gave Andi yet another one of his endless supply of drugs, Rahuna and Abukawal rushed around the end of the restaurant building, the cleric carrying a drowsy Sadu, the Shenti warrior towing a vacant-eyed Lysanda.

Waving the newcomers toward the cargo hauler, Tom pulled Andi toward the car. She had to wait while Rogers squeezed himself into the back. He'd have to ride in a half-crouching position, so he could work the weapon rigged on a crude turntable in the rear of the much-revamped speedster.

Handing Andi into the driver's seat, Tom shut the door. "Start the motor and be ready." He ran over to the cargo hauler to confer with Mitch and Abukawal.

Once she got the car's engine idling, she craned awkwardly to check on Rogers. "Will you be okay back there for two hours?" She eyed the very small space and the gigantic gun. The soldier was built on the husky side.

"I'll be fine, thanks. I'll sure be glad to get back to the city, ma'am." Rogers was shoving extra charge capsules into the side of the weapon, feeding them into the magazine. "This has been one hell of a patrol." Pausing for a second, he flashed a crooked smile. "Wish we had the APC instead of an old truck, though."

"You and me both." *I'd also like a clear road back to the capital, please.* The trip so far had been nerve-racking and often terrifying, but the idea of driving on the center line of the transportway, visible to any pursuers, gave Andi the shakes. But there were no other viable routes left to them.

Tom opened the passenger door and jumped in, slamming the door shut. "Let's go. Accelerate when you hit the on-ramp. The truck will follow."

Automatically, she reached for the controls, then had a second thought. "Should I use the lights?"

He checked the sky above. "Can you manage with just the moonlight?"

She nodded.

"All right, no lights then," Tom said. "Now punch it."

Doing as she was told, revving the engine, Andi wasted no time. Her passengers were both jolted back by her rapid acceleration out of the yard. At the controls of this fast groundcar, she felt good, more in charge of her own fate.

"Don't get too far ahead of Mitch." Tom checked behind to see how the cargo hauler fared. "We worked on the truck for hours. I guarantee it's never been so babied in its life span, but the thing's still a damn mud crawler compared to this beauty."

"Can't get eight people in here, sir," Rogers said.

"Not if they're all as big as you, soldier." Tom laughed.

Andi found a speed at which she wouldn't pull too far ahead of the massive truck and set the cruise control. *I just want to push the engine to the manufacturer's limit and then some. Mitch could never keep up, though.* She eyed the readouts, checking the fuel levels before her gaze drifted to the badly dented com console. "Do you think the com will work after you beat it up? Maybe someone else is on duty, someone with more sense."

Tom's smile was sheepish.

Probably regretting that earlier loss of control.

"We can try," he said. "For as many credits as Tonkiln spent on this car, it should be able to take abuse and still function." He checked the time. "Shift change would've been a little while ago. Here goes nothing." Activating the com, he reset to the military frequency and the unit produced a reassuring hum. "Patrol KJ123, calling Command." Tom repeated the call sign twice before a powerful return broadcast cut across his words.

"Captain Deverane, it is so good to hear from you. Give us your coordinates, and we'll send an extraction team. Is Miss Markriss with you?"

Quietly, Tom thumbed the comlink closed.

Surprised and annoyed, Andi stared at him, not the road, for a second. "Why didn't you answer him, tell him where we are?"

"Because it wasn't Sectors Command on the link. The Betang like to play tricks. You were right. They must be close to come in so clear. Damn, I wish the truck could go faster." Tom twisted in his seat to stare behind them at the cargo hauler. "Accelerate a bit. Let's see if Mitch can coax anymore out of the old girl."

But when Andi sped up by a few more miles per hour, she drew away from their companion vehicle.

"Never mind, slow down, come even with them on the passenger side," Tom said. "I need to talk to Mitch."

"I'll try." *Slow down?* Andi concentrated on her driving for the next few minutes. The entire transportway stretched eerily empty on both sides, except for their two vehicles. The last medinject had numbed the blaster sear, leaving her calm and loose but clear headed. *How long do I have before the effect wears off? Mitch said he couldn't give me anymore for forty-eight hours.* Remembering the crippling pain she'd been suffering, she blew her breath out through her teeth. *Make me an addict—I don't care! I'll detox later.*

Tom leaned across her, shouting out the window at Mitch across the nerve-rackingly small gap between the two vehicles as they barreled down the transportway. "The Betang tried to decoy us into giving away our position on the com a few minutes ago. I figure they must be following us."

Mitch grimaced, keeping his eyes on the road. "Not too hard to guess where we're headed."

Tom jerked his thumb over his shoulder to the rear. "We'll drop back and see if anyone's coming. You keep going as fast as the hunk of junk will motor, okay?"

"Got it, sir. Good hunting." Mitch waved as Andi slowed even further and fell behind the cargo hauler, looping the car around in a big U-turn to return the way she'd come. She had to grit her teeth to make herself drive *into* the possible pursuit. Her hands were shaking on the wheel, so she tightened her grip till her knuckles went white.

Tom reached over and pried one of her hands loose from the wheel, rubbing it softly. "Take us five miles in this direction." He looked at her face, eyes narrowed. "You're doing a great job."

She frowned at him. "I hate this, you know. Every instinct I have is telling me I'm crazy to go back toward South Amri."

"I have to see if there's any sign of pursuit," he said patiently.

"Oh, I know. I'm just telling you—"

Searing pain stabbed across her skull. Raising both hands instinctively to her forehead as the mind touch of the Betang drilled its way into her consciousness, Andi forgot all about driving. The contact was stronger than when she'd awakened from her nap in the South Amri vehicle servicing bay. Her chest constricted, and she heard herself wheeze. Veering sharply to the left, the car decelerated.

"*Andi*, snap out of it! Take the controls." Tom's voice sounded as if it was coming from a long distance.

Her vision narrowed. The pressure and buzzing flooded her mind, further inhibiting each strained breath and fluttering heartbeat.

Speaking right next to her ear, Tom said, "You have to drive this thing. Breathe."

Andi squinted her eyes open but was still in too much pain to move, other than to hit the brakes. She watched, paralyzed as the vehicle slewed across the transportway and bumped over the edge of the road, coming to a stop about three feet onto the shoulder, just short of the drop-off to the drainage canal running alongside. Hunching over in the driver's seat, she clutched her temples, her whole body trembling. She had to fight to get any air into her lungs.

"Now what?" Rogers yelled.

"Keep your eyes open, soldier. Watch your tracker readout." Andi heard the passenger door lock disengage, then cool air brushed over her as Tom popped her own door open. Awkwardly, he embraced her in the confined space. "Sweetheart, you've got to fight this off. You're the only one who can drive us out of here."

She opened her eyes but blinked them shut again as even the faint moonlight sent stabbing pain through her eyeballs. Stomach heaving, she leaned around him and retched. "I can't breathe. My head hurts like it's going to explode."

"The Betang must be coming—we have a narrow window of time to escape. Try to hold it off, concentrate," Tom said.

Moaning, she let her head fall forward onto his shoulder. Stroking her hair, he kissed her cheek.

Andi leaned on him for a minute, trying to absorb his strength. Her chest loosened up a little as she breathed in the spice and musk of his scent. Pulling in more oxygen reduced the headache slightly. Moving as if her head might fall off, she straightened. "I'll try."

"That's the Andi I know," Tom said, patting her on the shoulder before sprinting around the car back to his seat.

Fumbling, vision full of blank spots and squiggly lightning bolts, Andi managed to get the car into reverse, bumping onto the transportway again. Turning in fits and starts, she pointed the nose away from South Amri.

"*Punch it*," Tom said in Andi's right ear.

She slammed on the acceleration, trusting him to steer. The little sports vehicle responded in an instant, pinning her into her seat and probably leaving poor Rogers jammed against the rough edge of his makeshift moon roof.

"Tracker readout shows targets, sir," Rogers shouted.

She thought her heart was going to pound its way right out of her chest. "Distance?"

"Fifteen miles out, coming steadily."

Gritting her teeth, Andi put her head down and activated the final power reserves. The car hurtled along the dark transportway.

"Are you still under attack or has it eased?" Tom stroked her cheek. "Vision improving, I gather."

"Some. My eyesight is clearing. I can breathe again. I still have a hell of a headache, though." She checked the rearview mirror. "Rogers, are the targets gaining?"

"Not on this baby." Rogers' admiration for Gul's expensive car was clear in his voice. "Wish I could drive it, ma'am."

"So do I."

"Watch for the cargo hauler." Tom pushed at the phantom brake on his side of the car. "We'll overtake it faster than you think at this speed. When we do rejoin them, I'm going to transfer Rahuna and the boy into this vehicle then I want you to head straight for the capital."

"I'm not going to leave you." She whipped her head to stare at him in shock. He might as well have doused her with cold water. "*I won't.*"

"Eyes on the road. You have to go on ahead. Those targets are going to catch up with us once we're traveling with the clunker cargo hauler. As soon as the Betang gets within mind-scan distance again, it *will* kill you."

"How? How can it sense me from so far away, let alone kill me? It touched me at Iraku's compound, before it tried to kill me. Did it get my DNA then?" Andi strove to make sense of the danger.

"I didn't want to scare you unnecessarily before, but yes, the Betang was sampling your DNA when it touched you. Remember I said earlier, once it's tasted a human's genetic makeup, it has the power to kill that person when it gets close enough," Tom said. "Even if we manage to fight the rebels off with our heavy weapons, you'll die. I won't take the chance." His gaze was steady, unblinking. "Don't argue. You hightail it to the capital. Between you and Rahuna, you can persuade Command to send us a rescue team."

"I don't want to cut and run." Stubborn as she felt at the moment, she could see his logic. A little.

"But you know I'm right, don't you?" He sounded relieved, probably because she'd implicitly accepted his argument.

She drove at frantic speed for another minute before sighting the cargo hauler ahead.

Stopped on the side of the road.

"*What the hell?*" Tom put a clenched fist on the dashboard and stared ahead with narrowed eyes.

"Maybe their engine's slagging, sir." Rogers' voice held resignation.

Fuming, impatient, hand on the door, Tom was poised to move, as soon as Andi brought them to a halt beside the cargo hauler.

"Keep the engine running. I'll get Rahuna and Sadu over here in a minute." Tom bolted from the car, striding across the transportway to meet Mitch as he walked around the front of the stopped cargo hauler. The two men talked, easily visible now in the gray predawn light. Tom's shoulders slumped the longer the sergeant went on.

Not a good sign.

Rogers leaned over the seat. "Doesn't look promising, ma'am. That cargo-hauler engine's still running. Wonder what's going on?"

A wave of cold dread washed through Andi. "Corporal, can you please take another read-ing on your tracker?"

"Targets still approaching, ma'am." Rogers looked up from the tracker and pulled his shirt collar away from his neck.

"Try taking a reading ahead of us, *toward* the capital." *Oh, I hope I'm wrong...*

Flipping his device, the soldier scanned in the direction she'd requested. He whistled, eyes opening wide. He showed her the readout while talking so fast he was spitting. "Big target, stationary, multiple vehicles. Roadblock. You called it, ma'am."

"How far?"

"About five miles ahead." Chewing his lips, he stared at the readout.

Tom came back to the car, sliding into his seat. Andi could see from his lined face and hooded eyes how reluctant he was to tell them what he'd learned.

She touched his arm. "It's okay. Rogers did a forward scan. We're cut off."

"Yes." He sat for a minute then flipped the comlink switch, as if to try one last appeal for help. "*Fuck.*" Stress and worry etched his face as he turned to her. "We'll figure out something, I promise."

"We've made it this far. I have confidence in you." Leaning over, she gave him a quick kiss.

"What now, sir?" Uneasily, Rogers shifted in the cramped rear compartment.

"Rahuna says there's a rock formation of some kind about two miles ahead. Guess he travels this road a lot in his ministry, huh?" Tom tried a lopsided smile.

Nodding, Andi shifted the car out of idle. The motor roared. "I think I know the place he means. Shall I follow the truck?"

"Right, stick close. I told Mitch it doesn't matter if we burn out the truck engine now, once we make this rock formation. At least the heavy weapons we got from Iraku provide us some edge." Tom raised his eyebrows and rubbed his forehead, then his neck. He sat on the edge of the seat, fingers drumming on his thighs.

"The Betang brought the rebels several haulers' worth of weapons, not just the ones we took from Iraku," Andi said.

"Unusual for the Betang to show such desperation, as far as tracking us. Their campaign on Zulaire must still be in the early stages, fragile enough for the Sectors to be able to stop it." A tired smile was all Tom could muster. "No pressure on us, right?"

Nodding, she matched his grin.

Mitch drove the cargo hauler off the edge of the transportway ahead of them, steering over the uneven ground toward an isolated upthrust of rock. The massive formation was the remnant of some violent geological episode in Zulaire's long-gone past, rising out of nowhere in the middle of the flat plains. Andi had seen the natural wonder on the way out from the capital—the Knives of the Under Spirits, so-called because of the formation's jagged shapes and resemblance to a bundle of ceremonial knife blades. The Knives towered at an angle about two hundred feet into the Zulairian sky.

"Not a bad spot, sir," Rogers said as their vehicle began the bumpy trip off the transportway and across the hard-packed, dusty plain toward the rocks.

"Don't let the car get stalled in the dirt," Tom said, voice tense. "Pull in front of the cargo hauler and angle it just a bit when you park, so we have a vee formation to take cover behind."

Andi did as she was requested then shut the motor off. The sudden silence surprised her, but a moment later she heard the sounds of approaching vehicles coming from the north. The rumbling was faint as yet but unmistakable, giving her nervous chills up and down her spine.

"Come on, time to get you to a safer spot." Tom tugged her out of her seat, hurrying her around the back, squeezing between Gul's car and the nose of the cargo hauler. Mitch, Latvik and Abukawal were busy placing heavy-caliber weapons at intervals along the barricaded vehicles.

"Wish we had the APC." The sergeant loaded a full pack of ammo into the gun he was preparing and moved onto the next one.

"Don't we all," Tom said. "Take charge here for a few minutes, would you? I've got to talk to Andi."

"No problem, sir. I think a few minutes are all we've got, though." Slamming the cover down on the massive gun, Mitch set the safety to off.

"Hold on a minute." Andi pulled her hand from Tom's. "I can shoot. I can fight. I want to be here on the line with you, not hiding in a rock crevice like Sadu and Lysanda."

She expected him to argue, had her own counterarguments ready.

He stood staring at her for a long minute, hands on his hips, saying nothing, face drawn. Then he nodded. "Okay. We can use all the firepower we can get. But you tell me the instant you feel anything from the Betang, understand?"

"Of course."

"Help me get the Tonkilns and Rahuna settled." He held out his hand to her.

Lacing her fingers through his, she went at a quick pace to the rock wall where Rahuna stood beside a sobbing Lysanda, arm around her shoulders. Sadu watched his sister's face, thumb in mouth, deciding whether this was something he should cry over, too. As Andi approached them, the toddler's little face crumpled, and he began to howl. She reached for him, to offer what comfort she could. Lysanda forestalled her, gathering her baby brother into her arms and croon-ing a song while she rocked back and forth.

Rahuna met Tom, holding out a hand. "I should like a weapon, Captain."

Unclasping his blaster from the holster, the captain handed it over. Andi gaped at him, then eyed the cleric with raised brows, horrified that things had come to this necessity. *Rahuna with a weapon? Rahuna prepared to kill people?* His Serene Holiness took the weapon gingerly, studying the sleek, black Mark 27 blaster with a judicious eye. Tom reached over and shifted the weapon in his hands, adjusted Rahuna's grip.

"You click off the safety here." Tom pointed with one hand. "Aim, depress this." He demonstrated. "And it shoots. Plenty of charges left. Any questions, sir?"

"No. I'll manage. Sanenre does not forbid killing in a good cause. I must be responsible for the Tonkiln children." The cleric experimented with aiming. "I won't allow Lysanda and Sadu to fall into the hands of these killers, trust me."

Tom assessed Rahuna with a long, measuring gaze then nodded. "All right, on my command, or if the rest of us are neutralized, agreed?"

"Agreed," His Serene Holiness said. "And, Captain, Sanenre's blessing on us all in the next hour."

"We'll need it." Tom saluted before he and Andi jogged back toward the defensive line of vehicles.

Opposite their group, back on the transportway, a motley convoy of ten assorted vehicles had come to a halt.

"Pretty overpowering odds." Andi stared across the dusty plain, her eyes narrowed. *Looks like the entire contingent from the village, all armed to the teeth.* Drawing her blaster, she clicked the safety off. "Where do you want me?"

"Between Mitch and me." Tom drew her to the indicated spot.

Andi swallowed hard. "Orders?"

"Just shoot the bastards." He gave her a quick kiss. "Stay hunkered down as much as you can." He strode away, calling to Mitch for another blaster.

Crouching behind the rear flank of the car, Andi found a position where she could get a clear line of sight without being too exposed. Tom brushed her back as he moved to take his place.

Strange how the enemy is so silent. Why aren't they yelling demands or something? Sweat trickled down her neck. Her legs were cramping already. Inaction was so much more torturous to endure than action. She wanted to stand up and run toward the trucks, attacking them, just to get the combat underway.

"Remember, make each shot count," Tom said in a tense whisper.

She nodded, moistening her lips with the tip of her tongue, afraid to try her voice.

Suddenly, fifty or sixty rebels poured out from around the ragtag, dilapidated vehicles that made up the convoy. Screaming oaths and curses, the men ran across the plain, firing their weapons uselessly since they were still out of range. Whatever heavy armament the insurgents had mounted on their trucks shot a barrage of covering fire, bracketing the Knives harmlessly on the first round.

"Fire at will!" Tom shouted.

His command startled her. Reflexively, she pressed the firing button, and the beam went wild. Her companions' blaster fire erupted around Andi. She swallowed hard, took aim and shot again, but her next blast also went wide. Pinpointing a single enemy soldier rather than trying to sweep across the mob, Andi controlled her weapon, letting off a short burst. The man stumbled and fell as her shot hit him.

Andi swallowed. *Don't think, don't feel, just shoot them before they can shoot you.*

She settled into a rhythm of aim, fire, move on to the next target without waiting to see if she'd been successful. Totally focused on her own battle, Andi hovered in a zone, aware of the others beside her, hearing the boom every time Rogers fired his energy cannon, blocking incoming blasts, but her senses had narrowed. She focused only on the sights of her own blaster.

At first the insurgents were easy to pick off as they sprinted in a disorganized mob. The attack failed, and a few minutes later the next wave came at them using a pair of slowly moving cargo haulers as shields.

"Disable those trucks, damn it," Tom yelled over the din. "Don't let them get close."

The Sectors party would have been overwhelmed in short order without the heavy weapons they'd found in Iraku's truck. As it was, Rogers and Latvik targeted and knocked out the oncoming trucks with relative ease. A short lull fell. Andi's hands were sore, her legs shaking. She slumped to the ground, back to the car and lowered her head. Tom moved along the line of his makeshift fortifications, checking the need for recharges, checking for injuries.

"*Incoming*," Mitch shouted. Andi, Tom and the others hit the dirt as an energy charge exploded harmlessly behind them, striking midway between them and the spot where Rahuna and the Tonkilns huddled in the shelter of the Knives.

Tom took up a position where Gul's car and the cargo hauler met. "Return fire!"

Andi pinpointed the location where the energy grenades were being launched. "Rogers, see that ugly green flatbed over there? That's the one to take out, quick."

"With pleasure, ma'am." Swinging his cannon around on the makeshift turntable in Gul's backseat, Rogers unleashed an intense barrage of energy. The designated truck blew up in a huge explosion, setting a couple of the other vehicles on fire. A number of the enemy fell, either from the concussion or from shrapnel. The rebels in the field hesitated, before withdrawing in a ragged wave.

"*Yes!*" Andi pumped her fist in the air and slapped Rogers on the back. "Great shot."

"They've got reinforcements, sir." Mitch pointed out three more trucks driving in from the north.

"Keep an eye on them." Tom crouched beside Andi. "I'm proud of you."

She stared at the newly arrived vehicles. Unexpectedly, a slimy sensation rippled down her arms, as if she'd been stroked by a tentacle. *The Betang must be in one of those trucks.*

"Andi?" He put his arms around her, turning her to face him.

Reaching up, she wiped a smear of blood from his cheek where he'd been grazed by shrapnel, her hand trembling. *What if he'd been seriously injured, or even killed? That was a pretty near miss.* "I'm cool as a cucumber when they're attacking, but I have the shakes like crazy in the lulls like this one."

"That's normal. Adrenaline rush. Are you okay? No injuries?" He eyed her up and down, running his hand along her arm.

Andi hesitated.

He glared at her. "Answer me. You're hiding something."

Gesturing at the enemy convoy, she said, "The Betang is here. It must have come in one of those new trucks. The sensation is faint, but I can tell the creature's there."

"You need to see this." Mitch crouched next to Andi's side, viewers in hand. "To the left, by the red cargo hauler. It's nothing I've ever seen. Betang projecting a false image maybe?"

Grabbing the viewers from him with a curse, Tom took a long look, then passed them to Andi. He waited while she adjusted the focus and tried to find what the two men had seen. *There it is. And it's got those horrible red stubs turned in this direction.* Instinctively trying to hide, she dropped the viewers and shrank back. "That's the creature all right. Oh, Lords, now it's probably seen me. What can we do? Could you give me an inject, knock me out?"

Tom shook his head. "You'll just die faster. You can't fight it if you're unconscious."

"*Fight it?* Fight it with *what?*" She clamped down hard on the rising edge of her hysteria and sucked in a deep breath before she started again. "Look, I don't *want* to die, but there's nothing else we can do then, is there? At least I wouldn't have to suffer." Unable to meet his eyes, she swallowed and looked away. "I'm not a coward. You know I'm a fighter, but it was excruciating when the Betang tried to kill me before." She looked at their grim faces, struck by a new worry. "Can it kill all of us with a mental blast?"

Shaking his head, Tom took her arm, rotating it a bit so they could both see the imprint of the Betang's suckers. "You're the only one at direct risk from the Betang." He drew her to her feet, stopped her next anxious remark with a fierce kiss, then held her away from him. "You know I love you. Do you trust me?"

"Of course I do." *And I don't want to die here, in the dust, where you have to watch.* Trembling all over, Andi felt a cold sweat beading her arms and legs, despite the heat of the day. "Are you sure a knockout inject won't work? Has it ever been tried?"

Face lined with worry, he nodded. "It's been tried. We're not going down that road, not with your life at stake. There's a Special Forces technique to defend against mental assaults like the Betang's. I can teach you, right here, right now."

He expects me to master some complicated mental trick here? Now? Skeptically, Andi holstered her blaster. "How long did it take you to learn?"

"My experience isn't important." He scrutinized their defense line, the battered, shot-up truck and car. "We need to get you to a safer place to try this." Tom exchanged a glance with Mitch. "You're in charge."

"Make it quick, sir." The sergeant had retrieved the viewers and was studying the enemy. "They're having a confab. The Betang's doing a lot of gesturin', pointing at us. Working the mob up pretty effectively."

"I'll be right back." Tom flicked an assessing glance over at the rebel throng on the road. Squaring his jaw, he picked Andi up and carried her toward the Knives.

Listening to his strong heartbeat as she lay curled against his chest, she said, "I love you."

"I love you, too." He paused in front of a short outcropping of the glossy, black rock, setting her down in the small alcove between it and the main body of the Knives. As she tried to sit comfortably on the ground, Tom knelt in front of her, keeping her hands in his. "Concentrate on what I'm going to tell you."

She scooted back a little, to have the rock wall of the Knives behind her. She studied his face.

Tom's green eyes locked onto her. "First step. Identify a mental focal point that implies defense to you. Think of something symbolizing protection. A wall, a fire, something. Do you understand what I'm saying?"

"I guess so." Andi shrugged. She chewed her lip and looked away from him. "How is this going to help?"

"Whatever you decide on, make it real in your mind. Clear everything else out. You can't afford to think about anything but your defense. You hold the picture, no matter what. Don't think of me, don't think of the Betang, except in the sense that it can't get through to you, no matter what it tries. Have one focus, on your defensive point, and only that thought. Try it now. Close your eyes and try it," he urged.

Hearing shouts from the barricade, she tried to peer around him. "The men are calling. You'd better go." *He's wasting valuable time on this. I can't let him sacrifice the safety of the others just to try to comfort me.* "You've got to get back. I don't want you to watch me die." She tried a small smile for him.

Tom gave her such a rough shake that her head rocked from the force. His fingers clenched on her arms. Andi was shocked back into attention by the small amount of pain. He spoke low and fast. "Never mind them. Mitch is in charge. He's fine. Worry about yourself. Close your eyes and visualize, now. *Do it.*"

Obediently, she shut her eyes, trying to empty her mind. She ignored increasing pressure in her chest and flashes of pain from the Betang's mind scan but couldn't settle on anything to use as a mental defense. *What says protection to me? Right now, being somewhere else! A wall, as he'd suggested? No, walls crumble or fall down. No good. Fire?* Andi shivered, remembering what it had been like, caught in the burning Tonkiln mansion. *Definitely not fire.* How pathetic and ridiculous she was to hope this emergency meditation would work! If her life wasn't at stake she'd be laughing at the mere idea. With a sigh, she opened her eyes, shaking her head.

"This isn't a game." Tom shouted at her, releasing his grip on her and flinging his arms out. He stood, turned away from her, hands on his hips, head tilted, and was silent for a minute.

I'm letting him down. Andi stared at his back. *He really believes this should work for me, and I can't even pretend I'm taking it seriously. He knows I'm not trying.*

As if he'd been eavesdropping on her thoughts, Tom spun around. He hunkered down and smoothed her hair away from her face with both hands, before giving her a lingering kiss. "I know what I'm asking seems absurd. I've seen it work. It *can* save you." He pulled her so close to him that their noses were nearly touching. Andi breathed in his musky scent, and her head cleared a bit. He kept talking, his voice low and hurried. "You have to fight for yourself. You have to believe in yourself, like I believe in those heavy blasters over there. And I believe in you just as much." Tom gestured toward the barricade behind them where his men were rearranging some of the meager defenses. "But blasters aren't the right weapons for this kind of a fight. You have what you need inside yourself. Try again."

Overwhelmed, Andi laid her head on his shoulder.

"Andi...for me, for *us.*" Tom's voice sounded gentle, but she heard the tension underlying the calm words. He hugged her, his arms warm and strong around her shaking body. "If I didn't think this was a real chance for you to survive, I'd be saying a whole lot of other things right now. I'd be saying good-bye, okay? And I would've had Mitch put you under so you wouldn't suffer. Hell, I'd give you the inject myself. But I won't. You can do this."

She took another breath, savoring the moment. Fiercely, she hugged him. *If Tom thinks it can be done, then I need to believe in him.* Leaning against the rock wall, trying to get com-fortable, Andi didn't want any distractions, however small. She'd already found one chink in the Betang's armor, possessing a genetic ability to see through its illusions. So perhaps she could fight off its other powers as well.

Something on a nearby slab of the black rock caught her eye. Brushing the patina of dust away, she uncovered a small painting, faded, aged with the passage of centuries, but the figures seemed clear enough. *An urabu. No, a herd of urabu.*

This time when she closed her eyes, the peaceful glade came to mind imme-diately. Had it just been a few days? She'd been leaning against the tree and the urabu had wandered into the clearing. Drawing on the memory, Andi tried to re-create all the small details in her mind's eye—the cool meadow grass, the rough tree bark against her back, the little insects buzzing around the purple and white flowers. And, of course, the urabu. The majestic buck, with his glorious horns and those luminous emerald eyes. She realized now his eyes were the same bright green as the glow from Sanenre's emerald healing device.

The image of the sacred urabu buck came to her mind fully formed, gazing at her. She was sure if she opened her eyes, the creature would be there, standing in front of her on the dusty plain. The buck observed her for a long minute, then swung his elegant head with the rack of crowning antlers around, facing away from Andi, guarding her as he would guard his own small herd of does and fawns.

The urabu bugled a challenging cry that echoed around the glade now existing in her mind's eye. No one was going to think *him* to death. He'd go down fighting and inflict grievous harm on the opponent. Hooves, antlers, teeth—all fearsome weapons. Even the alien Betang would be hard put to get past an enraged urabu if unarmed.

Two more urabu bucks walked from the forest, joining her first protector. The trio stood together. A gentle pressure nudged against her spine. The fawn had come to her, pushing her, trying to get her to stand.

The fawn can't be behind me. I'm sitting with my back to the Knives. Andi was tempted to open her eyes for a reality check. The alpha male turned his head and snorted at her, shaking the impressive rack of antlers.

Eyes closed, going by the vivid scene in her mind, she rose and took three steps forward.

She was in the vision, but her peripheral hearing caught snatches of what was going on around her.

She heard Rahuna ask Tom, "What are you doing to her?"

"She's doing it herself, sir. Don't touch her. Don't distract her."

Leave me alone. Andi didn't know if she said that or merely thought it, but the sound of the men's voices faded. She stood in the glade on soft grass. The fawn nestled next to her, its velvet fur tickling her arm. A rough tongue licked her hand as the fawn gazed up into her face with its green eyes. Swinging their heads from side to side, the three urabu bucks made a circle around her, shaking their impressive antlers in open challenge. The Betang's inexorable mental pressure remained steady on her chest, accompanied by pounding in her head. Dark clouds ringed the urabu circle, swirling around all of them.

Three wheezing breaths later, she could no longer see the glade itself, only the ominous sooty clouds. The air crackled with tension and rumbles of distant thunder, as if a giant summer storm approached. The hair on her arms rose, and a spark of static electricity stung her hand when the fawn nuzzled her again. Tendrils of the smoky fog attempted to reach out toward her, but the urabu kicked them away, trampled them underfoot, or fended the wispy tentacles off with their long, sweeping horns. From time to time the leader of the urabu swung his head around to look at Andi, his eyes glowing more and more green as the eerie, silent battle went on. She concentrated all her strength on supporting the bucks in their efforts, trying to will them her energy to fight off the attack.

Outside the magic circle in Andi's mind, out in the real world of Zulaire, she knew the Sectors soldiers and Abukawal were still waging a furious fight against overwhelming odds. *I hope Tom is all right.*

The deadly smothering pressure from the Betang wrapped her body in its grip and tightened like a clenched fist. Heart stuttering, she fell to one knee, the fawn staggering under her weight but managing to keep her from a complete collapse. *Can't think about Tom. Can't think about anything but this battle I'm in.* The fog redoubled its efforts to reach her. One tendril brushed her cheek before the fawn leaped up to butt it away. Her cheek burned where the fog had touched, the pain somewhat soothed as the fawn licked the spot.

Andi was on her knees. Her chest wouldn't expand to take air in. Her vision was blurry, black spots at the edges. Extremely agitated now, the urabu kicked, lashing out, shredding the fog with their horns. With his nubby horns, the fawn butted her hard in the ribs, right on the blaster sear. A jolt of extreme pain shot through her, clearing her head. The little urabu looped his head under her arm and encouraged her to stand up again.

Breathe in, count five, breathe out. Just breathe. Just count the breaths. Relax. Renewed energy circulated in her body. Planting one foot under her, Andi pushed to a standing position, leaning on the fawn. She stood there a minute, breathing more easily, surrounded by the mythical defenders.

Time to take this fight to the enemy. Grinning, Andi straightened, squaring her shoulders and walked to stand next to the urabu alpha. He acknowledged her with a look. She marched forward, all three urabu falling in beside her. Faster and faster she went, running now.

The fog swirled away from her, dissipated. The glowing red core of the smoke loomed ahead of her. *I need a weapon. No, I* am *the weapon—my thoughts, my mind.* The red thing ahead of her retreated deeper into the clinging fog as she advanced with her urabu. Determined to catch her enemy, to kill the foe, Andi sprinted.

In the distance, voices shouted her name, the sounds faint. *Ignore that, don't be distracted. They don't matter right now.*

The Betang stood in front of her, wreathed in the black fog, which twisted and writhed in concert with the creature's tentacles. As the alien slithered backward, its red eye stalks quivered and knotted. One urabu ran ahead, lowering its antlers and shaking them in an unmistakably threatening gesture, cutting off the Betang's avenue of retreat.

Andi slowed down, finally walking up to her enemy and taking a stand just out of reach of the curling, whiplike tentacles. Hands on her hips, eyes narrowed, she studied the Betang. *I can see it through and through, nothing hidden. Maybe this is the way it sees humans.* Frantically, the Betang moved back and forth on the green grass. Andi raised her hands, palms facing the enemy, which stopped and shrank back, tentacles wrapping around itself defensively.

Staring at the twisted red stalks, Andi stepped closer. *You will die now, you fucking thing from a nightmare.*

As if her thought had been a signal, the urabu paced forward on stiff legs. Locking their stance, lowering their thick, muscular necks, all three drove into the Betang's soft lower body with the sharp tips of their antlers. As the three bucks thrust and tore, the alien crumpled. Rearing high on its back legs, the alpha urabu came down full force on the Betang's upper carapace shell, cracking it wide open. Disgusting viscous gray matter flowed sluggishly out of the fractures. A high-pitched screaming noise filled Andi's ears. Blinking, she clapped her hands to her ears.

In the real world, Tom caught her in a close embrace, snapping the spell. "Lords of Space, when I saw you walking right into the field of fire, I thought I was going to have a heart attack."

She would have collapsed without his arms holding her up.

I'm standing on the transportway. How did I get here? What is he talking about?

She stared around. The broken, oozing body of the dead Betang lay in front of her on the road, beside the destroyed cargo hauler. She kicked aside a limp tentacle trailing across her foot. Mitch, Rogers and Latvik made a defensive circle around her, facing outward, weapons drawn. Her vision came and went, alternating between the dead alien and burning trucks in front of her and the urabu in the lush meadow. *The urabu are leaving.* She reached out to them. *"Don't go. Come back!"*

Tom lifted her off her feet. Andi's vision went to a pinpoint, then black. The world faded away.

***

When she came to, she was half-reclining, leaning on the black, striated rock of the Knives. A lumpy pack cushioned her head, and Tom sat next to her, holding her hand and calling her name softly. His eyes were damp with emotion. Andi reached up to touch his cheek. "Hey, it's all right, I'm okay."

Crushing her to him, Tom kissed her long and hard.

Safe in his arms, she looked around. "What happened? Was I really out there on the road?"

"*Mitch.*" He summoned the sergeant and the ever-necessary medkit. He turned back to Andi. "Yes, you were out on the goddamn road." Swallowing hard, he hugged her. "I lost ten years off my life when you strolled past us out into the field of fire. We scrambled to make a protective cordon around you, tried to keep the rebels from killing you. You really spooked them, and a lot of them ran. There was some kind of green aura or glow around you, like a force field. Then when you got up on the transportway and confronted the Betang—"

"It *is* dead?" Feeling free of the insidious pressure, she knew the answer even as he was speaking.

"Oh, yeah. I don't know what you did to it, but the body looks like it was worked over with blunt instruments and knives." Rubbing the back of his head, Tom gave a little whistle. "I mean, I was standing there while you did it, and I can't explain what happened. You never actually touched it."

"The urabu saved me." Andi stroked her fingers over the ancient symbols on the rock face next to her. "They killed the Betang for me."

Tom stared at her for a long minute. "Well, *I* don't have any better explanation. When the rebels saw what the Betang really was, and realized you'd killed it, they fucking *ran*. Just threw down their weapons and took to their heels."

Now Mitch knelt next to her, reaching for her wrist, taking her pulse. Easing back against the pack, Andi felt all her aches and pains and suppressed a small moan. Next minute she looked around in alarm as a new sound arose overhead. "What's that noise?" *Please, don't tell me the rebels have air support now.*

"We've got guardian angels above us." A big grin on his face, Tom pointed to the sky.

Two Sectors Aerial Support Craft hovered above the Knives, and a third was taking up position over the burned-out trucks on the transportway. Andi watched heavily armed commandos slide from each ASC, floating down on their anti-grav boots.

Walking over from their pitiful line of defense, Rahuna held out the borrowed blaster. "Allow me to return this, Captain. Thankfully, I didn't have occasion to use it."

"Lysanda and Sadu are okay?" Andi tried to peer around the cleric to check on her charges personally, but Tom was in her way.

Rahuna bowed. "Thanks to you and to Sanenre, yes. I saw His green glow around you as you went to the enemy. You were in His Grace, child."

Checking the safety, Tom holstered the weapon. "It was close, let me tell you."

"Captain Deverane?" yelled one of the commandos who had just arrived, as his fellows dispersed themselves along the defensive line. Weapon at the ready, the man stared around.

"Here." Tom held up his arm, clenched his fist and waved as he shouted. "We're sure happy to see you guys."

The soldier ran up, saluted. "Lieutenant Andrews, sir. Glad to be of assistance. We've notified Command. They'll be sending an evac unit for the extraction."

Crisply, Tom returned the salute. "There's a dead Betang over there in the middle of the trucks." Putting his hand on the lieutenant's shoulder, Tom forced him into a half turn away from his view of Andi, pointing across the plain toward the road. "Command will want to preserve the body for scientific analysis. You need to let them know what we've got for them."

The young lieutenant had been eyeing Andi appreciatively, but now he went pale as his jaw dropped, and he rocked back on his heels. "A—a *Betang*, sir? Here on Zulaire? This Sector hasn't been penetrated."

"Yeah, this Sector is compromised now, trust me." Reaching out, Tom snagged the canteen hanging on the other man's belt, handing the cool container off to Andi. "Here, you probably need some of this." He smiled at her, his eyes softening, facial muscles relaxed.

She laughed at him. *You didn't like him giving me the once-over, did you?* Running one hand through her hair to try to restore order to the wild curls as she raised the canteen to drink, Andi thoroughly enjoyed the moment.

As Andrews talked into his com, Tom and Mitch conferred next to her. Not paying too much attention, Andi listened with half an ear, more interested in slaking her raging thirst with cold water from the canteen. After drinking deeply, she poured some of the water on her hand and swiped it over her face, drying off with the hem of her tunic.

Tom clapped the lieutenant on the shoulder. "Glad you guys showed up when you did."

"Well, the way I heard it, when the shift changed the comlink operator mentioned how he'd gotten a crank call from someone claiming to be you, sir. The watch commander is an old friend of yours, I guess? Anyway, the word is the Old Man went orbital because the contact hadn't been reported. So next thing we know, the entire base is on alert, and we're on a sortie to look for you. Appreciate you being so easy to find, sir," Andrews said with a wry smile. "I had specific orders not to come back without you. Most action we've seen since we got to this planet."

"You'll be seeing a lot more action now that the Betang have infiltrated." Tom's face was grim. He turned back to Andi and Mitch. "She okay?"

"Your lady is good to go, sir." The sergeant gave her one last inject and made a thumbs-up sign.

"Thank you." Rubbing her arm, which felt like a pincushion peppered with small purple bruises, Andi leaned back, closing her eyes. No urabu appeared. She didn't know if she'd ever see them again, in any form. *They brought me so much luck. Maybe their job is done.*

The end of her ordeal drew closer by the minute.

I hope…

CHAPTER NINE

Less than half an hour later, Andi watched as the giant evacuation ship came in for a landing in the open plain slightly to the east of the Knives. Tom straightened from where he'd been lounging against the cool black rocks, close to her. "Here we go. Things will move fast from here on out."

An officer with armed escort headed across the dusty plain from the evac ship. Tom strode off to meet them, Mitch on his heels. Crisp salutes were exchanged, and the two officers fell into an animated conversation while the sergeant chimed in occasionally.

Returning to Andi and the others gathered by the Knives in what shade there was, Tom said. "We're going to the civilian terminal at the spaceport. I've asked Captain Kenyatta over there to call ahead and make sure some of His Serene Holiness' staff will be waiting. Lord Tonkiln will meet us there as well to collect his children." He gave Andi a conspiratorial smile. "I told them you'd be coming to the base with us for medical attention, okay?"

"Fine with me," she said. "This blaster sear really aches. I want that promised time in the rejuve resonator."

"Sure thing. You're entitled." Tom beamed at her, his green eyes warm, then surveyed the three remaining members of his squad. "Get your gear, soldiers, and make tracks for the ship."

"Yes, sir." Mitch saluted. "Not all that much gear to get." He winked at Andi. "Medkit's about empty of anythin' useful by now anyway."

Tom just nodded. "Collect the packs and our personal weapons, Mitch. That'll be fine. The troops from base can bring the other gear in. See you at the evac ship."

"I must get something from the cargo hauler." Rahuna slapped his forehead. "Andi, can you manage the child?"

"Of course," she agreed wearily.

"Whatever you forgot may not be in good shape any longer," Tom said to Rahuna's retreating back. "The cargo hauler took an amazing amount of punishment during the firefight."

Waving his left hand to indicate he'd heard, His Serene Holiness continued doggedly down the slight incline toward the battered vehicles.

"What do you suppose he left that's worth retrieving?" Shading her eyes against the glare, Andi watched the cleric circle the truck, moving out of view.

"I don't really care. It's his problem. You're *not* carrying Sadu." Tom's tone brooked no disagreement. "Not with that proximity wound. Abukawal, you carry the boy."

Sadu was so worn out he didn't seem to care anymore who hauled him around, as long as no one expected him to walk on his own power. With a big yawn, the toddler allowed the tall Shenti warrior to pick him up, Sadu leaning his head on the man's broad shoulder.

Hoisting Andi effortlessly off the ground, Tom got her situated in his arms, trying to avoid bumping her wounds, before striding toward the evac ship. A loose cordon of heavily armed Sectors troops fell in around them as an escort. Their ride sat poised for takeoff, engines humming at a subtle pitch. She kept glancing over her shoulder at the scene of their dramatic last stand.

Staggering as Tom set her down at the base of the on-ramp, Andi was grateful when he and Mitch reached to steady her.

"Watch your step, ma'am." The sergeant's familiar drawl penetrated her fog of exhaustion and pain.

Once inside the ship, she sank into a cushioned seat near the front of the large craft. Leaning her head back, she closed her eyes, more tired than she'd ever been. Andi couldn't even summon the energy to make sure that Lysanda and Sadu were safely aboard, or that Rahuna had found whatever he was after in the cargo hauler. When she heard someone slide into the seat next to her, she opened her eyes reluctantly.

Flattering concern reflected in his face, Tom studied her, reaching across to take her hand. "You okay? Should I ask Mitch to give you something else?"

Andi rolled her head side to side against the seat back. *I don't care if I never have another inject as long as I live.* "I'm tired. Nothing more serious." Her voice sounded weak and whispery even to herself. Clearing her throat, she tried to exhibit some interest in what was going on. "Any reason why I shouldn't take a nap?"

"Go ahead, but flight time won't be more than half an hour. Command is eager to get us back. A debrief is top priority, I'm sure."

"Wake me when we land." Keeping her fingers around his warm hand, Andi curled up and drifted off to sleep.

***

Tom shook her awake all too soon. "We're at the spaceport. Come on, we need to join the others outside."

"I'm going to sleep around the clock, starting sometime soon." Standing up with effort and smoothing her dress over her hips, Andi sighed.

He led her toward the exit door. "I wanted you to rest as long as possible." Holding her elbow gently, he escorted her down the off-ramp and away from the ship. The big craft lifted off again, straight up as before veering across the spaceport, heading for the Sectors base on the other side. The backwash from the takeoff blew Andi's hair around her face, and she flattened her palms over it to keep the waving tendrils in some semblance of neatness.

"They're waiting for us over there." Tom nodded to where the rest of their party stood closer to the terminal.

As Andi got within a few paces of the group, a door opened in the side of the building and Planetary Lord and Chief of the Obati Tamir Tonkiln emerged, surrounded by guards and retainers, a Sectors general by his side. A bevy of priests in black religious habits followed at a discreet distance.

Sadu, recognizing his father in the vanguard of newcomers, struggled in Abukawal's arms. The Shenti warrior managed to hold the squirming toddler a minute longer before setting him safely down on the pavement to make a wobbling run to his father. Reaching Lord Tonkiln, throwing himself the last half a yard and twining his short arms around the Obati's neck, Sadu made it clear that things were right with his world now that he had his father close by.

Blinking back tears, Andi leaned into Tom.

The Planetary High Lord hugged Sadu so tightly that the boy squeaked. Tonkiln regarded Lysanda, still clinging timorously to Abukawal. She appeared torn between a desire to go to her father and a reluctance to release the warrior's strong hand.

"Sanda?" Lord Tonkiln held out his free arm to her. The girl hid her face in Abukawal's chest. "Will someone please tell me what's going on here?" The Planetary High Lord braced Sadu on one hip and scowled. "Why is my own daughter afraid of me?" He pointed at Abukawal. "Who is this?"

Quickly, Rahuna took Lysanda's hand, escorting her and Abukawal to Tonkiln. "Your daughter has been through a tremendous ordeal, my lord, her life spared through miraculous intervention by Miss Markriss, Captain Deverane here, and his soldiers. The rescue party included this fine young Shenti man. May I present Abukawal, son and heir of the Shenti chief of the Western Ranges?"

Andi hid a smile. *Smooth one, Rahuna. You just forced Tonkiln to observe the customary civilities in front of all these witnesses and recognize Abukawal's rank and standing.*

The Planetary High Lord made the traditional Clan sign of greeting and peace. Abukawal bowed. "It has been my honor to be of service to your daughter and son in their time of peril and hardship."

Wiping her forehead, locking her knees to stay upright, Andi spoke up. "We're all tired and thirsty. If you and—" She glanced at the high-ranking Sectors officer who stood by, and who had so far been silent "—the others want to hear the whole story here and now, I suggest we move inside, out of this blazing sun."

The Sectors general smiled. "She's giving us good advice, Lord Tonkiln. Base Commander General Chang-Wilkins at your service, Miss Markriss. It's a pleasure to meet you." He came to shake her hand. "Your grandfather and I are old friends. Glad we could oblige him by extracting you from the compound."

So Grandfather Loxton was the one who'd exerted pressure on the military to rescue me.

Andi refocused her attention as High Lord Tonkiln said, "I owe you more than I can possibly repay, Miss Markriss. In this time of terrible loss and death, you preserved two lives more precious to me than my own." The Planetary High Lord glanced around impatiently. "Where is that officious portmaster? We require a privacy to conduct these discussions."

The general was still staring at Andi, eyebrows pulled together in a puzzled frown. "Miss Markriss, I understand you somehow killed a Betang infiltrator embedded with the rebels? I'll be eager to get a debrief on that."

"I'll tell you all about it in return for full treatment in the base hospital rejuve resonator, sir." Andi winced as a piercing twinge traveled through her nervous system. "Soon."

Tom swept her up in his arms. "I think you've had enough for one day." He glared over at Tonkiln and the general. "Can't this debriefing wait until tomorrow? She's about at the end of her orbit."

"No, no, I'll be all right." Twining her arms around his neck, Andi leaned against him. "Lord Tonkiln shouldn't have to wait any longer to hear about what happened in the summer colony. Then I'll rest, I promise. You can even *order* me to rest."

Tom gazed at her, his green eyes reflecting his loving concern. "That's an affirmative. Believe it."

The portmaster bustled up, surrounded by his own subordinates, and bowed so low his nose nearly touched the ground. "I have a conference room and refreshments ready for you, High Lord."

As the portmaster led them to a well-air-conditioned, large meeting room, Tom carried Andi, and the rest of the group trailed after them. Andi settled into a chair, Tom drawing another one up to sit beside her.

Tonkiln stared at both of them and nodded. "We'll keep it brief for today."

Andi couldn't control the shaking in her hands. Exhaustion and deferred stress, she supposed. Together, she and Tom told the story of the events that had begun a few days ago. Abukawal or Rahuna chimed in on occasion with some detail they considered essential.

Lysanda fell asleep in Abukawal's arms while the debriefing continued. The Planetary High Lord handed Sadu over to a nursemaid, a woman who'd worked for his family in years past, apparently recalled from retirement for this emergency.

Andi blinked away sudden tears as the nanny carried the drowsy toddler off, remembering the sweet girl who had been Sadu's nursemaid in the summer compound, now dead in that burned-out village. Three massive, armed Obati guards accompanied the elderly woman and the toddler as they left the room. *Distant members of Tonkiln's own sub-Clan, by the tattoos. I'm glad the Planetary High Lord isn't taking any chances with his remaining son. Sadu's going to rule Zulaire one day, after all.* As he was carried from the room, Sadu gurgled in his sleep, thumb firmly stuffed into his toothless mouth. Andi grinned. *Hard as that may be to imagine right now.*

"An amazing tale altogether." Rahuna set his wineglass on the table when Andi and Tom had finished. "I lived through most of it, and even I can hardly credit our good fortune. But much work remains to be done, my friends."

"Yes, you're right," Lord Tonkiln agreed, clenching his fists. "Even if this one alien sentient has been eliminated, and we're fortunate enough that there were no others, we have to clean out the pockets of rebellion. Rebuild trust between the three Clans. A divided Zulaire will fall to the enemy."

"If there are any other Betang on Zulaire," General Chang-Wilkins told them, "it'll be a major operation to save the planet. Highest priority. We must work in unison on this. The Sectors can't afford to cede a planet in this Sector to the Mawreg so you'll have our full cooperation, Lord Tonkiln, I assure you."

"Captain Deverane, I'm told you're eligible for retirement now?" The ruler toyed with his wineglass, swirling the ruby liquid.

"I've served enough years to retire." Tom raised his eyebrows as he shifted in his chair and drank some wine.

Startled by the turn the conversation was taking, Andi glanced from one man to the other. *Why would Tonkiln care about Tom's career decisions?*

Steepling his fingers, the Planetary High Lord peered at the captain. "Zulaire isn't open to outside settlement via veterans' acres claims, but I can make an exception in your case. A *substantial* exception." Rising and pacing in a tight circle, Tonkiln said, "Zulaire and I owe you much already, but I ask for more. We need someone with interstellar military experience and strong connections to the Sectors to take charge of the unified planetary defense force I'm going to establish. We must find a way to blend Obati, Shenti and Naranti in one strand and build on that, creating a military capable of protecting this world and my people." He paused in front of Tom's chair. "Would such a challenge interest you? Compensation would be commensurate to the task, I assure you."

Setting his glass aside, Tom rose to his feet. "An incredible offer, sir. I'd definitely be interested. It's an honor to be considered, but I'd have to discuss it with Andi."

Smiling, she gazed at him. "There are so many things to commend that plan I can't begin to list them. There can't possibly be a better-qualified candidate for the job."

Tonkiln nodded. He put one hand over his heart, fist clenched, and bowed slightly to Andi. "You're welcome to return to my home to recuperate after your medical treatment. From this day forward you are a daughter of the Tonkiln House, a member of the Obati Clan, with all the rights and privileges that pertain."

Lords of Space, he just made me a princess of Zulaire. Stunned, she was almost at a loss for words, stammering as she said, "I'm grateful, sir, and deeply honored.

As far as tonight, though, I'd prefer to go on to my own home." *The mere idea of being in the busy Tonkiln household, even with my newly acquired status as daughter, isn't appealing in* any *way. I want some peace and quiet.*

And time alone with Tom.

Grinning, the captain winked at her.

Andi knew she was blushing as her cheeks grew warm. *A lot of time.*

Rahuna stepped forward. "Would you permit this much, Andi, that while you're at the hospital on the base, the High Lord and I will direct our staffs to open your house, lay in supplies, make all ready for you?"

"Thank you, what a lovely idea," Andi said, much relieved. *Tactful Rahuna to the rescue yet again.*

"All right then, now that's settled," Tom declared, "I'm getting her medical treatment without further delay." Taking her tea cup, he set it on the table next to his wineglass. Crouching down so he could study her face, he asked quietly, "Can you walk, or would you like me to carry you?"

"I can walk." Taking his outstretched hand, Andi stood, favoring her left side, which ached abominably. She was halfway across the room, heading to the exit, before Lord Tonkiln's imperious voice stopped them. "Tomorrow, we have business to conduct, Andi."

"Business?" Leaning heavily on Tom's arm, she turned to face the ruler. "What business, sir?"

"I have ore piling up at the mines." Tonkiln waved vaguely to the west.

Bewildered, Andi shook her head, holding up a hand to stop the flow of words. "Why are you talking to *me* about this? I'm not the resident Loxton agent."

"Either you're ratified as the Loxton planetary agent or Zulaire takes all of its considerable business to another company. *Immediately.*" Tonkiln's tired smile softened the stern lines of his autocratic face. He shook a finger at her. "I know who really kept the office running smoothly, made sure all obligations were met and the terms were fair. None of this was accomplished by Mr. Flintmay. He would have been lost without you."

She swallowed hard. "I'm honored by your confidence in me."

Sipping his wine, Tonkiln waved a careless hand. "As long as I know you're going to be in charge, I can wait a few days more. Yes, Captain, I see your impatience with this talk of commerce while the lady stands injured. Be gone then, off with you both."

Other than Tonkiln's impassive guards, the hall was empty. At the first turn in the corridor, safely out of sight, Tom pulled her into a fierce embrace, kissing her passionately.

Footsteps sounded behind them. Andi stepped back, Tom taking a defensive position in front of her, hand on the blaster at his side.

Dusty black robes flying, Rahuna was hurrying to catch up. "I have something of yours, something you'll need, I'm sure." When he reached them, he knelt, fumbling with the unfamiliar closures on the backpack he'd brought. Unsealing the flap, he withdrew the shimmering bride's shawl. Clambering to his feet, the cleric made a little ceremony of holding the garment out to her.

Andi knew she was blushing again, afraid to look at Tom. He pulled the fabric from Rahuna's fingers and wrapped the shawl's gauzy folds tenderly around her shoulders. When she glanced up, happiness suffused her at the warm expression on his face.

Eyes bright with approval, Rahuna clapped his hands. "Yes, my children, I predicted you'd need this when I met you the first afternoon on the transportway, did I not? I prefer officiating at the early fall weddings, you know. Officiating at yours will give me great pleasure." He beamed at them.

"I'd like to do my own proposing, if you don't mind." Tom put his arms around Andi and pulled her closer.

"Ah, I've been premature in my congratulations. I see." Not the least bit embarrassed, Rahuna smiled, wagging a finger at him. "Or else you've been tardy in asking the question, Captain." Chuckling, he walked away.

Andi looked at the floor. She could feel the heat in her cheeks.

"Hey." Gently, Tom forced her to turn around, putting one finger under her chin so he could see her face. Shyly, she tilted her head and raised her eyebrows as his gaze locked onto hers.

Swaying, Andi let herself melt into his strong embrace.

Tom kissed her before asking, "You will marry me, won't you? You're my heart and my home, the only thing that matters to me in this life."

"Put like that, how can I possibly refuse?" She smiled.

He crushed her to him as he claimed her in a kiss that left them both a bit shaken. Groaning in frustration, he took her hand. "We've got to get you through that rejuve treatment and find some privacy before we both go crazy. How far did you say your house is from the base?"

"All the way across the city." She laughed. "Of course, now that I'm a Tonkiln daughter, I don't have to pay attention to speed limits or traffic laws."

"Good. We'll set a record."

They resumed their walk toward the spaceport exit, where the general had promised a vehicle and armed escort would be waiting. Mitch had gone awhile ago to ensure the arrangements were made.

"Does everything on this planet happen so fast?" Tom held the door open for her.

"What do you mean?" Andi strolled past him, emerging into hot sunlight.

He followed, touching her elbow and pointing to the waiting military convoy. "I'm retiring. I'm cured of the incurable bhengola. There's a new job." He stopped and embraced her again, staring into her face. "I'm getting married." Head resting comfortably against his hard chest, Andi could hear his heartbeat. "Ten days ago, you were only an obscure name in a pre-mission briefing."

"And now?" She held her breath for his answer.

"And now—" He gave her that genuine smile, the one that reached and warmed his eyes. "I can't live without you."

"I can handle that. Try to remember one thing, though—I don't take orders very well."

He grinned. "Not a problem."

She closed her eyes as he moved to kiss her, and for the last time she had a vision of the alpha urabu, gazing at her quizzically, head tilted. *Thank you, my friend,* she thought, addressing her legendary champion. *My journey is complete. There's nothing more I need or want.*

The buck tossed its majestic antlers once in farewell and was gone.

***

For the rest of her years on Zulaire, Andrianda Deverane was the possessor of such good fortune that she became a legend herself. For it was said that the urabu of Sanenre had bestowed their blessing on her…once upon a time.

ABOUT VERONICA SCOTT

Best-selling, award-winning author Veronica Scott grew up in a house with a library full of books as its heart, and when she ran out of things to read, she started writing her own stories. Married young to her high school sweetheart then widowed, Veronica has two grown daughters, one young grandson and cats. You can usually find Veronica on Twitter, at her blog or on Facebook:

http://veronicascott.wordpress.com/
http://twitter.com/#!/vscotttheauthor
https://www.facebook.com/pages/Veronica-Scott/177217415659637